CONTENTS

AUTHOR'S THANKS

I f I may just take the opportunity, I would like to express my Gratitude and thanks to everybody who helped me in the process of writing, editting and bringing the book to market.

Especially worthy of mention is Anoop in India, who designed the cover of the book for me. And to Freelancer.com for enabling the process. It is hard to interpret my ideas, and yet you did just that.

My extra special thanks goes to Nicky Hatherell for proof reading, during her leave. I honour you as a great person with the kindest heart.

And my thanks also goes to Daniel Gurney, (my nine year old son and co-editor,) who listened as I read the story to him, and offered input that was invaluable.

And lastlyI extend my thanks to the Great Creator, who I believe flows through me. Without him, non of my creative efforts would exist.

NOTES & DEDICATION

Dedication

This book is dedicated to my two brothers, who never made it this far.

Authors Note

This story is made up and my own work. Celtishia and the Green Dimension does not really exist.
Any similarity of characters in the book to persons in real life is purely co-incidental.

1. THE LETTER

I t was an early Monday morning, and little Sarah Salter, aged thirteen, sat in the solicitor's office with the family lawyer. She was there for the reading of the "last will and testament," of her dad. Her late father, Jonathon Salter, had passed away one month earlier, (aged only forty-five.)

The death of Johnathon Salter had been sudden, after a lung collapse. The funeral that followed was full of stress and arguments within the family, as relatives all poked their noses into the arrangements.

However, now it was over, and other formalities were beginning. This was the first time the family got to find out how things were divided. The immediate family saw it as a chance to put things to rest, and move on.

The now late Mister Salter had worked most of his life in a garage fixing cars, so he had only a modest estate.

For the most part, there were no surprises. The house went to his surviving wife, Carly Salter, as did the car, the money, and most of the remaining assets. The letter from her dad, that was read out by the solicitor, described Carly Salter, (nee Shields,) as "the love of his life, and worth sacrificing everything for." Sarah thought this statement was odd, but dismissed it out of hand, and the will reading continued.

Sarah's brother 'Michael' was left Mister Salter's motorbike, which had been his pride and joy. The big 'Harley Davidson' was a valuable, imported monster of a machine. Sarah thought it was a cool bike, as it had been modified by her dad.

The wheels of the bike had been sprayed gold, and all the metal around the gas tank and other parts had been painted a red, with gold flames. She had never admitted that she liked the bike to her dad, and had avoided getting on it whenever possible. But Sarah knew it was the ideal present for her brother, who had just left the British Army with a medical discharge. The bike had always attracted the attention of a certain type of girl. (Mostly the wrong type.)

"And for my lovely daughter, Sarah," the lawyer continued to read, "I leave the contents of my security locker. The details are deposited with the lawyer in trust. You may access it on your 18th birthday onwards. I would also like her to know, that I love her lots, and am proud of her whatever she decides to do. As for the gifts inside, while their financial value is negligible, they are very special to me, and had been passed down the generations. Guard them well, and may they guide you home."

Sarah was not impressed, as she was secretly hoping for some money. Although she had loved her dad, and known him to be a bit of a joker.

The years came and went, and Sarah forgot all about the deposit box, and her father's gift. Life went on as usual, until she got a letter from the lawyer; reminding her about it.

And so, on the afternoon of her 18th Birthday, Sarah Salter stood inside her dad's security locker. She now wondered what her dad had left her, and now the waiting was over. The security locker was not what she had expected. It was a large cubicle, which when opened, revealed another large locker the same height as Sarah. There was also a mirror on the wall, and a large round table. And nothing else.

She entered with the guard. And they stood there looking at the locker. The guard approached and turned a key in its lock. The door opened and he reached inside.

After a bit of a struggle, he produced a large metal box. It was about 2 meters long, by a meter wide, and a meter high, and was placed on a table by the guard.

"We will leave you in peace," said the security officer. "This could be a private moment. And by the way, the locker is prepaid for another ten years, if you wish to keep the contents here."

And then he left the room.
Sarah turned the key, and opened the box slowly.
Then she peered inside.
Inside were three objects and a letter.
The letter read,

"Hello Sarah, and Happy Birthday."
"If you are reading this, then I am probably dead. I am aware my heart and lungs, do not function at their best and need better air, but I chose to remain here in Britain."
"I enclose three items for you. They are an ancient shofar, (or "ram's horn,") that belonged to my Jewish grandmother. It is an odd thing I know, but I can guarantee your friends won't have one. (Ha. Ha.)
I also enclose my favourite necklace for my favourite daughter, and my gran's bag of old rare silver coins. These items are special to me, and I have treasured them my whole life. I believe that you are meant to have them, but I don't know why."
"Anyway I love you. I will always be proud of you, and hope you get to do great things." "Lots of love, Dad."

She looked at the letter, smiled and said quietly "I loved you too dad." Then she inspected her presents.
The necklace was eighteen inches long, and appeared to be made of silver. It had thick eight millimetres curb chains, and a silver clasp. It

looked very strong. Sarah put it on, and looked in the mirror. It looked more like a man's necklace, but she liked it anyway. She decided that she would look for some kind of pendant to go on it.

The second object she inspected was the horn, which was initially wrapped in an old and dirty green cloth. It was a small round animal horn, and Sarah wondered what the ram would have looked like. It was mostly black, but some parts of it were green and grey. It was also clearly very old, and had holes in it.

She put it to her mouth and tried to blow it, because she wanted to see what sound it made. Unfortunately, she could get no sound from it on the first attempt. Eventually, she got it to make a noise that sounded like a long trumpet blast.

"Yes," she thought to herself, "my friends definitely won't have one of these. And why the blazes would they?"

Sarah had no interest in spiritual things, and religion especially. Her father had had nothing to do with the Jewish faith as far as she knew. Sarah had never set so much as a foot inside the local synagogue, nevertheless, she thought this was a quaint item to have and decided to keep it.

The biggest surprise however, was the bag of coins. The bag was made of old molding leather, fastened at the top with a drawstring. It contained about identical thirty coins in all.

She chose one of the mysterious coins at

random, and studied it in more detail. The coin seemed to be made of silver, and was not one Sarah was familiar with. On its rim was a language she was not familiar with, although she thought it looked vaguely Spanish. She looked more closely, and could just about make out the numerals 'MM' before the word 'Shekel'. But she had no idea whose currency this was, or if it had any real value. She returned the coin to the purse, and placed it in the locker, for safe keeping. She then picked up the small ram's horn, and placed it in her rucksack, although she had no idea why she wanted it on her.

She then went home, wearing her necklace. When she got there, she told her family what her dad had left her. She even showed her brother the ram's horn. Her mother looked on in horror.

"Good heavens," she said, "I thought I had seen the last of that thing. I never liked the sound it made."

2. THE STORM

T he story continues on a Monday evening, and an autumn day in Plymouth. The leaves were turning yellow and brown, and were falling from trees. The time of year meant the days were getting noticeably shorter, and the weather was always changing.

Of course, the British weather is renowned for being unpredictable, and this day, was no exception. One minute it was raining heavily, and the next there was bright sunshine. This had confused and annoyed everybody, because the weather forecast had predicted sunshine all day. But now a lot of people were travelling home soaked through to the skin, and taking shelter wherever they could find it.

For Sarah Salter, this meant catching the bus home. It was not a prospect she was looking forward to, as the dreaded 'Number 117 Bus' was nearly always late. And the storm coming in from the sea was not going to help.

The rain was getting heavier, and the wind had started to blow. People jostled for shelter. However, the bus shelter was too full for them all, but some of the elderly people were trying to force their way in anyway. Their comments, like "young people these days have no consideration", weren't helping either. It just put the young and old against each other, and resulted in exchanges of dirty looks.

By the time the bus arrived, the commuters were getting more and more angry. The dirty looks now threatened to erupt into disagreements, as the queue got longer.

When the bus finally arrived there was a sense of relief from everyone, and it seemed to express itself best in the comment, "at last! Ten minutes late again!" Sarah didn't think that this was so bad, and got on and paid the fare, before taking a seat on the upper deck.

"I tell you something is amiss", said an old man, behind her, when they were all finally under way. He was talking to his wife.

"You do keep talking nonsense", replied the old woman in a local accent, "just a thunderstorm about to come that's all". The old man didn't seem convinced, but he also looked like he was too terrified to push the matter further, for fear of being brought down to size again later. The submissiveness of the old man revealed that the woman here was clearly in charge.

However; Sarah know what the man meant. Nearly everybody had felt it. There was something in the air. A strange unsettling feeling was lingering, like someone was prompting her.

Something just wasn't right, and everybody was getting nervous. She was having this feeling that change was afoot, and that it wasn't going to be easy. "No" she thought to herself, "I'm just feeling anxious, and worried".

Perking herself up, Sarah smiled from her seat behind them, and sipped on the hot chocolate, which she had purchased and now carried in a disposable cup. It was slowly starting to warm and cheer her up. She needed cheering up.

The rain continued to tap against the window. But as the bus left behind the taller buildings of the City Centre, and moved towards Central Park, it was becoming increasing obvious that the it was getting even heavier, and louder. The rain was now falling at a slight angle due to increased wind.

In her mind, she started to replay the events of the day. This included losing her job in a call-centre, "due to cutbacks". Not that she really cared about the job anyway. Sarah hadn't been there long, and she knew that the money wouldn't last forever. She also knew that her mother would be all over her, giving her advice, in their attempt to motivate her to get another job. Her mother was keen for her to be constantly working, and bringing money into the house.

This was not the top concern for Sarah, because she was bright and had just accepted a place at medical school for the next academic year. At the moment, she was on of a gap year, and saving some money for her studies.

With this in mind, she had spent the rest of the day in the shopping mall, doing things she liked. This included window shopping, for books and the latest video games. However; she knew that the fun that day must come to an end eventually. So it was that at 6pm, she decided to purchase a takeaway drink and head home. Sarah loved her hot chocolate in the evening, and it was a great warming drink for days of bad weather.

Sarah was twenty years old, and always liked to dress in dark colors. Today, she was wearing a dark-red gothic dress, over her jeans. The coat she wearing was black with a hood. To finish the "Gothic" look, her face was painted white with excess make-up, and she wore scarlet red lipstick. She also carried a small rucksack, in which, (for reasons she didn't understand,) she carried the ram's horn her dad had left her. Her mother thought that this was "just macabre."

Of course, the way she dressed would cause others to look at her with suspicion. Sarah wasn't all that bothered about this, and it had the added advantage of gaining her mother's dis-approval. Her mother (meanwhile), would con-tinue to defend her, by saying that, "she is a lot friendlier than she likes to look".

Meanwhile, back on the bus, the park and ride terminal was coming into view. Sarah always got off here as it was close to where she lived, and started to walk the rest of the way home using the quickest route through the park. Her long hair was covered by her hood, but her face was getting soaked in the rain.

As she walked between the trees, the rain started to get heavier. She reminded herself that she must buy some more hair dye, as the ginger roots were starting to show through.

The first strike of lightning appeared in the sky, making clearly visible forks of light. Luckily for her the trees provided a natural canopy against the rain, and she was cheered up further by the sight of an old building made of concrete, amongst the trees. Then about five seconds later came the boom from the thunder, as sound follows the speed of light. Sarah believed that each second meant the eye of the storm was a mile away. All her life, she had been encouraged by her mother to count slowly to determine their distance.

Taking advantage of the tree shelter, she noticed that the building was some sort of old stone house with cemented up doors and windows.

There was a another lightning fork in the sky. The trees shook and some of the leaves began to fall allowing more of the rain through. The fork of lightning was followed four seconds later by a second crack of thunder. She had counted more accurately this time. She was starting to get cold and positioned herself as close to the building as she could to gain protection from the walls.

She knew the storm was getting closer, and more dangerous.

A third and a fourth lightning strike occurred, and their booms indicating that the storm's eye was getting nearer. First two seconds, then one.

Another lightning fork appeared, lighting up the sky. But this time it was different. The clouds and stars in the sky seemed for a few seconds, to turn the sky into a strong white light and Sarah could see plainly a planet, shaped exactly like the Earth come falling down towards her.

The sound of the boom should have followed immediately. But this time, Miss Salter heard the sound of what sounded like hand-bells ringing a mysterious peel as the earth in the sky got nearer. Simultaneously, the earth seemed to vibrate and Sarah found herself struggling to remain on her feet. The temperature seemed to drop, and her skin tingled and went numb like when you get pins and needles. This weird sensation lasted about thirty seconds.

Then as soon as it had happened, things were nearly back to normal. The rain was still falling heavily, she was cold, and the wind was blowing. She reasoned that her mind was playing tricks on her. But then she realized that she was surrounded by a light green mist, that seemed to make her feel more invigorated, and more alive than she was used to.

Then, (about 30 seconds later), there was another crack of lightning, and she saw what looked like a man with a pale-green face. He was about the same height. He wore what looked like a leather hoodie, and was carrying a modern fibreglass looking cross-bow in pale-green hands.

Sarah wondered if she was imagining him. He seemed normal but for his face and hands. She couldn't help but stare, and he now stared back. She averted her eyes, and wondered "was his face really green?" So she looked again.

He was gone, but the rain still poured. There was another crack, followed by another flash in the sky. Then a strong gust of wind caused some fallen leaves to blow up around her. Then there was a different sounding crack, and a nearby tree started to fall towards her and the boarded up house.

Once again Sarah saw the peculiar green man. He looked worried, and ran towards her pushing her out of the way of the falling branches. Falling onto the grass, they rolled a few feet down a slope and landed safely.

Sarah got to her feet, and looked around, trying to get her bearings, in the heavy rain.

"I don't understand", she exclaimed with good cause.

The fallen tree was there. So was the green man, and so was the storm. But, she could no longer see the tree covered path she knew and loved, as she seemed to be in a muddy clearing with forest all around. The darkness that was upon them had been replaced by a twilight.

The man pointed the cross-bow at her menacingly. "What are you, and what are you doing here?" he demanded.

3. GREEN PEOPLE?

S arah stared at the green man in disbelief, and then noticed he was shaking. She ventured to guess that he was in his forties "But with a green face" she thought, "who can tell?"

"What am I?" she asked. "Are you serious? You're green."

"And you are white. You know White? W.H.I.T.E?" he responded.

"That's make up, my skin is really sort of pink. You know like PINK? That's P.I.N.K by the way."

Returning sarcasm was something Sarah excelled at, especially when someone irritated her. And this man had irritated her by assuming she couldn't spell.

"Watch your manners pink lady," He replied, looking very angry yet confused. To attempt to hide this, the man once again pointed the cross bow at her, motioning an attempt to use it.

Sarah just stood there, quietly, scared, but even more confused. And as the moments passed, the man became yet more irritated. Finally: he called out loud, "Adah, can I have some help here? Back me up, its urgent!".

He paused, and then yelled, "Freida, quick now. Fetch the guard, tell him we may have caught an Egyptian spy here!"

"A what? An Egyptian spy", said Sarah, "you can't be serious". She paused, then a smile crossed her face. "Oh I get it! This is a joke for the Comic Convention right?"

The green man looked totally baffled, and asked, "What's a Comic Convention?"

"No idea, and this is no joking matter young lady", said another voice, interrupting their conversation from behind her. "Spying will land you up to ten years in Boudicca's prison. That's high security in case you don't know".

"This must be Adah" thought Sarah. Sarah noticed that she was tall, curvy and in her forties. She also had green skin, but with red freckles, and her cropped hair had black curls. She wore a little black dress, which exposed most of her legs. There was a sense of flirtatiousness about her.

"That's right. Ten years" said the man, bringing her back into the conversation. "Now answer my question. He pointed his crossbow at her again, and repeated his original question, "What are you, and what are you doing here?"

"Wow", said a very nervous Sarah. "No need for threats. My name is Sarah Salter, and I was taking a walk home in the park. Just trying to mind my own business and avoid getting struck by the lightning. Talking of which: it seems to be getting better now, so I'll just be on my ..."

Sarah never got to finish this sentence, because the woman now drew out what looked like a large metal gun and pointed it at her legs. It was enough to stop her talking.

"Well look around you Miss Sarah Salter," she said, "there is no park right here is there? Just our little farm".

Sarah looked around again in the twilight, and could see that the park had just vanished. However, suspended between the trees on natural vines, she could see what resembled a small white umbrella-like object. It seemed to be made of a kind of fibreglass.

"No" she thought "there cannot be?"

Sure enough, there were little hammocks beneath the umbrella-like dome. She could make out at least eight. They were suspended from the edge and made their way into a central wooden floor. And there was a boy and a girl, both aged about ten, with green skin, watching what looked like a film being projected on the dome's surface.

A rope ladder descended to the surface, where some fruit trees were. In addition, there was a posh looking barbeque for cooking. Indeed, there was yet another man in green skin, who seemed to be turning some meat on it. It provided a strange aroma, due to the herbs it was being cooked on. There were loads of them. And this smell mingled with the smell of the mist which seemed to smell of oregano, and sought to overwhelm her.

It was like there was a surge of energy in her body, and her ears were suddenly in great pain, like someone was rubbing them on the inside lobe. Her eye sight was also acting peculiar, for the sides of her vision were blurring white, enabling her to see only what was immediately in front of her.

Whatever was happening, it just made no sense. She was scared, confused, and also soaking wet from the rain. She felt dizzy, and fainted.

When she came around, Sarah had been moved into the strange farmhouse. She was laying sideways on a hammock suspended by four ropes, but her feet and hands were tied in front of her. She seemed to have some kind of medicinal mask on her face.

A slender young woman in her twenties was standing above her, with long black curly hair. She also had blue eyes and a green face, with blueish freckles. In fact, the only observable differences were her age, and the black tattoo on her arm in the shape of a six pointed star.

As if trying to provide some assistance, the girl gently removed Sarah's mask. "It was to stabilize your oxygen levels, decrease the amount; until you got used to our levels gradually," she kind of

explained. "It should be ok to remove it now."
Sarah just looked at her with suspicion.

"So, you are awake then?" said the mysterious young woman. Sarah suspected that she was trying to start a conversation.

"Yes, just now."

"And I understand you are called Sarah Salter? Is that correct?"

'Yes?"

"Good! Because I was kind of expecting you, Sarah. Or someone like you. And you could view it as lucky that I was here today."

The girl was observing Sarah, and she could tell that Sarah did not look convinced by this, so she continued with some sort of medical explanation. "To help you with the oxygen levels? You have been exposed to too much, and too quickly. I assume you experienced tunnel vision and a ringing in your ears before you passed out?"

"Yes," said Sarah.

"That was the result of the extra oxygen," the girl explained, "but you are stable now."

"Who are you?" Sarah asked her but not entirely convinced. Although she realized that her ears were no longer hurting and ringing. "And where am I?"

"Well, my name is Freida Sophia Smith. Freida means "Peace and tranquility", and this is my parents'...". She paused for a few seconds, then restarted her sentence. "This is the Sub-Holding

of my adoptive parents, Benjamin and Adah Sophia-Smith. The children are called Enoch and
Ruth, after the old stories."

"Nice to meet you".

Sarah looked over Freida's clothes, and noticed
that she wore a short sleeved green and brown
hoodie. But on closer inspection, she noticed
that the green was in the form of small leaves
forming a mist like patterns, that got increasingly greener around her breast area.

On the lower part of her body she wore green
and brown body hugging jeans. Despite being up
to date with fashion, Sarah had never seen jeans
quite like these. They had a pattern that resembled spiraling green leaves over the black. The
effect of the green skin against the green and
black clothing had a look of sexuality about it.

She looked again and noticed that the hoodie
had one sleeve slightly rolled up: only one. It
was like she wanted to show of her left arm,
which had been toned from exercise, but was
hiding something on the other right arm.

Around her neck, she wore an unusual silver
necklace. Attached to her leg, she was sporting
what looked like a plastic gun in a holster. There
was a menacing knife strapped to the skin of her
left arm.

"So much for peace and tranquility" thought
Sarah, as she looked at the gun.

"I need to tell you," Freida started to advise
her, "that my pistol, the one you are looking at,

is armed and can kill in one shot. I also need to inform you that several armed police officers are down below on the surface. They act on my command. They know me as Captain Sophie-Smith."

"Ok", said Sarah, realizing that Captain Sophie-Smith was not to be messed with.

"My torc," Freida pointed to her necklace, "is confirmation of my status within the government, and proof I am allowed to ask you questions. So, let's talk."

Stalling for time, Sarah studied the necklace. It was made from a long piece of silver bar metal. It was bent around Freida's neck, and welded together with a small clasp. It looked like it was not meant to be removed.

"Don't I have rights?" She eventually asked.

Freida smiled, "Yes, you have the right to be honest, and let us help you."

"I mean what about a lawyer?"

The smile faded from Freida's mouth. "You mean an advocate? But nobody needs one of those at this stage of proceedings. I assumed you would know that."

"Well apparently not" said Sarah.

"You are not from here, are you?"

"It would seem that way." Sarah paused, then asked, "Where is this farm anyway?"

"You mean the sub-holding? Well, it is in Dumnoni."

"Never heard of it," Sarah bluntly replied. She

was trying to be brave and show no fear.

"Have you heard of Celtishia?" enquired Freida, with more hope than expectation.

"No. I come from the City of Plymouth, and I am British."

"That's a start. But I am not sure we are getting anywhere though. Besides we call it 'The City of Devonport'." Having corrected her, the girl known as Freida, looked at her in a strange knowing way, before she continued. "You seem to have no idea what I am talking about, do you?"

"Look" said Sarah getting suddenly very angry, and trying to kick her questioner. "I don't know who you are, you weirdos, or why you are kidnapping me. But I won't say anything more. Just please send me home".

After avoiding a series of attempted kicks, Freida turned and left the room. She looked both upset and angry. But she said nothing, and just started to climb down the ladder to the floor below. Her silence unnerved Sarah.

Sarah listened as Freida reached the bottom of the rope ladder, and started talking to some colleagues below. Generally, it seemed to Sarah from the conversation, that she had in fact, misjudged Freida, for she was arguing a case to have Sarah released.

"I am telling you now that the girl is no spy. She just doesn't have the capabilities, or deviousness; for one thing, Look, I know it is unusual to meet a pink woman" Sarah could just hear Freida saying, "but she doesn't seem to understand where she is, or what is going on. She is clearly delusional, and judging by the sight of her very ill. We need to get someone to explain things to her, and check her health if you like?"

"Ok", came another voice, "that is the right thing to do here. But we must update the Regional Mayor. Seek alternative means to contain the situation, but for security reasons, I advise the guard remains. And if she is not the spy, then there is probably another out there."

"We'll make sure she is fed, and looked after, until a counsellor can arrive," Freida reassured him.

"Very well, the counsellor will be here on the train tomorrow morning. Just make sure, she doesn't go anywhere."

All Sarah could do was wait for the morning, and hope that whoever this counsellor was, she would at least be friendly and tell her what they wanted with her. So far all these weird green people had done was point guns at her, tie her up, and ask weird question.

Freida came back an hour later with a meal covered by a tray. Freida assured her this was to keep her 'strength up'. When she promised not to try and escape, Sarah was allowed to eat it with her hands untied. Her feet remained bound to the end of the bed.

The meal was the most unusual plate of food

Sarah had seen her life. The first course made of a variety of green beans in the form of a soup, with some sort of weird greenish bread. It was obviously fresh, as it was also warm, and tasted a bit like a narn bread with parsley and chives.

The second course brought about 15 minutes later was something Sarah was not pleased to see. "Freshly caught river snails, cooked in garlic and clover, and what Freida called 'Brachai-Moss.' Sarah couldn't face this, but agreed under Freida's persuasion, to take some more of the bread.

As she sat up and ate she noticed that the wooden floor, while resembling a treehouse, held a series of wooden rooms including a portable toilet. After the meal, Sarah asked Freida about using it. Freida agreed and escorted her there, and back safely.

On her return, the bed shackles were replaced with what resembled a copper electronic tag (in the shape of another torc), "to enable you to move about more freely", Freida said. Freida then apologized, that this had not been done earlier, saying she felt 'guilty for the use of shackles,' and that this 'electronic security torc' was now available as a more humane form of tracking her. It was attached to her ankle.

For the rest of the evening, Freida continually spoke nicely to her, and even asked if Sarah would like a bowl to wash in. This surfaced a few minutes later with a hot steamy towel, and a small glass mirror. The bowl was filled with warm water and some unusual looking pink flowers. Freida informed Sarah that this was called soapwort, and that it gave the water a lather useful for cleansing. Sure enough when Sarah tried washing her hands, and pressing the flower as advised, it lathered just like soap and left her hands smelling of fresh clover.

After the meal of green beans and bread, Sarah cried herself to sleep, and dreamt about the rain, the lightning, the bell sounds, the mist, and the Earth that fell from the sky's bright white light, and ten years in a strange prison cell eating snails.

Then all of a sudden, she awoke with a start, and a scream that woke of the rest of the canopied farm house. Her whole body was tingling like in a kind of spasm, and she remembered once more the same sensation after witnessing the falling planet. For about a minute she felt that everything was vibrating once more.

It took about five minutes, before Freida came up to the hammock, with some nice words. Freida spent a long time offering Sarah reassurances that sick people in Celtishia weren't sent to prison at all, as Adah, (Freida's mother), had threatened. Apparently, it was a tendency of the older generation to use scolding threats, and talk nonsense. Sarah thought that this had a been a mistake by the parents, and now suspected that they were behind an abduction of her, helped by the mysterious people downstairs.

Freida agreed to stay, and keep Sarah company, and so over time they started to bond. Freida also made her a hot chocolate, which Sarah thought was nice and kind. And so they eventually began to talk about the dream, and the park, and the bus journey.

When the Light and the falling Earth was mentioned, Freida said nothing, and for a short time a silence filled the air. However, the conversation resumed until she went back to sleep, and dreamt the whole thing all over again, with one difference. In this extra part of the dream, she was at home with her dad, once more. They were watching television, and arguing over a science fiction episode.

The following morning, she awoke at seven am. Sarah knew something was odd, as soon as she looked at the sky, and realized that the evening twilight was still there. The green mist providing a supernatural presence.

This time, she had a developed a totally different idea about what may have happened to her, because of the two near-identical dreams. The extra detail in the last dream had set her thoughts ablaze, and she remembered the argument in question.

The episode she had been almost forced to watch, as there was only one television in the house, was about an alternative dimension. In this episode, a group of people met themselves in another dimension, where things were similar, yet different. People had different outlooks on life, caused by their different circumstances. They had somehow managed to return to their dimension, but the details were hazy to her.

The argument was all about whether such a thing, as an alternative world, was even possible.

Sarah had argued alone, against the rest of her family. They clearly believed in them, yet Sarah was advocating they were scientifically impossible. "Science fiction is called science fiction for a reason," she had argued. "Because it is fiction."

But that was then, and this was now. And now the question was burning in her mind.

"Have I somehow transferred to another dimension like in that sci-fi episode, I saw before on television? Like I dreamt about last night?"

Her skepticism meant that this was very unlikely, and yet things were definitely different. (Green people, twilight, security torcs were all visible to her, even as she thought). So, it occurred to her as she lay in the hammock, she would need to think it over some more, and gather some kind of proof. The whole theory sounded like madness to her, and would seem worse to the investigator, that they called 'the Counsellor". And yet she realized, if there were counsellors, it would make these people real, and natural. And if they were natural, with their green skin, they were also normal. And this meant that she, (Miss Salter), was the odd one out, and somehow, she didn't belong in this world.

She was still in the process of working all this out, when Freida came by at 7.30am smiling. The purpose of her visit was to announce breakfast down below in the clearing.

"I will be cooking eggs to go on some bread you like, and we have enough fruit to make a smoothie," she reassuringly announced.

"Eggs", though Sarah, at last something that isn't green. But she was in for a shock. The eggs were green duck eggs with brown speckles. They were bigger than the eggs she was used to. When they were cracked open, they were indeed white, but the yolks were green. But they tasted like eggs, and they fried like eggs on the barbeque. So she reasoned that, "they must be eggs."

Freida picked up on her uncertainty, and pointed out that the duck they came from was now 'free ranging in the clearing.' Sarah looked across and could see the duck in question. It was the size of an enormous turkey, but Sarah thought that it looked cute with its black feathers.

Freida made the smoothie fresh from the farm's own apples, locally grown kiwi, pears and mint, and claimed it was good for a balanced diet. It tasted nice and refreshing, and she said "Thank you," as best she could. But deep inside Sarah was thinking that she would give anything for a bacon sandwich, and tomato sauce instead of all these weird green things.

When she didn't eat much, the others looked worried for her. She was able to brush this off, however, by saying she was "obviously a littles anxious about meeting 'the counsellor'".

Freida and Sarah, sat and ate for about half an hour, and others slowly came over to join them. At first they seemed uncertain, (even scared of her), but in time they opened up and chatted away about eggs, ducks, and life in the canopy of the sub-holding.

Adah and Benjamin (Freida's parents) seemed less scared and more relaxed than the night before, and Adah even apologized for how they originally spoke to her. They then escorted her around the six acre site that they owned. She even seemed to be enjoy pointing out the canal on one side, and the monorail, near to the canopy. It was the most bizarre place she had ever seen in her life. Sarah noticed immediately that there was a combination of modern and old working alongside each other, whilst somehow attempting to respect the environment.

Sarah eventually excused herself for a second time to visit the toilet. This time she was not given an escort to watch her every move.

It was whilst she was sitting on the toilet that she got her next shock, because the speaker system in the house, suddenly screamed a warning to the house.

"Intruder alert! Unknown man in the trees. Cameras and drones marking his location."

The voice sounded slightly tinny, but was followed by what sounded like a large series of whirring noises. Then there was gunfire in the distance, and Sarah heard a bullet ricochet nearby in the house.

The guards were heard to run, and Freida screamed for them to "return fire", and to "chase him down."

Sarah peered through the toilet window, and could see five armed guards jump onto a series of passenger transport machines, and give chase over rough terrain. They branched out, and then circled back in, dodging between trees as they sped forward. Meanwhile a series of light beams were shining down from fast moving drones, indicating the location of the intruder.

The ground based machines were armed with built in laser guns, and these were used to open fire on this mysterious enemy. Branches ripped from trees, and earth exploded upwards in the air. The effect was instant and gave an immediate advantage over their opponent.

After several exchanges of gunfire, most of which seemed to be some kind of laser, she heard a voice come through a radio say, "the enemy assassin has been captured."

From a distance, she heard Freida's command.

"Put him in the cellar. I will talk to him later. Right now, my priorities are elsewhere.!" And by that it was clear, she was talking about Sarah up above her in the tree house.

After a few minutes, a concerned Freida yelled through the door, "are you ok in there Sarah?"

"Yes, but what is going on?"

"Just a security lapse, we are strengthening our security as we speak. Try not to worry."

Sarah could not believe her ears. "Try not to worry?"

"Yes, and you can come out now, all is secure."

Freida was waiting for her outside, looking as worried as she sounded. "I am so glad you are OK", she said. "It seems that someone knows we are here, and is not pleased."

"Well that's obvious! But who?"

"I am not the best person to explain, but the Counsellor will be here soon. Now I know you are ok, I am going to question the assassin, to see what I can find out."

For the next hour, Sarah lay down on the bed and tried to sleep. But down below her was a commotion that stopped her.

Freida was sitting at a desk, when the guards dragged in the accused prisoner. He was a thin man, with an orange and green uniform. On his face he had a scar that stretched from his ear to his mouth. He was wearing handcuffs, which tied his arms behind his back. He was made to kneel on the floor by the guards at the foot of

Freida's desk.

"Sit down," she said to him, and pointed to a chair.

The man got up, and limped to the chair, saying nothing. He sat down and stared at her in a menacing way.

"So who are you then?" She asked.

"My name is Scarabo, I am a soldier of Egypt, and my number is 401c-10-50D."

"Where are you from Scarabo?"

"Cairo."

"Why are you here?'

"No comment."

"I know anyway. You left your orders in your jacket. Which was very dumb by the way."

"So why ask?" Scarabo demanded.

"Just giving you a chance to come clean?"

"No comment."

Freida picked up a piece of paper on her desk. Saying nothing, she read the words, and looked at him.

"Well. The paper has just seven words on it. "Freida Sophie-Smith." Written underneath is a figure, "thirty thousand Egyptian dollars." What do you have to say about that?"

"No comment."

"Really? Because I know this is how assassins' notes are written. But I am disappointed, I seem to be worth so little. The last guy got twice that."

"What? That cheating bitch. And she said, you

'wouldn't be expecting me'."

"Oh! Princess Phillipa again. Not really surprising though. Always does things on the cheap, and in a shoddy way. Just will not pay for quality. Hence, why you are here."

The assassin jumped from his seat, and attempted to kick out at Freida. Freida however had seen this coming, and easily avoided the blow. The assassin was now laying on the ground, wriggling, and trying to get to his feet, His hands securely fastened.

Freida continued to talk in a casual way. "I will hand you over to the Regional Mayor for trial. The charge will probably be attempted assassination, and espionage. The evidence will be examined fairly. You will have legal counsel, and a fair trial. But expect to spend a long time in jail."

"Damn you," shouted Scarabo, now on his feet. "She will send someone else."

"Probably, but not you. And not today!" And she turned to the guards. "Take him away," she commanded. And Scarabo was dragged, kicking and screaming abuse at Freida, into a van, and away to the Mayor.

And Sarah just watched it all speechless. Freida had avoided being assassinated, for at least the second time. And she didn't even seem all that bothered. It was like this was all usual to her.

It was about 9.30am, by the time the counsellor arrived. He was dressed in a black suit with no collar, over his green skin. He wore brown leather ankle boots on his feet, and a pendant attached to a green cord around his neck. It was made from finely polished silver, with Celtic etchings all around it, and a glass stone in the middle.

It was obvious that he was considered an important man, by the way he walked and the tendency of all the people to congregate around him as soon as he arrived. The Counsellor, however, did not seem that worried about meeting the people of the farm or the security, but went straight upstairs to where Sarah was sitting on the bed.

As soon as he viewed her, it was obvious that his main priority was to confirm the reports about the color of her skin. After a few awkward moments of staring at Sarah, he spoke in a forced but soft way.

"Hello Sarah, I have been requested to come and look at y." He stopped and paused. "I apologize," he continued, "what I meant to say was, my name is Daniel, and I am here to meet you and assess your situation. But first, I am going to have a chat with the people you have already met. I need to get up to speed so to speak." And with this made his exit, and went to chat with Freida, Benjamin and Adah.

It was Freida who returned with an update about half an hour later, carrying a pile of mainly black and green patterned clothes, consisting of underwear, jeans, a top, and some brown ankle boots. They were neatly placed in a basket.

"Hello Sarah, I hope you understand that this is serious. You are either a spy, or a very lost sick person needing our help", she said. "The good news is he understands that you are probably not a spy for The Egyptian Empire. However, he needs to be sure, and requires you to change into these. You are also required to hand over all your possessions for inspection, by a female operative. You are allowed to be present if you wish."

"I would", said Sarah. "But why does he think that I am ill?"

"Isn't it obvious," Freida replied, "everyone else here is green. You are not, and that is very odd. It suggests an alternative diet of some kind."

"Is everyone here green skinned then?"

"Of course, even our enemies, in the Egyptian Empire. But, no spy would make themselves stand out like you do. And we now know that it was another Egyptian spy that has already been caught and questioned."

"So naturally, we want to find out about you, how you got here, and what, if anything, is wrong with you," replied Freida. "In addition, the Counsellor has used his pendant to empathically assess your mind to see if you are lying or hostile. Latest technology, only a few have. He has found you to be friendly and truthful."

Freida politely pointed to the clothes, and said,

"now please change your clothes, and put yours in the bucket. Its just procedure and nothing to worry about. I will leave you to change in peace. Yell when you are done." And with that, Freida left the room. And Sarah changed into the alternative clothes as she was asked.

The inspection went fairly smoothly, although Sarah had trouble explaining what certain things were for. The thing she expected to have problems explaining, seemed normal to them.

"Oh, how sweet," said Freida, "you have a Shofar. A goat's horn; I believe?"

There was, however, particular confusion over things like hair dye, tampons, and spare socks. These objects were clearly never heard of by anyone else who was present, but the thing that caused the biggest mystery was a paper magazine.

"Why don't you just download it to a tablet" asked the Counsellor.

"But I like the paper," Sarah responded.

"But what a waste", he parried. "You see paper is reserved here for only the most important things. It is second in importance, to what is set in stone. That is why most of what you need is found here on our hand tablets. They are lighter to carry, and fit in your pockets, although I wear mine around my neck."

He held up his pendant which seemed to have a glass stone in it, as if hinting she should reconsider. When the meeting was over, Sarah decided to ask Freida, where she might get a computer.

"May I borrow one of those computer things?" she asked her. She was taking the hint, and was awed by its ability to partially read minds.

"Of course, it might help you to fill in the details, or remember something. Just tap the glass of the screen and ask for "My instructor" And by the way, you may consider yourself no longer under house arrest, but for your own safety's sake, I advise you to stay in this area with people who know you until I can straighten everything up."

She was given a hand held device called a "Tech-Tab". Sarah was soon to learn that it was far more capable that anything she was used to, or imagined. The "Tech-Tab" was flat, but round in shape, and fitted in her outstretched hand. What she had thought was a pendant, was actually a glass screen surrounded by a shiny yellow frame.

"Its only low spec, I'm afraid," said Freida. "It is limited to three dimensional, virtual reality, holo-projected global internet access, and includes living nanite cells to speed up data transfer. And it can only manage to store two hundred petabytes of data. All basic child's play really".

Freida stopped for a few moments, because she suspected that Sarah was dubious about the last part, but continued anyway. "Of course, the manufacture of this particular model was stopped about ten years ago, as they have a tendency to learn, and use initiative for themselves.

This is not considered a good thing."

Oh? Asked Sarah, wondering why machines using their initiative was a bad thing?

Freida wasn't entirely sure either, but answered as best as she could. "Apparently, it gets us one step closer to something called the singularity? When machines don't need us, or something."

They both stopped to reflect on that one.

"Anyway, I could lend you mine from tomorrow, if you prefer," Freida continued. "Once I get clearance to do so. t is secure to my finger print only at present, and I would need permission to include another user".

"That's more complicated and advanced than I am used to", admitted Sarah, who was feeling overwhelmed by the scientific terminology.

"Well don't worry", she replied, and handed her some headphones. "Just tap the screen. And if you get stuck, place on these headphones and it will read you mind, remove them when you are done. All perfectly safe and tested technology."

Once again, Freida left the room, leaving Sarah alone to think things through.

"If I am in an alternative dimension," she thought, "their technology is clearly more advanced than ours." And with that placed on the headphones, and a holographic set of glasses appeared in front of her. Next, she tapped the screen, and said "the instructor please".

4. KNOWLEDGE

"Hello, how can I help you?" came the reply, and a holographic man with green skin, appeared in front of her. He had a young looking face, and tidy black hair. On first impressions: he reminded Sarah of the typical business executive, that you would find in a bank, or accountancy office. He even had the suit and tie, that matched.

Sarah paused in shock, because she hadn't expected this.

"Hello", said Sarah, "who are you".

"I am the 'Virtual Information Nanite Computerised Empathic Neural-interface Technology" System, or VINCENT if you prefer," said the holographic green man. The words had appeared in black above his head, the letters clearly visible.

"I am visible to anyone in your proximity, and anybody present can interact with me," Vincent Continued. "However, I remain here for you, and will go at your command.".

"Well Vincent, I am confused...."

"Please explain?" asked Vincent, with a sympathetic tone, "and I will do my best to try and help you".

"Are you aware of my situation?"

"Yes. You were under house arrest, and now you are not," Vincent replied.

"And is this conversation personal and confidential?"

"Of course," he assured her, "as long as nobody is listening in. I never repeat anything myself."

She thought for a while about what to ask. Finally, she took the plunge.

"Well I think I have travelled here from another dimension which of course seems mad, so I need a brief description of this country and the planet we are on. A few minutes only".

"My pleasure", replied Vincent, and a green planet appeared the size of a giant beanbag, and it looked exactly like the one in the dream and the park. Vincent pointed at a small island with looked similar to the British Isles she knew, only there was a river where the Irish Sea should have been, which started in the place Sarah knew as the Isle of Mann.

"The planet you are on is called 'Twilight-Earth'. It is the third planet of nine rotating around its sun, which we call "The Bright Star". Bright Star's planets are called Mercury, Venus, Green Earth, Red Mars, Jupiter, Saturn, Uranus, Neptune and Plutos."

Vincent now pointed at both Mars and Earth. "The planets of Green Earth and Red Mars are very close to each other. Identical in distance to the sun, they both are in the range capable of producing life. They both reside in perpetual twilight. Mars however has a red mist."

The images returned to a solar system rotating the Sun, and then zoomed in on the Green Earth.

"Yes, in the case of the Green Earth, it is partially shielded from Bright Star, by Venus. And it is at an annoying angle meaning that planet doesn't benefit from the full rays."

Sarah watched the holographic movement of the planets in their solar system. After a polite pause, Vincent continued his initial speech.

"Well as I was saying, the planet is called Green Earth. It has a diameter of 12710 kilometers. It takes the shape of a near-perfect circle. The Green Earth has three moons, nearly equally apart. These moons, (called Lunos, Brexos, and Zaitos,) reflect Twilight to the sides of the moon not facing the sun. Where the Green Earth spins we benefit from the perpetual twilight."

"Furthermore, as you will notice there are two layers of cloud. The first is the mist level, which you are in now. This is trapped water vapor, which helps the oxygenization of the planet, and guarantees an average human life expectancy of one hundred and twenty years. The green is a re-fraction of the light and greenery surrounding the planet, and the high degree of chloroplast content"

"The second layer is the stratosphere that breaks up the light from the Bright Star, and has the occasional green cloud."

Sarah waited a few seconds before asking her next question.

"Does everybody on this planet have green skin?"

"Yes, it is down to the distance from the sun and the angle of Green-Earth. Humanity as we know it, adapted within its species at an early stage, by eating mostly green food. This influenced their skin pigmentation. The melamine that caused the green skin, is now believed to be firmly planted in the DNA of Humanity."

"The League of Nations has copies of the D.N.A. of every major group on the planet. They can verify that there is ultimately only one human race."

"The League of Nations?"

"The League of Nations (or L O N,) is a talking shop mostly. Originally it was set up to provide a basis of agreement between the many countries that exist. When a situation is recognized by the majority of the League of Nations, its status is generally not opposed by others. They also make international trade agreements official. It helps keep the peace when the majority are able to put pressure on individual rogue states."

The Green Earth stopped spinning, so that Vincent could continue.

"Right now you are here, in island country called 'Celtishia'. It is a self-sufficient green land, named after the Celts, who were the indigenous people. It is a country with full League of Nations status, although it is being challenged via political means at present, in that same chamber. The people of this land, however, have remained here for millennia defeating all rivals, including the Romans, Vikings, and more recently The Germanicas Empire."

"The Germanicas?" questioned Sarah. But then she paused. "No, that probably doesn't matter." She had decided not to ask.

There was another pause before Vincent continued.

"The population also includes the descendants of people who have fled other countries. The biggest influx included a large tribe of Hebrews, like the Sophie-Smiths, who descend from people who arrived nearly two thousand years ago, when the Romans flattened Jerusalem to the ground. They have managed to keep their racial distinctiveness by only marrying other Jews. This natural tendency or trait, is so strong that less than one percent of the Jews will marry outside their culture. Over the millennia, many groups and tribes have sought sanctuary here, as they have fled from other lands."

"The official population of Celtishia is about eighty million, but unofficially Freida told me there are many more. She has access to these kind of things, and has previously advised me to grant you sufficient clearance to know this as well"

"Anyway, the country is run by a Grand Queen, who delegates responsibilities to the Regional Mayor Regions, all of whom have elected governments. This region is called Dumnonii, and the Regional Mayor reports directly to Boudicca herself.'

Sarah paused stunned, and knew instantly, that in her dimension Boudicca had failed to lead a revolt. And then vanished without trace, never to be heard from again. She realized that this was a key moment where she could see a divergence in the dimensions.

"So how does this country function?" asked Sarah, ignoring the blatant difference between the Green Dimension and her own.

"Well... The legal system is based on ten basic absolutes, and all other legal decisions are expected to comply to them. If you want a copy, all you need to do is ask for a cartouche. In addition, there is much respect for a book called "The Book of Comparisons", which features a series of old sayings that apply to everyday life. These are believed to encourage sensible life choices, and therefore, are free to anybody who wants them."

Vincent projected an image of both a cartouche and "The Book of Comparisons" to Sarah's holographic glasses for her to see. After a pause for her to take in the details, he continued.

"The main language of Celtishia is "Celtic", which you seem to speak as well. However, there is a second spoken language called Rabbinic".

But over time, however, the Celtic language, became the dominant tongue".

"Indeed, even now, the vast majority of people live in peace, and have contributed to the defense, science and agriculture of Celtishia. In days gone by, the country imported and genetically modified seeds. Therefore; it has leant to produce a variety of crops, like chili, cocoa, rape seed for oil, and various beans. By working both above and below ground, they get a high yield every year.

"Below ground?" asked a puzzled Sarah.

Vincent projected another holographic image to the glasses. "Of course: only about eleven percent of the population live above ground in the trees. The remaining eighty-nine percent, live in large underground caverns."

"The tunnels of Celtishia are some of the most fascinating in the world. They are found all under Celtishia, from Lands' End, to John O Groats. They are often interconnected, and sometimes go on for miles. In the most densely populated areas, they may go down for many levels."

"But why don't the tunnels collapse? This would be unsafe surely? And how far down below ground could you go anyway?"

"Well Sarah, they are well designed and mapped. What is more, the deepest we have gone below the earth is only twelve miles, which is merely scratching the surface. They have also developed a means of strengthening the tunnels, using a sort of greenish glue, that seals gaps and adds considerable strength to the structures. The utilize advanced construction technology to strengthen also ensures maximum stability above ground, and keep the trees growing".

"Many have living quarters, and others have recreational facilities. But mostly, they are used for growing a whole series of genetically modified underground crops, which utilize vertical farming techniques. The main development was the use of aeroponics, that uses mist and no soil to grow crops, without pesticides. Consequently, the country usually has food and medicines to spare and export. Some we just give away. Every year, we used to spend a little of our export money to import a few resources only, but things now are different."

"You see, we have designed the tunnels to provide safety and homes, but elsewhere in the world they are viewed as "Catacombs," or escape tunnels. They are not portrayed as architectural achievements, but as the means to a sub-standard quality of life. They suggest the tunnels are full of disease."

"Some of our biggest critics, including Egypt, tend to refer to us as "the cave people". They use our lifestyle choices to suggest that Celtishia is full of primitive people, who lack the desire for change. Freida used to tell me that 'big empires view what is different as dangerous."

"And Egypt regards Celtishia as a threat?" asked Sarah.

"Yes. And they run a continuous campaign, using viral media to discredit the nation. We have even been called 'a nation of rats with little civilization.' Of course, they make their assumptions only by what they see at the surface level."

It appeared that Vincent wanted to say more, but instead he paused for a while. His tone changed to a something more apologetic. "Sarah, I am sorry to interrupt your learning, and leave you, but it would appear that there are some official people here to see you. If you need any further help, hit the top left hand of the screen again."

And with that the Vincent and the holographic images vanished. Instantly she was thrown out of the fantasy-virtual reality world she had been in. Sarah realized that she was back on her hammock, where she started, and had been all along.

5. NEXT STEPS

Minutes later, Freida was sitting beside Sarah, with an arm apologetically around her shoulder. The Counsellor known as Daniel, was standing next to the door looking worried, by a vast array of armed security intent on some kind of official business. Sarah had the feeling that she was probably on official business.

After a long pause, it was the Counsellor who spoke first. "It would appear that there is great concern for your safety, and welfare. The earlier disturbance would suggest that enemies of the state are already aware of your arrival. So these men are here to escort you to a secure Centre later today. You are not under arrest, and are free to refuse, but I would advise against it! You do of course, remember the exchange of gunfire?"

Sarah looked at Freida, Freida nodded.

"I can come with you if you like?" she kindly offered.

"Ok," Sarah reluctantly agreed, "but just one thing, can I have a cartouche, and a copy of the Book of Comparisons before I go? I would like to learn more, and get up to speed with what is going on. I would also like to keep Vincent". She felt that she must explain. "That personal computer you lent me that is."

The counsellor smiled with approval. "That should not be a problem, I will see them issued along with seven sets of clean clothes, starter currency and a backpack," replied the Counsellor. "This will be a standard refugee pack."

"But I am not a refugee?" Sarah tried to argue.

"I know; but you have arrived with only the clothes on your back, and what is in your pack."

"By the way," he continued, "our 'Queen Boudicca' has heard about all about you and wants to meet you. It would be a great privilege for you to attend, and probably very informative. Again, this is something you must choose to do, and will explain a lot I suspect".

"I will leave you to rest now", he finished, and then left the room. Sarah had noticed that Freida had shown some repressed excitement, at her meeting Queen Boudicca; and that the counsellor looked jealous.

This left Sarah and Freida alone to talk. And so for the first time, Sarah opened up to Freida about the world she knew, and how it was different. They also talked about her theory of coming from another dimension, thinking Freida would deem her mad. But it wasn't so.

"This would kind of make sense," she replied, in a matter of fact way. "I mean I can think of no other explanation as to why you are not green.

Besides your clothes are odd, and the dreams you had?"

"Is she for real?" thought a perplexed and baffled Sarah. Eventually she spoke, "I just wish that I could make more sense of this."

"I think meeting Boudicca will explain some of it to you. She probably knows things we do not. I mean she has top advisors, and a whole library of classified documents at her disposal. Of course, she also has other problems now."

"Should I be worried," asked Sarah.

"Not at all, she is known to be kind and gracious, a fair and discreet ruler. The country is slowly healing under her rule, after the previous ruler." Freida paused, wondering if she had said too much. "And she is also a personal friend of mine. We speak regularly."

The items arrived within about two hours. The clothes were mostly black with green edges, and made from a kind of cotton. The boots that arrived were designed to cover the ankles, and were a dark shade of brown, with matching laces. When Sarah looked around her she could see within the mist, that most of the grass and bushes were long, and the boots were obviously meant for protection.

The cartouche was about six inches long, two inches wide, and an inch deep. It resembled a small tube, and was made of silver and had writing in an ancient language. Sarah looked baffled.

"The point," Freida explained laughing, "is that

you learn the rules, in both languages, off by heart and try and apply them."

"Will you help me?"

"I would be honoured," said Freida, and with that she passed Sarah the book.

The book was the only paper book in Celtishia that Sarah had seen since swapping over to this dimension. It was made from fine white paper, with a definite green tinge. It was bound in a high quality green leather skin, and on it was emblazed in gold lettering, its title "The Book of Comparisons". Its sub-title was "Wisdom for life".

An introductory commentary explained that while this was not a seriously religious book, it contained advice for living the day to day aspects of life. It was set out in a series of matching expressions. It talked about marriage, sex, money and even getting along with others.

The commentary also indicated that, "Its advice will seem timely to the reader. Many have used this book to discover "The Whisper" in the details of their lives".

The first time Sarah opened the book at random, and read aloud some random words. "It is better to get wisdom that gold, to get insight rather than silver."

She paused, and said, "I don't get it," to Freida. "Why would wisdom be better than gold?"

Freida replied, slowly and patiently. "Well I guess that wisdom is how you apply things. You could use gold to buy a degree for example, but what is the use if you have no skills to match your qualification. You may even keep a better role, and get more money, but the time will always come, when you are found wanting, or to be just plain useless."

Sarah must have looked a bit unconvinced, because Freida continued. "For example; The Egyptians love gold, and buy qualifications, and do a lot of pretending. And it does fool some people. But in recent years their businesses have got into trouble, due to bad management and designs. They are losing customers, and are having to outsource or bring in expertise from other places to correct things."

"Not only that it is also affecting their military. The mass denial has affected the reliability of weapons and machinery. Although nobody truly knows how much so, they joke about the army with only a few weapons that work."

Sarah was a bit shocked for she had not expected Freida, (of all people,) to have this level of insight. Neither had she ever imagined that religious books could be applied to everyday situations. "Okay," she said in surprise, "I can see that this book will take some getting used to, maybe I'll read some more later."

As Freida left Sarah alone to her thoughts, that is exactly what she did. And there was one set of verses that stood out above all others. Although written hundreds of years previously for an unknown King Lemuel, they seemed a challenge for her in this alternative twilight world. So much so that, whenever she tried reading something else, these words just would not leave her mind.

The verse in question simply said, "Speak up and defend the rights of the poor, vulnerable, destitute and needy." It was all she could think about. It was like a voice in her head just kept repeating it over and over. And the words were like commands, that formed into questions.

"What poor and needy?" she wondered. "And why can't they speak for themselves. What is going on here? What rights are they being denied?"

"Is this," she wondered, "the reason why I am here? And if so, could I have done this back in my version of reality? Why here, and why now? And can I get back to my world. And do the rules apply there too"

"I guess" she reasoned to herself, "that why I am here is the first riddle I must resolve. And I wonder if meeting Queen Boudicca will have any answers to all this?"

Sarah didn't have long to ponder this great question, because within minutes the armed guards arrived to take her on the next step of the journey.

6. THE FLIGHT

A fter making their way to a nearby clearing, Sarah was taken to a helicopter pad, where she could see a big green and white striped helicopter, with a six pointed star on its tail. Freida explained that this was because it was a military helicopter, that doubled up for hospital trips.

She could also see, (what at first glance was a cave with a door), but soon realized it was a doorway to some catacombs below. It clearly also served as a control base for the helipad.

There were many guards there by the helicopter pad, all armed and clearly alert in case of trouble. The first guard motioned Sarah's party towards the huge flying machine. As they approached, another guard opened the door, and politely beckoned her to get quickly inside.

Once inside, Sarah saw that there were twelve seats in the passenger section. Four rows by three. Next to that was an enclosed section for transporting injured people. Sarah tried to take a window seat, but was politely urged to one of the centre seats, by the military steward. Freida first showed Sarah how to fasten her seatbelt, and then proceeded to fasten herself in and make herself comfortable.

The plane soon filled up with officials and guards. Then the pilot spoke through a speaker system to everyone aboard.

"Good afternoon all. And a special good morning shout out to our guest Sarah Salter. Sarah, my name is John Steere, and I am here to fly you, and your escorts to the Celtishian Secure Transport Bay. I am instructed to remind you that you are not under arrest. You are free to request us to you down at any time if you so wish."

Sarah wasn't so sure about this. After all it was a military air craft, being flown by a military man. It was being flown to a major secure location, and to the current location of the head of the realm. Sure, the helicopter was also used for emergency service work, but that didn't change its military ownership. And it was this that made her uneasy, about the idea that they could put down on her request.

Sarah must have, somehow, indicated this as much, in the way she presented herself. Because the Captain once again spoke into the speaker system.

"I re-iterate that the only purpose of this flight is of course to see you safely away from those who wish to harm you," he continued. "I am of course trained in all forms of evasive maneuvers. The chopper we are flying is a 'Celtishia x4", and is among the fastest in the known world reaching speeds over six hundred kilometers per hour if needed"

"The weather today is reasonable. There is no expected rain, and our lovely green mist is hanging low. We will be flying below the clouds, and cruising at 100 kilometers per hour. In addition, we will be heading North East to our destination, in what is likely to be a smooth journey."

"In the air we will be joined by two other security choppers, who will escort us further, and provide interception if necessary. There will also be a series of midi-drones, that will shadow our heat signatures, and provide additional air support if needed. Do not be alarmed their presence is precautionary, and proof of our concern for you Sarah. So get ready, and we will be off."

After a few seconds, the engine started, and the two big green blades started to whirr into action. Starting to rotate slowly, they got faster and faster, until they merged into a giant circle, and then the helicopter started to lift from the ground.

Higher and higher it rose into the air, and as the trees got lower and lower beneath her, they also got smaller and smaller. Eventually, the trees and disguised houses below became almost invisible to the eye, as they were covered in the green mist. Above her, Sarah could make out a layer of clouds. Some of these were also a pale green.

For the next hour the helicopter flew steadily at the same altitude. As the ground beneath occasionally rose, Sarah could make out some trees. And the drones, continued to provide an escort at a respectable distance.

At another point of the journey, the convoy flew over a major city, called "Ringham," where trees intermingled with vast circular skyscrapers. Freida lent Sarah some binoculars. As she looked on in amazement, Sarah kept her thoughts to herself, but realized that she had never seen such an amazing combination of urban and rural design in the same place. The buildings were cylindrical and made mostly of red brick, but all had roof gardens with trees on top, to match their surroundings. They were linked by rope and steel bridges, making giant canopies in the sky. As Sarah looked further through the telescopic lenses, she could make out people enjoying life and the views within the green mist.

She was brought back to reality by John Steere - the pilot. He spoke through the loud speaker with great concern. "Fasten your seat belts, please, for it seems that we have company."

The helicopter on the right was abandoning its original position flying alongside, and was now heading behind and to the right. There was another clearly visible yellow helicopter in the sky, now being intercepted by their chaperones. The drones now sprung to life, and flew off to intercept their target opponent. It all happened very quickly, but Sarah could see that they had formed a pincer movement, and honed in on their prey.

There was a short exchange of gunfire, and an explosion in the sky. The yellow enemy was now a load of loose metal falling down onto Ringham.

Sarah looked on in shock. Even though she had seen similar scenes in the movies; this was the first time that she had seen it happen in real life. And it wasn't so exciting. It was terrifying. And for a moment, Sarah thought about the loss of life for the crew of the enemy yellow chopper.

"I know," said Freida, with a note of concern. "I hate seeing things like that too. But honestly, it was them or us."

"I understand", she replied, "I just hope that the falling debris doesn't kill anybody else as well."

"Hopefully people will have taken cover when the fighting started. There would have been alarms as well."

"That's ok then," said Sarah, using her best sarcasm. And she wondered how many times Freida had witnessed such things? She seemed to be taking them in her stride, as an everyday thing.

Meanwhile, the drones, circled back around, and returned to their original position, encircling the helicopter. This made the people on the helicopter feel temporarily safer, but nobody dared to ask the question that was on their minds.

In the end, it was Freida who broke the silence, by speaking into the speaker system to the pilot.

"What is going on? Why was there an Egyptian chopper in Celtishian airspace?"

"They have been testing our airspace for weeks now," the Pilot explained. "It was feared that one may got through the radar defenses a week ago, and hid somewhere for a period. It seems that the armed escort was a good precaution."

"But all is ok now, so sit back and relax for the rest of your journey. But keep your seatbelts on as we are going to increase our speed drastically."

Sarah looked at Freida in disbelief, she knew that not all was ok. But she also knew she was in the best possible hands. Sure enough five minutes later they were joined by two other flying escorts. Only this time they were clearly planes.

"Celtishian Air Fighters," explained Freida. "Very good at interception. They have extreme air attack capabilities, and can take off vertically using their own thruster jets."

At the back of the helicopter, Sarah could hear a female passenger groan. It was horrific, loud and resembled a sound of shock and despair, like the person making the noise had lost all hope.

"She cries out of madness and despair" said a strange voice in her head, "and yet she does not even know who too. I hear this all the time, it is getting more common now, and they fear that nobody listens or understands their plight".

The voice was right, for over the next two hours of the journey, Sarah heard many such groans. Some were female and some were from men, and yet they all had the same things in common. Despair, hopelessness, rejection, and confusion. And Sarah was worrying about these groans, and the voice that kept speaking to her.

And just when it seemed things could get no worse, a news reel flashed up on the ceiling from a projector on the wall. A good looking green faced female sat speaking from behind a desk.

"Good Morning," said the presenter, through surround sound speakers. We interrupt what you are now doing to inform you that the stand-off between Egypt and Celtishia has come to an unfortunate end. Jules is near the scene to tell us more."

A new face appeared. This time it was a man in a sharp suit, overlooking some kind of marina. Only Sarah could tell she was looking at hundreds, even thousands of floating fibreglass domes, built on top of small pontoons. They were moored together to form some kind of giant floating city, which was protected by an enormous breakwater.

At first it seemed like a picturesque view. But this effect did not last long. In the background some military gunfire could clearly be heard.

"Thank you Delores," said the man. "Yes, just an hour ago, the Egyptian Empire raided 'Sea Town'. It appears they were after food, and slaves. This is a well-known swamp city, that specializes in the production of eels and edible seaweed. This food is much sought after overseas, and a major export for our economy."

"It is a quiet area with hard industrious people. Being a hard area to farm, the people here have adapted to build houses out to sea, to advance the fishing and seaweed industries. However, the Egyptians have long been claiming that this impinges on their new water territory. Celtishia however, claim they have owned these waters for millennia, by reason of the fact they surround our island."

Images appeared showing the first attack, and people running scared and confused.

The first raid started one hour ago with shelling of the homes of innocent people. As people fled the local militia started to mobilize. The officials put out distress calls to the government. However; it seems that the area, and the government has been wrong footed, and help is not expected in a hurry."

"The fighting continues, yet sources here reveal that the resistance is not going well, and the advantage is clearly with the raiding army". No sooner had he said those words, a Celtishian helicopter could clearly be seen falling from the sky. The people on the carriage covered their eyes in fright, and groaned in despair at the holographic images they were seeing.

Over the next few hours the broadcasts continued, until finally it was clear that Egypt had performed a successful raid and had taken over one hundred female slaves, plus their children before retreating. The news broadcasts continued to put a brave spin on the event.

"While this is an incursion into our territories for the first time in over 1500 years," they said, 'it is not an invasion as the Egyptians have left. Further attacks are feared in other areas. There is a call for all coastal communities to be aware, and permission is given to defend yourselves against overseas aggression."

"In the meantime, the Celtishian Forces are now being mobilized. All service personnel are ordered to report to duty officers, and return to their barracks. And anyone needing work may find it in our drone factories."

"If you feel loyal and ready to fight for your county, we are asking for volunteers to head to Cardiff for now, where emergency military training is being offered"

The holographic images were soon replaced with a message.

"This broadcast encourages everyone to take a minute's silence in honor of those taken. Meanwhile the government will request the return of the captives through diplomatic channels."

"Our Queen Boudicca urges you to keep calm, and be brave. The government also assures us that anti-raid defenses are being developed and implemented."

"Keep calm and be brave, she means arm yourselves," said a passenger.

"More like they are planning more appeasement measures" said one of the other women on the

Helicopter, "And Egypt will demand a lot".

Sarah thought back to an earlier part of the announcement.

"Slaves?" she asked.

"Yes, the Egyptians run their empire using slavery, while here we are free. In every case where Egypt has conquered, slaves were taken as surrender payment from the defeated nation. Officially they are used as builders, but everyone here knows that they now serve their masters in Egypt in unspeakable ways."

Sarah sadly knew what she meant for she had studied 'History.' She knew that slavery always meant abuse by those in power. She had noticed that the abusers were always able to justify it, by saying that that their victims were somehow better off this way.

Clearly, the idea of more oppression, and future slavery, caused much fear on the helicopter. Outwardly Freida was trying to keep people's spirit up, with a few nice platitudes, like "not far now", and "should be there soon."

Deep inside, Sarah knew something was wrong, and the fear prevailed. And it appeared that she wasn't the only person listening to their instincts, as arguments erupted.

"We should have remained in the treaty, and this would not be happening. Blooming old people wanting to leave", screamed a younger person. "Why antagonize them. Now we will be in it, but have no say on what happens."

"But the treaty demanded no arms, so this would have been worse eventually. It is proof that Egypt can't be trusted, and then we would have been defenseless, like the Iceni before the first Boudicca" the oldest looking guard replied.

"What would you know? She wasn't like us"

"I know that their idea of more Egypt meant less Celtishia, more monetary demands plus trade and land grabs." She pointed at Sarah, "Besides look around you."

Clearly she was meant to be a reason for optimism, although at this moment, Miss Sarah Salter failed to see how she could help. She was soon brought back down to earth however, as somebody disagreed with the man.

"Now we're done for," was the reply, and it was obvious that they were looking at her pink skin, which stood out in contrast to their green. Naturally, Sarah didn't like that, and was confused by it all. However, the race row was only broken up by the pilot saying, Attention ladies and gentlemen, we are about to land at "The HUB. Prepare for landing and disembarkation".

"Oh, and Sarah," he continued, "I have just heard that Queen Boudicca herself is there to meet you in person."

The helicopter slowed down, and came to a slow descent. Eventually, it set itself down on its landing pad, and everybody disembarked, mostly continuing to look at Sarah with suspicion.

Most of the passengers went through a blue door marked arrival.

However, Sarah and Freida were ushered to another door marked "Security Only," and into a waiting area.

Once inside, they waited where they were. Until they were told to enter.

After all she had seen, Sarah looked at Freida and knew she needed some answers. So indicating to Freida, what she was going to do, Sarah took her Tech-Tab and touched the screen. Within seconds, Vincent reappeared and asked, "Hello again Sarah, And hello Freida. What can I do for you?"

"Sarah took a deep breath and asked, "please, will you tell me about The Egyptian Empire? Everybody seems to be on edge about it!"

The holographic globe of the earth appeared once more, and spun round a little, and now Vincent pointed to another green region in the south west of the Mediterranean Sea, marked Egypt. In Sarah's mind, this was in the right location, but there should also have been desert there.

"The Egyptian people are descended from the Ancient Egyptians. They are ruled by a Pharaoh. The people of Celtishia have always been suspicious of them. They claim to be pro-women, but they impose many restrictions regarding what women can do."

"The original Egypt led by Cleopatra was defeated by Rome. However, when Rome too fell to the German Tribes, (in the year 4236,) there was a general, descended the same Cleopatra, who seized the chance to rebirth his nation. They have a strong army, but their key strength is in long range raiding boats, getting in and getting out."

"The Egyptian Empire grow gradually over time expanding and taking in weaker nations. However, the problems for Celtishia began 56 years ago, when Egypt suddenly produced a health oil, that could ease pains, like arthritis. I say suddenly, because up to this point they weren't known for success in pharmaceuticals. It is believed that they gained the technology from a raid".

"Anyway, this oil enabled them to create jobs and gain a head start on competitors, including Celtishia. It also started regional medical advancement and business start-ups. They utilized their extra funds to strengthen their military, and plan invasions of further weaker nations, (like Catalonia, Spain, and Portugal). The Empire stretches now from Egypt, proceeds along the bottom of the Mediterranean, and keeping to the coast reaching nearly all the way to Calais. But of course, while they have focused on controlling the coasts, they can then influence trade inland as well."

"Like all big empires they were able to justify

their actions to their neighbors, through intimidation. In addition, whenever they invaded, they would capture key people, and get them to confess to crimes, that justified their intervention. Basically they would try and portray themselves as liberators."

 "And as the Egyptian Empire grew, so did their influence. Other smaller and less threatening Empires, including the Germans and Scandinavians, signed treaties with them and the Med Alliance was born. The main player though is clearly Egypt".

The map now showed the region of Egypt growing to cover the coast of most of Europe. The name changed to read The Med Alliance. On closer inspection, apart from Celtishia, she could see only a few Scandinavian countries, Germany, and inland France, and an enlarged Russia on the map.

Vincent continued. "However, after 30 years of growth and dominance, the Egyptian Tiger was quickly and temporarily tamed when Celtishia (with its huge pharmaceutical industry) created an alternative and better mode of oil production. This treatment was based on an oil recipe, that could be adapted for patient needs and made using home computers. This rendered the Egyptian oil market almost redundant."

"This led to loss of their customers, business collapses, and the rise of an extreme government to rule the new established Empire. The Med Alliance feared collapse."

"The new government started to impose taxation and sanctions upon Celtishia, to make us pay for their luxury. Furthermore, through a series of trade and social agreements, (like independent Court rulings,) Celtishia has been hit by disadvantageous restrictions. To try and prevent escalation, Celtishia has attempted to appease the Med Alliance."

"Problems have arisen, because many here now resent funding the luxury of others while the Med Alliance attempt to demand more, and influence the everyday life of Celtishia. Having become fed up, with the failure of appeasement, and demands for more, Celtishia chose the rejection of many treaties."

"Nobody knows exactly why they chose this course of action, but it was a fair vote. The reasons put through of course vary, but it would seem to be a rejection of what Egypt offers and stands for. A quote you often here is "we don't need their tech, as love, laughter, caring and sharing, are all free.""

"So basically, Egypt is offering nothing to attract Celtishia?"

"Perhaps? Anyway, things have escalated further in recent years, for now the Pharaoh of Egypt (who thinks himself a God), is saying that our Queen Boudicca should not be allowed to rule Celtishia. 'As a woman,' he says, 'she is devious, weak and untrustworthy, and that she is the root of all our problems."

Vincent projected another holographic set of images, though this time they were like a news reel. A man wearing a gold and blue mask resembling a snake's head, was speaking a strange language. An interpreter next to him was offering the translation.

"People of Celtishia, why do you continue to defy your Pharaoh? You listen to an inferior woman, who is naïve and immoral".

"We have been more than fair, in the terms we offer you for membership of our club of nations. We accept that your circumstances are different, and allow you to contribute for the benefit of our wisdom and rules."

"It is obvious that if you join us in service to the Med Alliance this day, you will be better off in the long run. Only we can be trusted to govern fairly for we have the superior culture, language and intelligence. With more Egypt, we will see us all move forward together".

"So, I ask how you dare to vote to rule yourselves, and not succumb to our funding expectations? Do you not know that we in Egypt and our territories, need weapons, food, alcohol, and infrastructure? But we know the only route your independence can lead to is suffering. You would be better off belonging to something bigger."

"Boudicca claims she is acting according to Celtic wishes, tradition and faith, and is speaking for Celtishia and the Whisper. Instead, your God,

'The Great Deserter," he continued laughing, "is silent, and allows a weak queen to lead you. But, out of her prejudice, she thinks she can dictate terms to a series of other states."

"Pharaoh, and Egypt's Gods are generous, and impose fair rules for all. Under us you will prosper. You will be poorer without us, as you will be unable to trade, or develop."

The newsreel stopped, and Vincent spoke first.

"Of course, just to clarify, Miss Salter, the deity of Celtishia is called "The Great Designer", but that name is rarely used. Instead people refer to his voice alone, as "the Whisper.' Out of reverence for the name."

"But back to Egypt," Vincent continued, knowing he had to keep on track "Apparently all their other territories agree, and have even suggested another ruler. By coincidence, the recommended candidate is the royal cousin of the sheik called Mustapha Sword, who is also 115th inline to the Celtishian throne due to the previous practice of Royals only marrying other Royals in Europe".

"Mustapha Sword?" interrupted Sarah laughing. "Everybody Must have a Sword, where would he like it? Up his?"

"Really, Miss Salter?" said Vincent, formally to correct her etiquette. As he did so, Sarah noticed the guards, looking on in shock. They had heard her. Clearly speaking out on this, was not the "done thing," even in front of security.

Sarah felt embarrassed, but she continued the mocking anyway. Freida grew increasingly amused as she did so.

"All hail Prince Mustapha Sword, the puppet ruler. He will keep Egypt happy by making us give them everything they want, because he will use the sword to back it up".

"Precisely, and the majority of the Celtishians have bravely rejected him outright in the referendum. Although there is a following in Glasgoer, that is now getting militant," Freida informed her.

"However, with the rejection of Mustapha," Vincent interjected, "the Egyptian Empire started saying that Celtishia has offended their honor, and committed blasphemy against The Pharaoh. The Med Alliance fell in line behind their superior ally, and has staged troops at Calais looking across, and are forming a naval blockade to try and intimidate. Their helicopters are currently blockading the skies over the Med Alliance territories. They say that as we are not part of them we cannot have their air-space either."

"What? So Celtishia is poised on the brink of war?" asked a shocked Sarah.

"Yes," interrupted Freida, "but at the moment it is more of a stand-off scenario, with neither side making the first military move. Some believe that Egypt fears the involvement of former Celtishian colonies, notably America and Ghana, and has persuaded the Sheik to take a long term approach. However: Celtishia is starting now to feel the pain, and fish stocks in particular are getting rarer. The goods for export are piling up."

"Well," said Sarah in a kind of righteous anger. "Maybe something should be done about it! This new Pharaoh sounds like a right prat, and his Egypt sounds like a nation of bullies and must be stopped."

"Unfortunately, that is looking very unlikely at present", said Vincent. "Unless you have ideas. In which case, it may be an idea to tell somebody. But for now, we must end this conversation."

And with that Vincent switched himself off, as the guards were ushering Freida and Sarah towards the next room, which was marked by a large metal door.

The guards opened the door, and they went inside.

7. THE PROPHECY

On the other side of the door, stood an elegantly dressed woman, flanked on either side by two armed guards. Sarah noticed that she had her face turned away. As the mysterious woman continued to look through the window in front of her, she finally spoke.

"Hello again Freida. I see that you have returned, as I knew you would one day. I am of course glad about this. And I see that you have the guest we were expecting."

Sarah was stunned. What did she mean expecting? Freida gave Sarah an apologetic but embarrassed look. What was Freida hiding?

Freida took a step forward and greeted the Queen with a curtsey.

"Yes my Queen," Freida replied looking both amused and delighted. "This is Sarah Salter. From the City of Plymouth. And she has already worked out, that she could have come from the Mist-Less Dimension"

"A great start then, is it not," replied the Queen,

as she turned around.

The effect was clearly intentional but effective. Sarah stood and looked in awe, for the woman who stood in front of her was considerably younger looking than she had expected. And yet she showed a beauty and self-confidence well beyond her years. For Boudicca must only have been about thirty years old.

Boudicca had the usual pale green skin for Celtishia, only she had a diagonal bluey-green, arrow shaped effect, war painted across her face. Her hair was long, curly and ginger, and parted neatly down the centre. Her eyes were a dark brown

Her body shape was thin but slightly curvy, and provided a bell glass effect. Over a pair of pale-green jeans, Boudicca was wearing a cream coloured ball gown that stopped just above the knee, and exposed a little cleavage, and part of her shoulder. The dress had no sleeves, but was embroidered with a vast array of sequins, in another diagonal pattern similar to her face.

The round pendant she wore, however, was the most amazing Sarah had seen so far. It hung from a large solid gold chain, and was gold in colour. The centre stone was an emerald green. Sarah's first thought was regarding expensive it must be. This however, were not her only jewels, because at a forty-five degree angle on her head, she wore a jewel encrusted gold diadem.

But what really unnerved Sarah, was that Boudicca was smiling. This indicated that she clearly knew something, that Sarah did not.

The silence was momentarily broken, when Freida interjected with "really, she is a lot friendlier than she likes to look".

"Sarah Salter?" asked an amused Boudicca. "That is fascinating."

"Why?" asked Sarah.

"Well It seems that the whisper doesn't do things by halves. I had asked him to spice things up, and he sends a Salter." The Queen laughed a little.

There was silence as they both studied each other. Sarah could tell from Boudicca's face that this was clearly a complicated issue to explain.

"And why were you expecting me?" Now in anger, she turned on Freida. "And what are you hiding?"

More awkward silence followed. Freida was looking downwards at her own boots, trying to avoid the question. In the end, it was Boudicca who spoke first.

"I will explain more later. And so will Freida. But right now, we need your help. Now follow me," she said, and pressed a button revealing a secret passage in the floor, with steps going downwards.

Sarah, Boudicca, and Freida started the descent. Sarah was led down a tall spiral staircase for about one hundred metres. They must have passed about four levels, as there were various green wooden doors in the structure leading, from the landings to who knows where.

"Bear with me," said Boudicca, "I know this is all very unsettling. But all will be explained."

Sarah looked over at Freida, who was just behind her. Freida looked both embarrassed and guilty.

"You have some explaining to do to me," Sarah said, feeling that Freida had lied to her by failing to mention things.

"Oh she does", said Boudicca, "but I can assure you that her intentions were only for your safety. There are things you don't know yet. So don't be too hard on her."

They stopped about one hundred and fifty metres down, at a doorway on another landing. The door was painted yellow and stood out from all the previous doors, as it was made of metal. It also had a security pad and two guards protecting it.

"We're here," said Boudicca. "Welcome to the Hall of the Iceni". And with that she tapped in a code, and the door opened, revealing a long and lavish hall made of marble. It was lit by crystal chandeliers. Sarah thought it the most amazing room she had ever seen.

The room must have been one hundred metres long, and the ceiling was about twenty-five metres from the floor. The width of the room was about fifty meters and ended in half a semi-circle. The walls were made from a type of pink granite, and besides them were some tall trees in large pots These in turn were decorated with candle shaped light bulbs. The lavish effect was completed by banners draped from the ceiling. The primary colours of blue and black stood out in contrast to the pink, and offered some variation in the room design.

In the centre of the room was a large round solid oak table. There were twelve luxurious padded chairs around, but four were occupied by people sitting there. (Three males and one female, all dressed in plain black clothes similar to Sarah's. They were straining to catch a glimpse of Sarah). Boudicca entered first, but had to turn around to the other two, who were just staring in disbelief and awe. She didn't look amused, and verbally snapped at them both.

"Well don't just stand there, you two! Come in."

"Sorry," said Freida before entering with Sarah.

"Could everyone take a seat," ordered Boudicca. Sarah sat down on a comfortable chair next to Freida, (for protection, because she felt confused and nervous). The others took a seat too, but seemed less nervous.

"Well", said Boudicca, "now we are all here, let's begin."

And everyone leant forward in attention, and Sarah realized that this was serious.

"First of all, I would like to introduce you to Miss Sarah Salter," said Boudicca pointing at Sarah, "who has just crossed over from "the Mist-Less

Dimension.' Now we all know what that means, and yet, we don't really know do we?"

And Sarah noticed that the expressions on their faces was one of both delight, and amusement.

"So we just prepare as usual, until the Whisper makes his will clear?" asked the unknown female.

"Well that is basically it, Amy. But he usually does, in these situations." Boudicca now pointed at the others. "So Sarah, this is Amy, our PR Guru," sneered Boudicca. "The others you don't know are General John, Admiral Peter and Chief Airman Boaz.

"Boaz?"

"Yes, its a Jewish name," said Boaz. It means 'strengh."

"My name is Sarah, and it doesn't," she replied sarcastically.

Boaz just smiled, and said, "Oh touché, I love sarcasm, or I would do, if I knew what it was". And everyone laughed, while Sarah knew that her and Boaz, would get along really well.

"Ok, so why are we here then?" asked Sarah, realizing that she knew nothing about what was happening.

Boaz looked over his spectacles, and answered her. "To discuss the best strategy for dealing with the Egyptian menace. Notably, the ongoing raid situation. It is hoped that you may have a different perspective on things."

'But why am I here? I am not a soldier, or a general. Or a politician. In fact; I am not apparently, even from this dimension," pointed out Sarah. She was now more confused than ever.

"Precisely!" said Airman Boaz in a firm but polite manner. "You are from one of the other known dimensions. Your arrival signifies change".

Sarah was now even more confused, and it must have shown on her face.

"Its time I explained" said Boudicca.

Sarah just looked at her, as Queen Boudicca began the story.

"In the year 3820AM."

Sarah interrupted her to query this. "3820 AM?"

"Yes!" Boudicca explained, "In the year 3820 Anno Mundi, in the Jewish calendar. My descendent Boudicca, of the Iceni Tribe, went to war with the Romans, in both of our dimensions. But here, she was warned not to engage them in open conflict, and the reason for this was that the Roman fighting style was better suited to this. In your dimension, they engaged the Romans and were defeated, but Boudicca and her two daughters were never captured. Some believe she was killed in battle, and others believe she poisoned herself."

"Yes?"

"Well wouldn't have been told to you is that they managed to escape the conflict, in their chariot, which somehow crossed over to the Green Dimension, (this dimension), and crashed in front of our Boudicca's home. This happened when the Chief Bard saw a vision of two worlds colliding."

"Anyway, the two Boudiccas talked with the other tribes. The presence of a white Boudicca was like an omen to them, and so the strategy here was changed to continue the guerrilla war, and attack the food supply line. Unable to feed themselves, and weakened by the raids, the Romans were defeated slowly, demoralized and forced to leave the shores. Sadly: the original Queen Boudicca was injured by an arrow in a raid, and died. My descendants from the Mist-Less World, (your world), assumed her place."

"But didn't people mind? You know with her having a white face like mine?"

"A little at first, but she had helped defeat the enemy. And she was Boudicca. Besides, the color of your skin is caused mostly by melanin, but is also influenced by climate, and the food you eat. Celtishia's mist is green and so is our food, so the people on the planet assume various shades of green. Her skin eventually became like theirs, and so she was accepted as rightful Queen. In time, your skin will probably end up like ours."

"But what if I don't want that?"

"Well that may not be your choice. We can try and get food for you that more closely resembles your own, but that won't be easy. Even with Royal Connections," she added. "However: you are not in any danger health wise, so try not to worry. Actually, green is a cool colour to be".

"But first there's more to our story. Since then, there have been many incidents of these visions, and every time, somebody has come in a time of need from the Mist-Less Dimension." In some cases, they chose to return. And in others they stayed with us?"

"They returned?"

"Yes, after an incident in approximately 5010 AM, in which two children disappeared, we (the council only), have been aware of a secret portal that opens on occasions (like a red moon). It leads to a town in the country you call England. There is a secret organization there, who are able to contact us and update us on news. Don't ask us to explain that, it is complicated."

"When people pass through larger portals to the other side, they hide them, forge documents, and help them to lose their green skin colour, and gain a pinker tone. This is how we discovered that it is mostly all to do with the food you eat, that influences your melanin."

'Unfortunately, over the years some of our people have gone to your dimension, and have been seen. Like-wise some of your people have come here, and returned before being provided with an explanation. This has led to rumors in your world, of green lizard people living below the ground, in a place called "Subterranean Earth." I believe that this is just viewed as crazy conspiracy theory."

"We in the leadership of Celtishia know differently of course, but keep it secret. We are the green people, and there are no lizards."

"More recently we have become aware of similar links to the City of Plymouth in that same country. Hence we had Freida and her adoptive parents, locate to the City of Devonport and wait for your arrival ten years ago. You must understand that many have gone through as agents since. They have often stayed there and married local women they really liked. Although this was not part of any plan of ours, we accepted it. And we were expecting a distant relative to return some day. There is a prophecy about it."

"A what?"

"A prediction about the future that has been written down. A word from The Whisper given to a person to pass on," replied the General. "And it is about you!"

"Rubbish! It can't be. I want to see it now," Sarah demanded.

At this point every face in the room turned towards Boudicca. They all looked worried. Boudicca looked taken aback. Stunned even, by the sheer audacity of the request.

Freida interjected to assist.

"Sarah, nobody should make demands of the Queen like that. It is considered rude. Almost insurrectionist".

"I apologize then, but please if there is a prophesy about me, surely I should know about it."

Boudicca left the room looking angry, but could be seen as she started to pace around outside in the hallway. The only sounds that could be heard were her pacing up, and down, and occasionally hitting out at a wall, or throwing something. Freida and the officials just looked uncomfortably at the floor. Nobody said a word, for it was clear that the Queen was now in a rage. Eventually Boudicca returned to the room. She looked angry, but resigned to what she had to do. "Okay" she said slowly and with a deep breath, "Sarah and Freida come with me. I will show you both the prophecy, but we will need these."

She handed Sarah some cloths, and cleaning Spray. She then nodded approvingly to Freida. "The rest of you are asked not to leave the complex, as you will be needed in due course. I believe you can continue your work from desks here."

"Yes Majesty", they all replied, and left the room, leaving only Boudicca, Sarah and Freida present. "Let's go then."

So Boudicca led the way from the room, down to the section marked "Royal Archives." Three floors down the came to a final room. Next to it was a warning sign.

"The Room of Prophecy.
Entrance for top officials, with
Royal approval only.
Non-compliance is considered Sacrilege.

Penalty is Death."

Boudicca now spoke to them, with the utmost sincerity and authority. "I will remind you both, that like the sign says, this is one of our most sacred rooms. It is a key duty of mine to protect it. You are very honoured to see inside. Although even now, I am not entirely convinced it is wise of me to let you."

And with that Boudicca, felt inside the cleavage of her dress. When she removed her hand, she had a key. She looked embarrassed.

"I had to put it somewhere safe. After I decided to open the room for you, I thought my bra would be a good place," she explained. "Now. Not a word."

And they said nothing.

The key was old looking and worn at the handle. Boudicca placed the key in the lock, and turned. There was a click and the door opened.

The room was full of cobwebs, and was of course pitch black. So Boudicca pressed a switch by the door and the light came on. There were more cobwebs, but they could now make out the end of the room. Boudicca sighed, then pressed her gold and emerald amulet, and spoke into it.

"Hi, I'm outside the Sacred Room. Please can we have some cleaners here." She turned to the other two. "Well why keep a dog and bark yourself, eh."

"Its a phone too?" asked Sarah.

"Of course, so is yours," Boudicca replied, realizing that there was much Sarah had to learn

"Anyway let's get started." Boudicca pushed aside the first cobweb, and went inside. The others followed, and a minute later the house cleaners arrived as well. They started to clean the room. And everyone worked hard together.

Twenty minutes later the room was clean. And Boudicca dismissed her servants.

This room was designed to resemble a perfect dome. It had a diameter of fifty metres. It was twenty feet high with curved, but arching walls. The walls had been whitewashed white, with a series of wall lights. The floor was made from a yellow marble.

There were a series of shelves with parchments, behind a strong pine table in the centre of the room. But in the centre of the shelves, was what resembled a large ornate cabinet. The Queen opened it, and drew out a very old mahogany box.

"It is unusual to find a mahogany box like this. The wood itself is very rare. But it is the contents that matter here the most."

The box was about two feet long, by a foot wide and deep. The only decoration on it was a six pointed star. Boudicca released a clasp and opened it. There was a hiss of air releasing, and a cold draught came from the box. Sarah realized that the box was designed for keeping the prophecy intact over a long period of time.

Inside the box was a small vellum parchment. Securely held and fitted to perfection. Boudicca removed it, and then she unrolled it on the table, in front of them all. Then she looked out of the window, facing away from them as she spoke.

"This is the prophecy given by the Prophet Peter Barach, about seventeen hundred years ago! It is written as a "stanza poem," which was not unusual for then. You see very few people could read or write, so it needed to be memorable. But what is unusual; is that it was written in our language. Not Rabbinic."

The girls looked at Boudicca like she was talking a foreign language anyway.

"What's a stanza poem," Freida mouthed at Sarah, while Boudicca had her back turned.

"How would I know?" she mouthed back. Then Sarah realized that Boudicca had turned around, and spotted their ignorance.

"A stanza poem," she said very slowly, "is a poem where the first letter of sentence, or section, starts with a different letter of the alphabet. This one does not progress through the entire alphabet."

"This text: it is so sacred, so mystical: I haven't even looked at it for nine years now. Just felt it should be left alone. I don't know why? It just seemed too important to keep looking at casually." She paused and reflected. "Well gather round, and I'll read it to you."

They circled around the table, and using a

pointer, Boudicca read the prophecy out load.

8. THE GREAT DESTROYER

A t the mouth of the Amazing Plym River
By lightningy by-passes the Dimensional Barrier
Coming with Chaos and humour, the now girl is Chosen
Dreaming solutions the Destroyer gets Dragged.

Enduring the Empathic assistance
Following the Fortitude of a Foreign Mistress
Gaining Glory from all the help she is Given
How bizarrely Her practices give that impression"

In the age of Irksom and Irrational need
Jesting and Jovial answers she'll tease
Knowing evoking Key solutions
Learning to Love will bring Liberation

Mist-Less remedies out of long ago Missions
Novel and New for Now solutions
Our Oracle Ordained with no Ordinary soldier
Past scarred Paramour emprisoned by a Preditor

Queen Boudicca herself will be on the throne
Returning the Reign Right Round again
Slowly and Simply back to The Whisper
To show justice To all and To guide The Destroyer
Under the Unction of the girl who is pink
Very reliable missions are Visioned

When the Whisper speaks all Will seem Wrong
Xenophoes are eXercising plans for eXpansion
Your hero will speak as You burst into song
Ze Zillionaire Pharaoh let down by the Zebra

T here was silence following the reading of the prophecy, as nobody dared to speak. Freida and Sarah looked at each other. Sarah was having what could be described as a light bulb moment. Freida however, was starting to go a paler shade of green.

"What" said Sarah eventually. "Read it again. Please."

So Boudicca read it again, but this time more slowly. As she did so, she paused at the end of every sentence, and paragraph. At the end of it, Sarah was raging with questions.

"How can I be the 'New Great Destroyer?' Ok, so I am from the Mist-Less Dimension, and the 'Mouth of the Plym.' As in Plymouth? Right! And I am pink. We can't deny that. But surely it all has to be correct?"

"Or will turn out to be so," Boudicca gently corrected her. "Remember it even mentions me by name"

"But there is no victim and paramour here. I don't even know what that word means, so it probably doesn't apply to me."

And what is this about a zebra?"

"Well," said Boudicca, in a matter of fact way. "A Paramour is an illicit mistress to another. Often kept secret, but long term in nature. They are often a kind of second and secret relationship, and are usually sexual in nature. And as for the Zebra. I haven't got a clue."

Boudicca looked at Freida, who was getting upset. Really upset. Sarah had unfortunately missed the full extent of this, and continued pace the floor, and to seethe at what she had heard.

"And what is all this, about knowing 'key solutions?' I mean really? Me? What would I have to offer?"

Boudicca responded kindly and patiently yet again. "According to this prophecy, 'Mist-Less remedies' from your dimension."

Sarah wasn't satisfied. But she turned around, to find that Boudicca was starting to comfort Freida. And Freida was starting to cry. Although she was trying hard to control it. Then to Sarah's amazement, Freida, broke free from the Queen, and covered her face as if in shame, and fled the room.

Boudicca and Sarah stood alone around the table. Sarah was baffled, but clearly Boudicca wasn't. It was like she had expected this, and feared the poem for this reason.

"Wait, what is going on?" Sarah asked, now calming down a bit. "What don't I know?"

"Well," said Boudicca, looking worried for her friend who had fled the room. "As you can see the victim mentioned here is clearly Freida. She has an interesting past. And she will have to explain it all to you when she is ready. Just listen when she tells you. And please don't judge her. She doesn't open up easy, but she does consider you a friend."

"Well she is a friend."

"Good, then, when the time comes be support-ive. Because as the poem says, this is to be a joint effort, your ideas, and her expertise. Success and survival will depend on how well you two work together."

They both returned to the Devonport base the next day, but Freida didn't open up to Sarah that day, or the next. And the days became weeks. Sarah knew that Boudicca could order Freida to speed things up, but she seemed okay with wait-ing.

Meanwhile the raids continued. Mostly it ap-peared that the Egyptians were trying to turn up and ambush the locals of Celtishia. However: early warning systems consisting of drones were in place, so this rarely happened. Instead the boats would attack and be repelled by local re-sistance.

But despite the lack of success, the Pharaoh would launch his media PR, and boast every time they captured someone, by parading them on international television, and exaggerating the numbers. The wrecked boats laying in the harbors were never seen. But his voice con-tinued as an act of menace, and predicted his victory day would probably be in the next few months.

Meanwhile a menacing 'Med Alliance' army was

growing in Spain. Luckily the boats that were to be used to transport them were still being built. A major assault was being planned, and they knew it.

Sarah spent these few weeks in the tunnels below the City of Devonport. It was an amazing experience for Sarah. Not least because she was assigned to be in the same room as Freida.

What Sarah really enjoyed about the underground life, was that it was like living in a commune, where everybody combined their resources. Everybody appreciated each other, and there was a special point made about the weekly meeting in 'the community lounge,' where they gathered over drinks. Some of course were alcoholic, but most people just drank hot chocolate or coffee.

It was in these meetings that people sang, to modern tunes. It had a life to it that was catching, and Sarah started to learn the songs and joined in. In fact, most weeks, everybody contributed something, whether a reading, or a poem, or just led a song. It was as if everybody was motivated to be involved, and make things better.

Sarah found it hard to take her part at first, but she received some help from a young woman called Amber. Together they performed a well-known sketch from her dimension, which whilst old and tested for her, was of course new to them.

The tunnels were well lit, and smelled good. (Usually of oregano.) There were huge rooms that were used for aeroponics or vertical farming, with layers on layers of trays used for growing crops like lettuce, cabbage and cucumbers. They looked like huge full underground greenhouses.

But the mood in the tunnels, was depressing most of the time, especially when the singing stopped. The worst time was late at night, when the children had gone to bed. The children seemed to have a simple way of seeing things, and viewing the ongoing and developing problems.

It seemed that everyone knew, that Celtishia was effectively in danger. They also knew that the stand-off was no longer in place. There was that same feeling in the air, that she had felt in Plymouth during the lightning, and she sensed that things were not going well.

Practically, they continued to produce food for themselves, and life continued as normal. Sarah ran out of makeup. And the result of no makeup, was that she was forced to get used to her own skin colour, which stood out being pink, among only light green people.

In her spare time, she read the sacred poets. She even started to become interested in them and would discuss them with some of the older residents. It seemed to her, however, that the writ-

N.R. Gurney

ings were being almost forgotten, and ignored at times.

Over time, it became clear that most people were concerned only with their own survival. And with this in mind, the country was starting to arm itself. Consequently, in the little spare time people had, they made weapons like guns, using templates from the internet and three dimensional printers. And this was okay, on the surface. Deep down she was concerned that it would not be enough.

9. FREIDA'S TALE

For the next few months, Sarah would see Freida walking about pacing and trying to put together her words. And she knew Freida was preparing herself for "that conversation," they were due to have in the near future.

In the evenings, they relaxed together. Sometimes distracting themselves by going to watch Devonport Argyle play in the professional hockey league. Then they would go for a drink across the road in the Celtishian Arms, which was usually okay, except when boys tried to hit on Freida. This always seemed to make her uncomfortable.

Sarah was baffled as to what could possibly be causing Freida so much distress. But she knew it had something to do with the prophecy, and her past. Usually she was strong and assertive in how she handled life and people. But it was like she had been exposed in public, and humiliated into giving into her problems.

It was also now clear that her usual boldness was some kind of pretense she put on. Something perhaps, she had been trained to do by the military. However, she now knew, that the real Freida underneath was very different.

The first clue was the way she insisted on keeping her right arm covered. Whether she was swimming, or engaged in combat sport, she always wore a plastic sleeve to cover it, and hide whatever was below. And whenever Sarah asked about it, Freida would somehow change the subject.

Meanwhile, their friendship was continuing to grow. As mates, the two of them shared a twin room in one of the tunnels. At night, Sarah could hear Freida crying. She wanted to know what it was about, but knew it was something she would just have to wait to find out about.

Sometimes Freida would have nightmares, and yell out "please no more blood," or "don't make me do this."

And then there were some nights when Freida would come in late at night with bruises, from another kickboxing bout she had put herself through. She always invited Sarah to come and watch, as she was gaining a reputation and building towards a big professional fight. It concerned Sarah that Freida was choosing increasingly harder and bigger opponents. And while she never lost, and remained unbeaten; the fights were getting increasingly dirtier, especially when the combatants were men.

Boudicca was also getting worried about Freida, even though she had enough to deal with already. Despite the raids, and threats from Egypt, she made time for her mentee. Every day: she would ring from the HUB to talk to Sarah and how things were, on some pretext. Then she would ask about Freida, and Sarah would tell her some of what she was seeing, like how she was spending a lot of time by her bed praying for forgiveness.

The Queen said Freida was "probably dealing with a strange mixture of anger and guilt, but she needn't. Nobody really thinks she has done wrong."

The next thing Sarah knew was that Boudicca herself arrived at the Devonport Base, saying she was "just passing through." This was clearly not the case, as it was well known that Boudicca was her older mentor.

It all came to a head at breakfast one day. Freida and Sarah were planning on going out into the forest for a day's rest. But first they had some chores to do. This included dropping off some dirty bedding to "The Base Laundry Service."

As they waited for some new sheets to arrive, they sat silently on sofas out of view. It was there that they overheard a conversation between two staff members.

"She's out there now, you know," said the first voice.

"Who?" asked another.

"That bloody foreigner. She is with that white faced girl. Bloody Israeli tart she is."

"What do you mean? The white faced girl?"

"No not her. That Freida. You can't tell me that she is worthy of the Queen's friendship, and yet she sees her almost daily. A disgrace it is."

"Oh?"

"Well she came here under a bit of a cloud, about the time of that foreign King's death. I hear she is wanted for crimes there, and survives on the basis of asylum here."

"Now you mention it. I heard something like that."

"Well there's more, she has been in trouble with the law here too. Queen Boudicca kept her out of jail apparently. Gave her priority treatment, and helped her get the best jobs. Wouldn't do it for us mind. Don't know how its allowed, but something should be done."

Sarah was taken back, by the allegation of Sarah being a fugitive. Freida just went a very pale green. And then left the room.

Sarah quickly dropped off the sheets to their room, and went to find her friend, in the caverns, as that was where she thought Freida would go. Eventually, she turned around a corner to be greeted by an old lady she knew called Doris.

"If you are looking for your friend, Freida? She was down at breakfast with Boudicca, having previously been found crying in the corridor, and urged to go to have something to eat. I don't know what's happened, but she told the Queen something, and the Queen told her to wait where she was, before storming off."

"Really. Thanks I guess." Sarah thought for a second or so. "Are they both there now?"

"Well Freida is. It appears she did as she was told."

"And the Queen?"

"Well she left her breakfast untouched, and then went and fired two laundry workers. She even ordered them to leave the Base immediately. Most unlike her. Absolutely fuming she was. The Queen is normally very nice to her staff. Come to think of it, she has never fired anyone in the base before. Doesn't normally interfere that way."

"And is Freida still there, by any chance?"

"Yes she is, I believe."

"Thanks Doris." And with that Sarah went to breakfast.

When she arrived the food was ready, and Freida was sitting alone. Clearly she had been crying again. Sarah knew better than to thrust herself on her friend at this moment.

"May I join you?"

"You don't have to ask. Of course you can."

Sarah sat down next to her, and her breakfast was served. It included all her favourite things, like yoghurt, ducks' eggs, and green soda bread. After they had finished eating, Freida reached across.

"Can we talk later? I think I can't put off talking to you about it any longer. There are things you need to know, and I would rather you heard them from me."

"Of course. Let's go out to the forest like we planned, and be alone together, where nobody can hear."

The first thing they did was go to the barracks, and borrow a couple of All-Terrain Personal Transport Machines (or PTMs,) for the journey. Sarah had never ridden one before, but soon got the hang of it, and found them ideal for traversing through the unaltered natural terrain. What surprised Sarah after riding them, is how they had never gained popularity in the England she knew, and that they were banned from use on the roads there.

The two girls also chose a small security team to accompany them. This was something Boudicca was insisting upon, whenever they left the complex. And so, to please Boudicca, this small entourage set out together, for a clearing in the local forest.

When they finally arrived at a small wooden enclosure, Freida ordered the men to secure the parameter, and not interrupt until she asked them to. They spread a picnic blanket on the ground, and with Sarah sitting on one side, and Freida on the other. Freida handed Sarah a helmet and visor, which she recognized as suitable for Virtual Reality.

"I know your virtual assistant, because he used to be mine of course. Nowadays, my virtual assistant is called Ella. I wanted a female, because I have issues with men. She is more technically advanced, and thinks less."

Sarah found it hard to imagine replacing Vincent, but suspected there was a hint at Freida's reasoning in what she had previously said.

"Ok," Sarah replied, "but why are you telling me this?"

"If you are willing Sarah, I will not only tell you, but show you too?" Freida said, and indicated that they should join their tech tabs together. "This process is an advanced form of Virtual Reality, in which you see, hear, and even smell what I did back then. Basically, it will enable you to relive the memories with me. All we have to do is link our technologies."

"I am willing, and here for you," said Sarah. "Whatever it is, we will deal with it together, as friends do." She had decided that it was worth the risk.

They then connected their Tech-tabs together through a wireless connection, to allow Freida to show her what she was going to share. Sarah saw an image of Vincent combine with Freida's female, (Ella), who was clearly Freida's holographic assistant.

First the holorams kissed, and embraced, then they entwined in a spiral, before forming into a circular screen that totally surrounded them.

For the next hour, Freida cried almost constantly as she relived the following memory from her past. Clearly in distress, she struggled with every sentence, but tried hard to relay the key facts.

"It all started, when I was living in a small Jewish village known as Amicula, in the country the Egyptians continue to call Palestine. It was located to the North East of Egypt."

And with this the image of a beautiful small village with plain white houses appeared in holographic images around them. They reminded her of a typical postcard village from the Middle East.

Freida continued, "we always knew that we were under the control of the Egyptian Empire. And we were also used to soldiers, arriving to forcibly steal at least a third of our crops, even when there wasn't much to spare. This was normal life for me while growing up"

An image of a menacing and drunk Egyptian soldier, wearing red appeared in front of them and was seen beating a man in the village. Other soldiers stood on and laughed, while a young Jewish teenage girl, could be seen hiding in the background. Eventually, the images became more positive, the soldiers vanished. The village was seen working together, and getting on with daily life.

The focus now changed to how the incident was remembered by Freida, and Sarah found herself looking through her eyes, into the face of an attractive teenage boy. With flowing long hair, and busting biceps, Sarah could literally feel Freida's attraction towards him.

"When I was aged fourteen, I was living with my original parents, and dating a boy in the village called Simeon. I liked him a lot. We had grown up together and could talk to each other about almost anything. And I mean talk. If something was worrying me, I would tell Simeon; and he would confide in me over his problems."

"We were poor, but we were happy together. There were about one hundred and fifty of us there. A mixture of ages all working productively together, and sharing our resources as best we could. It was a community, where everybody ate, or nobody ate."

"I didn't realize it at the time, but my place in that shared community was what gave me a purpose. We all had roles to fulfill, and would set about doing so to the best of our abilities. We looked out for each other, and knew each other's business."

"Then one day a whole battalion of the occupying soldiers came, with a series of yellow transportation trucks. The trucks were emblazoned with the crest of the Empire. It was a horrible black Snake, with a forked tongue in its mouth. Its image represented everything we hated. Oppression. Immorality. Evil. Temptation. Empire! And here they were in our village."

The pleasant scene was interrupted by the holographic arrival of troops in army vehicles. It looked like they were there for a purpose. Sarah and Freida looked on as the troops started to point their weapons, and order about the villagers. Freida continued the story.

"Under threat of gunfire, they quickly rounded our village up. We were made to form into two lines, the women in front of the men. As a village we were used to this. In fact, it happened every fortnight. They turned up and flexed their weapons: and we complied. They inspected our details, then they took food and went. We didn't have the means to defend ourselves, so we just put up with it."

"It was usually one of two groups of soldiers who inspected, but we were not familiar with this group. More alarmingly, there were noticeably more of them than usual."

"Then they asked to see all our Identification Documents to make the inspection look official. These were produced quickly as usual. But it soon became evident from the questioning, that this platoon couldn't understand the ID, as most of the soldiers couldn't read anyway."

The scene got nastier, as Sarah and Freida looked on. The threats had now turned into acts of violence. Some of the troops were hitting the villagers with truncheons, and spitting in their direction.

"When they realized that we knew this, their pride was offended. So they started to get aggressive with some of the older ladies, and demanded they explain, or read things for them. They were particularly asking about the ages of the children, and were being

answered in a reasonable way. However, it was clear to me, that our older women were trying to conceal things from them to protect us."

"When the soldiers eventually decided that they didn't like the answers, they got rude and abusive. They started swearing, and pushing them.".

"I could hear Simeon behind me telling me quietly under his breath to "keep calm, and they will go away". I was not to draw attention to myself, and 'all should be fine'." However, all was not fine, and they did not go away."

A soldier was seen to grab a teenage girl, and show her to his colleagues. He then told a joke in a foreign language and they laughed. The girl was resisting, and looking very uncomfortable.

"Instead, they started to single out the younger girls, (who looked in their early teenage years). They said that we were needed for the pleasure of the local puppet King, (Chief Prince Asama Herodius). They said he was rescuing us so we could be 'servants' in his palace, "and the lucky girls might one day become concubines". We all knew what that meant, and nobody from our village was in approval."

From Freida's memory, the co-joined Tech-Tabs showed another memory, of one man bravely moving forward to reason with their oppressors. For a brief second, even the enemy stopped and listened to what he had to say.

"Our tribal elder spoke up, Freida explained, and said "real men, do not take sexual slaves."

"Shut up infidel," came the instant reply, and the

chief guard drew a gun and shot him in the head.

After witnessing this, the scene froze. It was clear from the tone of her voice that followed, that she was not going to see this in as much detail.

"When they saw our elder laying there, our people broke from their required lines, and started yelling. Some even attacked the soldiers, but were overpowered. Others ran into the trees."

"Then the soldiers started dragging all the teenagers forward towards a truck. There was screaming and yelling everywhere, as our people protested and tried to resist. The Egyptians drew their guns and fired in the air, and the resistance subsided a little, out of fear. Some of the girls managed to escape, but I was not so lucky."

"I was grabbed by my hair initially, and then after putting up a struggle, I was grabbed by two men who put my arms behind my back. I could hear Simeon yell at them, to leave me alone. Then I hear a thud. I turned my head to see him on the floor, but bravely struggling against a much larger man."

"Next thing I knew, another man had approached him and hit him with the butt of his rifle, and Simeon hit the ground. Before he could regain his feet, the first soldier, lifted his gun and fired. I saw my best friend die that day in front of me, his body remaining motionless on the ground, and the blood flowing from his head. The memory of it haunts me even today."

And there it was, the retained memory that

troubled Freida so much. Her former boyfriend, Simeon, dead on the ground. Freida could be heard screaming a long "noooo," in the background. It was one of the most gruesome things Sarah had ever seen. The blood flowing from his head, as the love of Freida's life lay lifeless on the ground.

"I yelled abuse at the man I had seen murder my boyfriend, and kicked out harder at my capturers. But they just forced me to the floor and held me tighter, until I could not move. I just didn't have the strength to fight them. Then another guard approached me, and kicked me in the jaw. I was knocked out.

The images turned into a white background. And then a new memory started to surface for Sarah to look at. This time, she was positioned above a young Freida. She was being transported in an old and smelly army truck, as some kind of prisoner. It seemed to recall a conversation between her and other captives, but there was no sound. Freida filled in the blanks.

"When I regained consciousness, I was in the back of one of the trucks. I was laying curled up on the ground, where I had been dumped. My hands were fastened with a cable tie behind my back."

"As I awoke, Suzie, another girl from the village, asked if I was ok, which of course I was not. She advised me that I should keep still for another girl had just been shot for attempting to jump from the truck after it left our village."

"I asked what else had happened, after I lost consciousness, and was told that my parents had also been killed."

"Suzie told me that as I was kicked in the face, my mother had objected but was shot in the leg, and placed in a neck collar for slaves. She was then dragged to the commander of the soldiers, who was holding a kind of sword, and made to kneel in front of him. The commander spat in her face. Then, in full view of the rest of the village, proceeded to chop her head off with a blunt scimitar. (Apparently, it took several blows)."

"My father, apparently, had been luckier, for he was shot in an earlier struggle for my safety. Our village had experienced many deaths at those Egyptian hands"

"The truck drove on through the valleys, past places I had never seen before. I was able to sit up straight and make the best of it, but I cried until my eyes hurt for most of the journey. The other girls cried too, for they also had all lost somebody. And like me they were also scared"

"The journey lasted about three hours for the roads weaved between trees, and the mist lay heavy in Palestine that day. The progress of the convoy was slowed further, by toilet and cigarette breaks for the troops. However, I could feel a sense of injustice in the air as we travelled onwards to whatever awaited us., The truck was slow and the metal floor, we sat upon was hot. We were given no water to drink, and thirsted until we reached the palace."

"When we arrived, we were bundled off the truck, and keeping our heads down and our mouths shut for fear of our lives. We were then forcibly marched to the front door, and ordered to look upwards."

The image of the army truck disappeared, and now a view of a magnificent small city came into view. It was situated on top of a giant slope. And it overlooked the sea. It was made of white marble and pointed upwards to the sky. The largest building had huge windows made of glass, with spectacular metal lattices for extra cover from the sun. The door was made of bronze, and there was a statue there of a man on a horse. Freida could tell through her virtual reality headset that Sarah was impressed.

"When we raised our heads, we could see the palace in front of us. Although it was a spectacular sight, it filled us with dread and loathing."

"Behind the palace was the Mediterranean Sea, and the city of Gaza. I know this because I had seen it in pictures at home. This city was considered a modern version of Babylon to us, because its people traded in things considered unlawful to us, like slaves, and narcotic drugs. It was ruled by an elite group of Arabs, who oppressed the majority".

"Most noticeable to us was the smell of marijuana and other weird exotic things. It was market day, and stalls were all over the square in the background. Some of the local stall holders looked in our direction, with looks of apology for not intervening. Clearly they were scared."

"I was soon to discover that to them, we 'Israelis', (or natives,) represented no more than servants at best. They would refer to us as 'the soul-less ones,' or 'primitive monkeys.' They regarded their wealth as proof of their superiority, and flaunted it at us, whenever the chance arose, and showing favoritism to their own kind first. In this city, the rich would get richer, and the poor were exploited for little reward."

"I could see that the palace was surrounded by a large marble wall, with palace guards patrolling the perimeter."

The Palace Guards were seen to pay some money to the soldiers who captured the girls. The palace guards then took charge of their shackles, and ushered them forward towards the door of the Palace, where they were made to stand in line.

"The guards frightened us. They were bigger and fatter. They were armed with the latest weapons, but wore dirty unwashed uniforms. They were even dirtier than we were, and clearly hadn't washed that day, as they stank of stale sweat and excrement."

"They pushed us around, and slapped our faces. Then they laughed at us, and made crude jokes about who would be first to be sent to them. They called us primitive, unbroken and inferior. Apparently we were lucky to be rescued from our poverty and filth. They disgusted us, and we tried to resist their advances."

"Yo! Stupid Israelis," yelled one of the guards at the girls, who really did look scared. "You are now under the protection of us Palace Guards, you obey us completely now, or else." And they laughed in their faces, with an indifference to their plight. They were forced into the palace as soon as the door opened. Some were coerced via an arm-lock, or hair-pulling, from a guard. *"The door closed behind us with a bang."* Freida continued. And Sarah could make out that they were in some kind of courtyard, with marble walls, and glass windows with a kind of lattice over them to keep out the sun.

"Once more we were forced into a line. There were about fourteen girls here, of which I recognized six. The others I assumed, at this point, must have come from other villages nearby."

"We waited in silence, because nobody dared to speak, except one brave girl from our village called Siobhan. She just couldn't handle the silence, and kept nattering about the dirty windows, doors and floor. All nonsense to help her cope."

The image of Siobhan in the lineup, was a strange one. Clearly the girl didn't fit. It was also obvious that she hadn't quite grasped the danger she was in. To Sarah, it looked like she was in denial of her situation.

"Meanwhile we could see other servants, and some of the nobility, appear at the window and view our arrival. They were mostly women. Some laughed, and pointed at Siobhan like they knew something. Others looked on with concern, and sympathy."

"Finally, the head of the guard appeared from a

nearby barracks. He was accompanied by two officials, one of whom was eating some kind of pastry in one hand. Both officials carried pink uniforms."

"They walked in front of each of us, and placed a uniform at each of our feet."

"Put these on," they ordered.

"Siobhan objected, 'but we have nowhere to change'." The guards did not look impressed with that. Nor did they seem to care. One of them drew a gun from a holster around his belt.

'Bang. Bang." And the girl called Siobhan fell over, and lay flat on the ground. Blood flowed red from her head, and Sarah who now saw this memory felt like she was about to be sick.

"The Head of the Guard had fired a gun, and Siobhan now lay dead. We could see two bullet wounds, one in the chest, and one in the head. Some of the women in the palace were cheering and laughing."

"I had always liked Siobhan. Yes, she talked a lot, but she had a kind heart, and would always think the best of people. Even the bad ones. She was naïve that way. But she was not particularly pretty, or athletically remarkable. And it was for these reasons, she now lay dead."

"And I realized, that there and then, that those laughing were the most smartly dressed. And they thought it funny to see a teenage girl shot in front of them. They thought it entertainment. However, the servant classes, (those wearing uniforms), stood silently with tears in their eyes. They were clearly shocked, and scared, by what they had seen. It was

only out of a sense of hopelessness, and fear, that they had remained subservient to their mistresses."

"I said, get dressed! Now!" The Head Guard re-ordered the teenage girls, and slowly, looking embarrassed, they started to remove clothing and change.

"And we did so. Right there in the courtyard. We stripped naked in full view of everyone, before putting on the new clothes. And none of us dared to speak, for fear of our lives, even though we felt humiliated by the jeers of the male guards."

"The pink and green clothes were clearly not designed for our benefit. They consisted of very short shorts, sleeveless tops that were too large, and underwear. They were thin, and made from a material that itched badly."

The next memory surfaced and joined up to the previous one, almost instantly. This time, Sarah was literally looking through Freida's eyes.

"You three over here," shouted the guard, who was pointing towards myself, Suzie and a girl I didn't then know. I later learnt she was called Emily, and had come from as far away as Cairo, where her parents were also slaves.

"Anyway, we approached the guard, and he introduced to one of the cheering women. She looked at us, like we were common filth. It was clear that she did not like us."

Sarah could see that the woman was a woman in her thirties, with slightly darker green skin than Freida. She was very tall, and reached a height of eight feet. She also had a curvy build, and a pretty face. Towering over the three teenage girls, she wore a black and white striped dress, which resembled a slain zebra.

And Sarah suddenly remembered the prophecy had mentioned *"Ze Zillionaire Pharaoh let down by the Zebra."*

The loathing for the Princess was now starting to surface. The white flat hat she wore just looked phony, and the flower resembled an attempt to look cute. But Sarah could tell that beneath this image was a dangerously sweet faced woman, with evil intent. The mostly gold and expensive jewels she wore, failed to impress Sarah. The Princess looked like she had no concept even of responsibility, and just flaunted her power in front of others.

"This is Princess Phillipa," said the Guard, with a voice of clear admiration. *"She is a Lebanese Princess, born into royalty. Her mother is the Chief Princess, and married to Chief Prince Asama himself. She will be your manager for the duration of your stay, and she will explain the rules of you being here. You will do as she tells you, because your lives are literally in her hands."*

"She knew this of course, and dressed accordingly with designers to help her maximize her features, and to cast fear into us."

"Is this the best they could find," she said, looking at the three of them, but talking to the guard. Even in the memory she could feel her con-

tempt. *"The quality gets worse with every year."*
She looked at us again."

"Come with me, you lot," she snarled down at them.

The images in the memory moved forward in time yet again. They were now in a kitchen. Or were they?

"No," thought Sarah, "I am looking in on the girls from a video camera."

"This," interjected Vincent "is the best recording that could be found from the time. It is of course a copy, as the original is sealed in the Egyptian records. They are not keen to release it and you will soon see why."

And with that, Freida continued to narrate over the recording.

We were taken to the kitchen. Here once more we were grabbed by some guards. Then one by one, we were taken over to the stove. Then Phillipa produced a poker from the grill, and used it to brand us.

Sarah removed her headset in astonishment and shock, to find out that Freida then lifted her right sleeve. She showed Sarah her arm, and the sight she saw repulsed her. Sure enough, there was the brand of a slave. The crest of Phillipa of Lebanon, was burned into her skin.

Freida put her head set back on, and signaled to Sarah to do the same. Freida continued her story, and Sarah wondered what she could say to help. She also wondered how people could do such cruel things, and how others managed to survive?

Meanwhile, back in the simulation, there was a series of struggles occurring in the kitchen. As one by one, the terrified young girls were dragged towards a stove. Here Princess Phillipa stood holding the brand, with an evil smile on her face.

All of the girls fought as best they could, but were overpowered. Then with delight, Princess Phillipa, would place the brand on their arm. And with every branding she said the words, "you are mine now. Slave. Never forget it."

Freida continued her commentary, *"I will never forget that pain. Or the powerlessness and humiliation I felt, as I was branded last. I tried to fight it, but was not strong enough against the guards. No matter how hard I tried, I was unable to resist, and I was overpowered into position. The poker came down on my arm, and I screamed in pain, as the smell of burning flesh wafted from my right arm."*

The next scene showed the guards pick them up, where they rolled on the floor in pain. The guards then dragged the girls by their armpits, and threw them into a tiny room.

"Immediately afterwards, we were taken to this small room you now see, with three mattresses on the floor. The soldiers just threw us inside and told us to sleep. I took the dirty mattress nearest to the door, and this became my bed for the next two years. We had no cupboards, and nowhere to put anything

we found. We were denied possessions anyway."

The memory continued as seen through Freida's eyes. They were back in the palace, but now working hard under the eye of the Princess.

"Over the next few days, we were put to work cleaning the walls and floors until our knuckles bled. We were given only three minutes for a shower every day, and never given anything for wounds, we incurred at work."

"Princess Phillipa turned out to be an even nastier piece of work, than we had first thought. She would walk around talking to everyone, if she deemed them worthy. Most people she would ignore."

"Most of the time, she was resting on a lounger, telling us the system in the palace over and over again. This basically meant a life of servitude until we were seventeen, the legal age of consent. Not that we really had the choice of consent, as we were only prisoners. By that time, they believed we would be "broken" and open to other options."

"Then, it was planned, at seventeen, if we were considered worthy by the Chief Prince, we could become a concubine. "But never a wife, like my mum is," the princess reminded us. "It would be an abomination for a slave to gain power!"

Sarah was now greeted by yet another memory. This one consisted of the Princess shouting in her face, at close range. It was followed by the appearance of an enormously obese green man, waddling down a hallway, in the background. This enormous and disgusting looking middle aged man, was wearing expensive clothes and was choosing to ignore them.

"You are just a slave. But you may be lucky to share the Prince's bed, as a slave. And you will *enjoy it."*

Freida continued as this memory froze. *"She made out that she had a say in our success, but we all knew that it was really the result of a Chief Prince's lust that would decide. None of us wanted to succeed, and we thought the Chief Prince mean and ugly, but failure meant we would be sent to the barrack to entertain the troops. We regularly caught sight of such girls, and they looked docile and numb: like the light had lost their eyes."*

"When she wasn't talking, eating, or resting, she would keep a loose eye on what we were doing. When she didn't like it, she would slap us about, then hit us with a riding crop on our backs, or hands. If the quality of our work did not meet her standards, she would push us over, kick us hard, then scourge our backs with a bamboo cane. If we answered her back, she would punch our faces over and over, and then scourge our backsides with a riding crop. It was usually six lashes, and we cried and bled a lot."

"Our mistress never learnt our names and never spoke to us nicely. She referred to us by "You", or "Slave." This went on for two years, until I became available for the status of concubine."

A new slightly larger dormitory appeared in the VR simulation of events. This one had six plain and simple single beds, and a basic wardrobe to either side. On first impressions, it looked like things were starting to improve.

However, Freida stopped talking here, and her crying got worse. Sarah put her arm around her, and in time the joint Tech-Tabs continued the tale on her behalf, using the female voice of 'Ella.'

"I was disgusted at the idea of becoming a concubine for the king. But I hated the idea of the barracks even more, because it would mean at least one different man every night."

"Of course, the Chief Prince option wasn't that much better. You can see that Chief Prince Asama was very fat, with layers of skin, on top of layers of skin. He also wasn't all that hygienic. I had seen him around the palace on occasions, talking very loud to impress others. Sometimes he would leer at us girls, and make obscene gestures."

The memories of the Chief Prince were replaced by the memories of more guards. And a series of green people in smart black suits, carrying clipboards, and looking very official.

"I remember the day the guards joked that "he likes young girls, but is surrounded by Egyptian officials, who would be jealous, and corrupt "League of Nations" delegates who would not be impressed." So for this reason he kept his distance until we were old enough."

"We tried to avoid him as well, but this was difficult as we had to go where his daughter in law told us. This was often where the Chief Prince hung out. On

one occasion he looked at me with contempt and said "I would pay for being such a tease."

"That evening, I got a very severe beating from Princess Philippa, for wearing the only clothes we were given by her. My skin smarted all night from the cane, and the bruises made indentations in my skin. But the following day, despite the pain I was in, we started to receive dance lessons on top of our duties."

The corridors of the palace were replaced by a small seedy bar. It was lit by red lights, and was playing slow music. There was a small stage, next to the bar, that had its own dance poles. Girls were practicing routines, looking like it was enjoyable. But at the front, another girl could be seen crying, and in great distress.

"We were taught belly dancing, and all other means of seductive dancing. However, the beatings were now restricted to non-visible and covered parts of our bodies, as at least once a week we were made to dance seductively before the Chief Prince and his guests, at supper time."

I knew that some of the other girls were turning seventeen now, and being forced to sleep with him. They clearly did not enjoy it."

"When Suzie was taken there, she came back a nervous wreck, and over the next few weeks, she turned into a living zombie, as the light went from her eyes. Emily must have had a worse time, because she never returned to our room. Apparently she displeased the Chief Prince, and was sent to the barracks for what was called "soldier sport." I never saw

her again. This was not uncommon, as many girls were sent to the barracks and others sold in Gaza."

Freida was crying uncontrollably now. And continued to do so.

Sarah knew which way this was going. This was child trafficking at its worst. It was abusive and sick to her. But she had already heard that this went on in this dimension from the media. Only this was a friend of hers. And the virtual reality made it more real than she would have liked. The pain of another person, she cared about was there in front of her. She could see, smell and hear all she had gone through. And because Freida hurt, so did she!

And in the silence of her own thoughts, she started to ask the questions like, "where was The Whisper when this was happening. And why did he allow it?"

In the simulation she could now see Freida praying whenever she got the chance for release from her suffering. And she could hear nothing except a silence, between Freida's sobs, as she continued to pray even though it was hurting her to do so.

Now in the anger of her heart, Sarah asked if "the Whisper was listening to the story as well?" And there was silence, and Freida became more composed, took a deep breath, and finished her story herself.

The seedy bar was replaced with only one image, the door to what was probably the Chief Prince's bedroom. It was made from expensive mahogany, and had a crown on the door.

"On my seventeenth birthday," she continued, taking charge back from Ella. "I was ordered to wear a white and green dress and veil, and was taken to the king. I pleaded as he did unspeakable things to me. It hurt, and I struggled to breath under his enormous body and weight. I cried into my pillow as he continued, with the lights out. He heard me, but continued, and didn't care."

"In the morning; I was tired, bruised and in shock. But that vile man said I 'would have to improve, or else.' And for that reason, he called for my services the next night as well. This was repeated for months. And I hated him. And I hated myself. And I wanted to die."

Sarah removed her headset, and straightened up. Freida had also taken her mask off again. Now as gently as she could manage, Sarah kindly took the crying face of Freida, and told her, "Now listen to me. This was not your fault. It was all theirs. They murdered your family, and probably your village. Then they abused their power, to abuse you more, over a long period of time. And you were their prisoner, so could not consent. This was wrong. In fact; it was sick."

"Since I got here," Sarah continued, "I have been reading your writings, and you have helped me, because you are kind. I know from even my limited knowledge of those writings: that people in power are meant to look after those below them. They are meant to speak up, and stop injustice, but they perpetrated it. Their acts were an abomination to humanity, and one day, they will receive their punishment."

She stopped talking, and Freida seemed to cry less. And Sarah thought for just a second, that she could hear 'The Whisper' agreeing with her. And in this moment she turned to her friend, and in compassion told her "Now listen, you do not have to tell me any more if you don't want to! I have got the gist. Although I am curious about how you escaped?"

The question of how Freida escaped her ordeal was the turning point of the story.

"Well I have gone this far," Freida replied, as memories of the palace emerged around her. They changed constantly as rooms were replaced by other rooms.

"I have already told you that I wanted to die. Well during this time, I lost track of who I was. I would wander around more, because the beating had virtually stopped. The king wanted me looking good, and bruises didn't fulfill that requirement, unless they came from him"

"Then one day, I was preparing myself in the mirror, when I suddenly realized, that I no longer recognized myself. I had made an effort that day, but I looked like a common hooker, and smelled of too much perfume. I was no longer the young girl, modestly dressed and naively in love, with a boy from my vil-

lage called Simeon. In fact, the mere memory of his face seemed more and more remote to me. And I felt as if I was never worthy of him, as all I knew were beatings from the Princess that had rained down on me for many years."

"Yet despite all this, I also knew that I was more, than what I was being programmed, to believe that I was. The Gazans would have had us believe, that we were just primitive apes, but instead here I was thinking for myself. My sense of self was growing, despite the pressures to conform, and I was now aware that I could resist my slavery. I don't know where I got the strength, as it seemed to just come from inside. If only, perhaps, in the smallest of ways."

"I realized that there must be an alternative, if I could just figure it out. For me though, most of the time, all I could think of was ending my life, and stopping the misery, by taking others with me."

The memories now focused in on a very large kitchen with lots of staff. Benjamin and Adah could now be seen in the background. They were looking on with sympathy, as Freida sat alone in a small office. She seemed to be helping herself to some food. The image froze.

"My status, as a mistress meant I was allowed into the kitchen where some of the best cooks from around the world were employed. There were two people there, a married couple called, Adah and Benjamin, from Celtishia, who noticed my unhappiness, and allowed me to hide down there, whenever I

wanted to escape my abusers for a few moments. But in time, I stupidly abused their trust."

"One day, I was down there hiding from those above. I sneaked into the store room, and stole a knife. I then gave myself a cut across the arm, wanting to bleed, feeling I deserved to suffer for the sexual acts I was allowing myself to perform."

"But Adah saw me, and ran to my aid. Then like my mother would have done, when I fell over through loss of blood. She bandaged me up. She sat me down, and gave me something to eat. It was just what I needed. A simple bit of love and concern."

"Over time, they knew that I could keep secrets, and confided in me that they were planning to return to Celtishia, and asked if I would like to go with them. Well of course I did. I was almost dead where I was."

"But I had one concern. And just couldn't go. The man who was doing this to me, would continue with others. In fact, a new shipload of girls had just arrived. Now that vile Princess Phillipa, was treating another three girls the same as Suzie, Emily, and myself."

"One day, I just lost it in their presence", and with that the images changed to a concerned looking Benjamin and Adah.

"I told them, I intended to go out in glory, so to speak. I want to kill the Chief Prince of Palestine, even though I would be impaled publically when caught."

"Now just hold it right there, daughter," Benjamin suddenly corrected her.

"And I was brought to my senses."

"He deserves to be punished, for rape;" he continued, "and this is possible under the influence of drugs. We will help you to drug him, and then photograph him. The shame it would bring him would be worse to him than death. We will train you, and you can escape with us afterwards.".

And once again, the image froze.

"They explained to me that in the Arab culture of this world, decisions are made in conjunction with status and a person's honor. A compromising photo, if made public, would effectively finish the regime there."

"Over the next week, I came to realize that Benjamin and Adah were agents, employed by a new foreign Queen called Boudicca, to help the Jewish people in Palestine. They got permission to teach me how to cook, and told me to take a baked cake every time the Chief Prince sent for me. But between eating, and mistress duties: (that would continue for the time being), they trained me to conceal a weapon, and use it."

At this point images of knives and cakes flashed around them, as the memories were clearly summarizing a few months in one go.

"It turned out that I was a good cook, and a fast learner. But I was even better with a knife."

"Now the Chief Prince started to make me a favourite, for he enjoyed the treats I brought him. (This annoyed Princess Phillipa, who could no longer touch me.) I made a special point of hand feeding him,

with a hint of subtle seduction."

"Benjamin and Adah had taught me to fake a sensual smile, and advised me to use it when with the Chief Prince. "Just pretend," they said. "He will never know the difference, as that is all his wives do anyway. Inflate his ego, and you will gain his trust. He is shallow that way."

"And so I did, and I took the cake, and I would feed it directly to him from my hand, whenever he lay down. Out of necessity, I became a good actor, and the Chief Prince started to fall for me, and called for me more. He really believed that I loved him, and really enjoyed his company. But that was the plan, you see."

The cakes faded into just one cake. It was round in shape, and covered in fruit and icing. It was being carried on a silver platter, by a younger version of Freida. She was wearing a very seductive green and pink spiraled dress, and a selection of fruit were draped around her neck, and attached to her body. Her green tights stopped just above her knee, and were supported by gold suspenders. Her hair was in pigtails, and she was wearing no shoes.

"Then we exacted our plan. One night, as I had done before, I approached the chamber with a cake. It was probably the best cake I have ever made. It was covered in his favorite icing, and laced with luxurious rum, and a sleeping drug. The idea was to only get him intoxicated, then take a photo for the internet, bringing shame on him, and an end to his reign

in charge."

"I wore seductive clothing, with fruit adorned in strategic places. This was quite usual. When they saw this, the guards made the usual rude innuendos about me being just the Chief Prince's mistress!

"You are just an Israeli whore, one of the guards was heard to yell," before they let into the Chief Prince's bedroom. It looked to Sarah that this had happened before, and they had no reason to suspect anything was wrong. Again the only image shown was the door of the room.

"I entertained the Chief Prince for about an hour, and hated every second of it. But I smiled anyway, and thought of nicer things, as best as I could. Then I suggested that he "lie down on the bed, and close his eyes, and I would bring him some cake in my hand." I brought him some, and he ate it from my hand, like he usually did. The rum relaxed him a little."

"However, it was obvious that things were not going according to plan, and the drug was failing to work. Instead of falling asleep he was just getting a little dizzy. I had to think fast, so I resorted to seduction, and suggested that perhaps the booze 'had gone down the wrong way.' I even said I would get some more, but he must keep his eyes closed, because I had a "treat" for him. So he closed his eyes believing that I was going do something he would enjoy. This time, though, I brought the knife, which was concealed in the cake, and kept it below the bed, just in case."

"This seemed to work, as he took his pleasure for about half an hour at my expense. But when he was

finished with me, he became angry, and the dizziness returned once more. And now knowing something was wrong, he told me he suspected that he was being poisoned by the chefs, and intended to call the guards, once he was dressed."

"Perhaps it was because I was covered in body fluids, and food remnants, that he never suspected me. Maybe it was because he thought I worshipped him as a man, and thought that what we did was fun. But he clearly thought I was innocent, and said I should "wait there", for he "would be back for more later."

"I knew however, that the game was almost up, and now he was getting dressed. Therefore, I knew the time had come to act."

The image of the door was now replaced by a new memory. This time Freida was in the bedroom and looking at the fat Chief Prince from behind. Sarah could see her arms in front of her, and feel the sweat of the Prince, as she embraced the man.

"So, I rose from the bed, and I approached him near naked from behind with a hug. I was attempting to distract him. To seduce my way out of the problem. He responded by gently laughing at me, as I then tried to urge him back towards the bed, pretending I wanted more, and he started back in that direction."

She was pulling the Prince's left arm, using both of her hands, that Sarah now noticed had been washed and painted with black nail varnish.

"But then he tripped and fell, and he landed on the knife, and it thrust into his back."

"What have you done to me," the Prince asked, as he wriggled in pain, trying to remove the knife. The scabbard of the blade could be seen protruding from his back, just out of reach.

"It was an accident," Freida pleaded to him, "but he got angry." Freida looked worried.

"You did this, so I am going to have you impaled.."

"But he never got to finish that sentence, and he gasped in surprise, when I started to fight back. In pain, he tried to call for help. But the use of my hand over his mouth, as Adah had trained me to do, was very effective. In desperation, he struggled, but all he could do was bite my hand. I continued to seize my chance despite the pain."

And Sarah saw it all like Freida had seen it. She could see the hand going down on his mouth, and the Prince biting while he fought for his last breath. He was clearly surprised that the girl he had thought loved him, was doing this to him.

"Eventually he started to fall onto the bed, dying right there and then. And because he was fat, the layers of his skin just drooped down and covered the knife; so it was no longer visible."

And Sarah saw the look of horror as the knife was twisted. And the Prince was seen giving his last breath, before his body went numb.

"I didn't know what to do, so I called Adah from the room, pretending to order room service. Establishing she was alone, I told her what had happened. And she talked me through what to do next."

"Under her advice, I then staged and took some photographs of the room, including my underwear on top of his body, the cake residue on the side of his mouth, and the Chief Prince naked on the bed."

Sarah was shocked. The younger Freida had killed her abuser. Benjamin and Adah who had later adopted her, had actually helped her. How could they have used her like that. But Freida continued, and answered that question as well.

"Now, this was what I had waited for about twelve months, but it felt awful. You see it takes a certain person to witness a death, and not be affected. But now I had to escape. So I did what I needed to do, and no more!"

"I made sure he was still on the bed, and placed him face up on his back. The knife in his back remained covered by the skin on his body, so I left it in there. I washed the skin surrounding it of any blood, and made him look like he was asleep."

"Now came the cold calculating bit. Some of the sheets had blood on them, so I placed these dirty sheets into a bin bag, and hid them under the bed. With new sheets and a blanket from the wardrobe, I then covered his naked body, leaving it dignified. His eyes were closed, as I felt he should be left looking as good as possible."

"I showered my body only to wash the blood of myself, then I dried myself with a towel. I smeared some of the food over myself make it look like I did before the attack. Then dressed in alternative skimpy

clothes, (which I tore myself), I simply left the room the same way that I came in."

"I told the guards outside that "Chief Prince Asama is now sleeping, and he does not want to be disturbed until ten am. The guards of course, suspected nothing, as they had seen me leave the Chief Prince asleep in his chambers before. I had even said that to them before. Besides, he was also known for getting up late at that time, and hated people who woke him early. Instead, the guards made their typical and sexist innuendos, like 'worn him out have you."

"And so, I now made my way down to our living quarters. There was a laundry hatch in the room, where the servants and concubines just dumped dirty linen through whenever they changed the bed. This was then outsourced to a business on the outskirts of the city."

"I jumped into the laundry hatch and came out in the laundry room, where Adah and Benjamin had planned to meet me. They had already disabled and tied up the one servant that was present. She was now struggling in a sitting position with a gag over her mouth."

"We apologized that we could not take her with us, and asked her to say anything that would help us escape."

"Half an hour later, the laundry van arrived, with a driver from Celtishia. It was stopped at first by Princess Phillipa. She was officially doing the rounds of the Palace to check that everything was ok. However, we had known for some time, she was visiting the

bedroom of an official late at night. She was tired herself and returning to bed in a hurry. The van was just waved on."

"We loaded in some of the laundry, including the sheets with the blood. Then the three of us jumped in. Then more laundry was loaded on top of us, by the driver. The door was shut. The van drove off. We were waved through at security by the lazy guards, and got out of the palace. It was as simple as that."

"The car took us to a rendezvous point. Which was a disused warehouse near the airport. The people meeting us were worried when they heard of the assassination at first, but carried on with our escape plan."

"We changed into different clothes, that made us look like posh officials. Then they gave us some fake identification, and a ride to the airport."

"After passing security, we boarded a private plane. This plane now took a short journey to Switzerland, where we got the connection to Celtishia. We landed at approximately six am in Celtishia, and immediately I put the request in for political asylum, claiming we had escaped a tyrannical regime, and telling the story of being trafficked."

"Adah and Benjamin had ensured that we would be expected. In fact, we were greeted by an official entourage, who were standing with the new Queen, Boudicca 11th. At this stage, she was aged only twenty years old, and officially under the control of a Royal Protector. She still, however, had the authority to grant pardons, and asylum requests at her *request, without the authority of her Council. This was done almost instantly, as an exercise in political maneuvering, and completed by eight am."*

Celtishia it turned out recognized the ancient principle of sanctuary cities for people who commit manslaughter by mistake.

"At ten am the Egyptians must have discovered the body, and by eleven am, there was a press statement.

<u>Breaking News</u>

Chief Prince Asama of Palestine found dead in compromising position Suspicion clearly pointing a fall and alcohol abuse

"The weeks went by, and we kept a low profile in Celtishia. Meanwhile our operatives on the ground continued to report back and update us. But nobody had expected things to turn out the way they did."

"It appeared at first, that the Palestinian Authorities were too proud to admit that they had been wrong footed by a small group of uneducated Israelis, as they saw us."

"However, in time, intelligence revealed that there was no evidence of me ever being there, as our abductions were kept secret, and strictly off book. Nor was there a record, (or even a photo,) of Adah and Benjamin, as the palace officially hired only local workers. Up to this point, the officials of his palace had kept quiet out of fear for their lives, but they were now talking. However, the trail quickly ran cold."

"It soon became obvious that things were slowly

coming out. Now international observers were everywhere. The death of the Chief Prince, was a big issue, but they could not find anybody to blame. Potentially it looked like an Egyptian interference, and conspiracy theorists everywhere placed the blame on Pharaoh, who denied everything as they expected he would. The Chief Prince's wife was also implicated as a woman who had an involvement in human trafficking, and therefore disgraced in the eyes of the world media before returning to Lebanon using diplomatic immunity."

"We became aware that, even though they had seen me leave, the guards had not stopped me, and this made them look incompetent. So they collectively said nothing about me. And so, nobody ever really told the truth, as they valued their own reputations more."

"And so, Princess Phillipa had become the potential new heir, but the international community to my great pleasure chose not to ratify this. It appeared that a rumor had spread, because she was known to be having an affair. The opposition had seized on this indiscretion to imply that she had been trying to manipulate herself to power, by sleeping with a rival of the Chief Prince. Nobody could doubt she would have done this, and she also wasn't liked. So this became an 'issue worthy of investigation'."

"New evidence emerged that suggested that she was prone to violence, with her servants. Many of whom were trafficked women, who were now dead. Further evidence was given implementing Princess Phillipa,

by the girl in the laundry room, who claimed that it was the Princess who had tied her up, and had intended to sell her later. The buyers fled when things went wrong. This testimony increased international concern."

"Her mother pleaded her daughter's innocence, but was ignored. In addition, it was perceived that the people in the region were close to rioting as no justice was being done for the villages that had been attacked and robbed of their young women over many years"

"Palestine is now ruled by an interim council, and has been for the last ten years."

"And well, I was granted asylum, and I was free to start afresh. But I was alone in the world. I was still legally a child, aged only seventeen."

"Luckily for me, Adah and Benjamin Sophia-Smith took me in. They said that "they would be proud to have me as their daughter." And so, they became my adoptive parents, and I am glad to be their daughter. For they have sacrificed the last ten years helping me to forget, and move on."

"Life was hard for me. I suffered nightmares for weeks on end. I lost weight through anorexia. I hated men, and sometimes got violent, whenever they approached me. I was constantly stressed, and even messed with my branding scar to try and get rid of it."

It was at this point Freida again removed the patch covering her right arm, for Sarah to see.

There were marks like scratches everywhere, cut into the skin some time ago, but still visible to see. Sarah looked at them, and knew instantly that they were caused by self- harm, probably involving a knife. Sarah now understood, why despite being Freida's best friend, she had not been allowed to view them even while sharing a room.

"Under security advice, I saw counselors in confidence at the military base where we were temporarily stationed. People genuinely tried to help, but I resisted wherever I could, and went into a downward spiral of self-harm, and being in trouble with the authorities, for petty theft and violence."

"Then one day, the young Queen Boudicca heard my story from some officials, and requested to meet me. She was aged only eighteen at the time, but had selected for herself the best advisors, including a rabbi, who understood my issues and advised her wisely."

"When we met, she was friendly, kind, and gracious, and came across as exceptionally intelligent for her years. She had already granted me asylum on the night I arrived, but knew that I needed more. And so in her Royal Capacity, she granted me a fresh opportunity, a full pardon and a clean slate, if I promised to stay out of trouble."

"There was of course a catch. Boudicca had trained in law at university. But she was required to do a year's military service within two years. She could also keep a close eye on me from there."

"However, this invitation made with concern for

my welfare from someone so high up, was challenging to me but what I needed. I accepted her offer, and she now promised to keep an eye out for me. And I cannot tell you how good it feels to have someone you admire tell you, that you matter to them."

"Then she offered our new makeshift family a homestead in Devonport, in the county of Dumnoni. This was generous of her, not least because Devonport is a sanctuary city, and therefore offered me legal protection, as long as I remain a tax payer there. But then she offered us extra free funds, as part of some 'Refugee Start Up" Initiative" to help us get started. This was very rare, but her right as Queen. I didn't fully understand her motive, until I saw the prophecy the other week with you. For I now know, that she must have read the prophecy and understood my part in it."

"Our family settled in well in Dumnoni, and our farm flourished. The extra funds enabled us to plant fruit trees, and prepare long term for the future. I received private tuition, and kept my part of the bargain."

"When I turned twenty, I served my military service with distinction because I was so well prepared. And of course Boudicca was breathing down my neck, spurring me to aim high and succeed. Despite having the authority to jail me within minutes if she had wanted to, Bou became a friend, and a colleague during this time."

On weekends off, I would return to Dumnoni, to spend time with my new family. My parents were so proud when I was later granted a place as in the special forces of Celtishia. I have advanced up the ranks, by hard work and by finding creative solutions to problems. Although, I know that Boudicca herself, has put in a few good words as well; along the way."

"Now that the queen has grown into her position more, I have become a trusted operative within her security team. I spend most of my time in Dumnoni, organizing defenses and reporting back directly to her. Having achieved the rank of Captain, I command just over two hundred people, and am often quoted as a success story."

Freida had finished her story, and Sarah sat up. She put her arm around Freida, and hugged her for ages, without saying a word. Sarah understood that this is what you do when you are concerned for someone; and want to show that you care. It was a sacred moment between them, and both of them knew that their friendship had just deepened. They both now had a best friend, that they could confide in, over anything.

From Sarah's point of view, she felt that she now understood Freida better. But she also felt guilty for the time she had tried to kick her when they first met. Of course, there was no way that she could have known about the mistreatment that she received as a child from the Princess.

She realized that while Freida would put on a strong front. In fact, she sometimes came across as being tough as nails, and could intimidate by just looking at you. But underneath it all, she was kind, caring and vulnerable. A young girl just trying to survive a bad ordeal as best as she knew how.

And Boudicca, she realized, was indeed a good leader, with wisdom well beyond her years. Even though she was the younger women, this had not held her back when it mattered. She was informed, dedicated and focused. For she had given Freida the help she needed, but allowed her to grow within herself.

And Sarah decided that stories like this should be prevented. She felt it was her duty to help, in whatever way possible, big or small. She just needed to figure out how?

Then she thought she heard a quiet sound in her ear.

"Go speak to Boudicca. She is Queen here, and she can advise you on the next step".

This thought had come to her. It was a realization that maybe they could figure this out. And that is why the Whisper had called her there!

10. CONNECTING

T he journey back to the base seemed like a long one, neither girl really having much more to think. But the PTMs drove quickly over the terrain, and they arrived back at the base in time for tea.

They ate and chatted as usual, then Sarah escorted Freida to bed early. They met Doris on the way, and Sarah asked her if she could wait outside their room, and Doris nodded knowingly. It appeared that she was also relieved that Freida was getting an early night, and had been worried that morning.

Sarah lay down on the opposite bed and rested, while Freida just drifted off to sleep. She was just exhausted from her emotional day. As soon as Freida was asleep, Sarah tucked her in with a blanket, then she left the room.

"Doris, would you mind going and asking Freida's parents to come and watch her, until I return?"

"Of course, she said, I will go and get them immediately. Leave it to me."

She returned thirty-five minutes later with Benjamin and Adah Sophia-Smith, and the two children, all of whom looked relieved. The parents saw Sarah, and went straight over and hugged her, before going inside to keep watch over their daughter.

The children followed saying nothing. But Sarah could hear Adah expressing concern about "how thin their daughter was looking." Sarah knew they were right, for she was eating noticeably less these last few days.

And with that Sarah tapped her Tech-Tab, and left a message that she was requesting to speak to Boudicca.

Boudicca was resting in bed herself, when she got the message. She had already been unofficially told that the girls had been talking, by one of the security team who had gone to the clearing with them. So she was kind of expecting contact from Sarah soon. She told Sarah to meet her in "The Prophecy Room," as they would not be disturbed there.

On the way, Sarah stopped and talked to a guard, but was not pleased by what she heard.

"Yes, the raids have continued. Three attempts today. It was on the news, so its official. A few casualties only on our side, but no successful slave abductions."

"Where were the attacks?"

"All in Dumnoni?"

"You mean Devon?"

"Do I?'

"No you don't. I'm sorry." For she had remembered she was in the Green Dimension. She paused and asked, "Where was attacked in Dumnoni?"

"Devonport, Exmouth, and Torquay. They were attacked by air, and sea. The cities have all received damage. But all repelled their attackers."

"Devonport! Any casualties?"

"A few, but non that were fatal this time. There is damage to key buildings and the naval dockyard though. It looks like these raids are meant to intimidate us only. And I don't know how long we can cope with it for."

"Then we need to start an offensive. Hit back somehow."

"I agree, but you need to convince the Queen," said the guard. "Only, she is committed to waiting this out for now. In fairness, this strategy has worked well for us for centuries."

"I know, and guess where I am off to now."

And with that she made her way to the Room of Prophecy to meet up Boudicca.

When Sarah arrived in the circular Room of Prophecy, she noticed that Boudicca was sitting on a chair around the large pine table. Sarah pulled up a chair next to her.

"I decided I would relocate my central cabinet," said Boudicca. "The prime Minister, and his key elected officials, will be here soon. There have been more raids we have to discuss. And I believe that more are coming."

"Good," said Sarah, "then it is a good thing that I spoke to you first. Cause I think that we need to do a counter strike. Hit at a critical point in their set up. But first I need to speak to you about Freida, if that's ok?"

The mention of Freida's name, indicated that Freida wellbeing was clearly a concern to the Queen. Sarah assumed this to be not surprising after what she had just heard and the mentorship Boudicca had herself provided her.

"You spoke to Freida then? She told you her story?"

"Yes."

"Is she ok?"

"Sort of, she got a lot of her chest."

Boudicca was not surprised by this, and enquired further. "I hope she is not alone now?"

"No. I got her parents to sit with her? Even though she is sleeping right now?"

Boudicca sounded relieved. "Great idea. They will look after her."

"And she told you everything, I assume?"

"I believe so. She mentioned abuse, revenge, murder, miscarriages of justice."

"Yep, that's about it."

"And she said you helped her."

"I have tried over the years. And I am quite fond of her really. I want to see Freida exceed her own expectations. That is why I helped her gain positions in her military career. But she doesn't know".

Sarah said nothing to this. Even though she knew Freida expected the Queens involvement. Eventually she spoke up. "Talking of the military, I want to see the raids stopped. I want to see the prisoners recovered and I want to see Egypt driven back to their homeland."

Boudicca looked taken aback by Sarah's bluntness, and sarcastically asked her, "and how do you think that we should do that then?"

"Pick a strategic location that matters to them and attack it hard. Somewhere that will hurt their ego. And cause them to make stupid mistakes as they defend their honour."

Boudicca paused, and started to pace the floor. Clearly she was weighing up her options before she eventually responded. "OK. I agree. But where would you hit?"

"I don't know yet."

"Then stick around here for the meeting, and maybe a target will arise."

The meeting involved all her chiefs of staff, and some of the elected government cabinet. Everybody there had something to say. It lasted about two hours. It was not much help. Mostly, the people in the room kept debating the same things over and over. They weighed up the advantages and disadvantages of their every idea, and jostled for their rights to be heard. No decisions were made, and even Boudicca eventually got bored.

When they had left, Boudicca turned to her and said, "I prefer meeting the military people. At least they come with ideas, and can get on with it, when they are asked."

"The problem with politicians everywhere," said Sarah, "is that they do like to sit on the fence a lot. And can be hopeless at making decisions."

"I have always found this room a great place to think," said Boudicca. "I just light a few candles, on the table, and reflect on the mahogany box. It helps me to focus. You should try it. Just sit here quietly and reflect, and see what comes to you. We call it 'Connecting'."

"Seriously?"

"Yes, and write what you come up with down onto paper. You can then examine it later, or check it with somebody else." And Boudicca nodded in a knowing way.

"Just like that?"

"Yes, here have the spare room key." And Boudicca gently threw it to her, and then started to leave. "And right now, I need ideas and solutions," she said. "Anyway, I must get on. Keep bringing your ideas to me. Just make them specific."

And so, Sarah lit some candles and just sat there. She thought that this was the most ridiculous thing she had ever done, and really couldn't see the point in it.

After half an hour, she got up and left.

Back in her room, she met up with Ben and Adah once more, as they watched over their sleeping daughter, Freida. The two children were asleep on the couch, and leaning into each other, oblivious to all that was going on around them. Once more the parents greeted Sarah with an affectionate hug.

Sarah was relieved that Freida's parents had come to approve of her, and asked them, "how is she?"

"Asleep," replied Adah. "She's okay, we think."

"She told me everything, you know."

"Really? Are you sure?" asked Adah.

"Well. What else could there be to tell?"

Adah and Benjamin looked at each other awkwardly at the mention of this. There was clearly something they knew that Adah would not discuss. Sheepishly, they looked in the direction of the two sleeping children. "Probably nothing really," said Adah, "just ignore us, foolish over protective parents that's all."

"That's all? You helped her escape. Then you took her in, and gave her a home. That's a seriously big all."

"Well we don't regret it. Never did. Even when the going was hard," Adah explained, with her arm now around Benjamin.

And so they continued chatting for an hour or so, about the green mist, and how Sarah was adjusting to the food they were getting.

"Mostly it is very good," she said, "I love the variety of raw beans, and cooked vegetables. I was not sure about the river snails, and the Brussel Sprout curry we had tonight though."

"Well I agree about the curry," said Benjamin, making a face of sheer horror. "That was one I will never forget."

Eventually the subject came around to the events of the night, and the meetings with Boudicca. Benjamin and Adah had the clearance to talk about this, and were able to offer some interesting insight.

"What you must remember," said Adah, "is that in the Egypt and Palestine Region, there is a lot more focus on "preserving honour," than on "honesty." Here we value honesty above all, and it is the cornerstone of all successful relationships." She looked lovingly at Benjamin, and continued, "so to dent the honor of Egypt, and humiliate them, as in 'really humiliate them,' is probably enough to see them go running back to their homeland. Shame is a great silencer that way."

"So any ideas?"

"I wish I had one. I want Egypt and their Pharaoh, to pay as much as you."

"What did Boudicca advise?" asked Benjamin, looking back lovingly at Adah. "After all you are probably the "New Great Destroyer" in the prophecy, that she loves?"

Sarah looked embarrassed. "She advised to reflect in candlelight. But, that's not really my thing, can't concentrate for long see. My mind wanders."

"It is good you tried. I imagine you thought it odd at first. I know I did."

"Yes, very!"

"That is usual. First, you need to stop trying so hard. Just empty your thoughts, and just be open to something else. Adjust to the silence. I find a simple mantra like 'I am listening, Holy Whisper' helps"

"But that room. It gives me the creeps."

"You are probably stressed after today, and tired. Why not try again tomorrow? You could also try using the Devonport Temple instead. There is more to do and read there, if you get distracted."

"Yeah, you are probably right."

"I am right, now get yourself off to bed," said Adah, "and I'll keep watch over you both."

And so, Sarah got dressed into night clothes, and lay down to sleep in the bed next to Freida. Adah sat alone in the chair next to them, and slowly let her drift off.

In her dreams that night, she saw once again the rain and the lightning. She heard the bell sounds, felt the mist wet against her skin, and saw again the Earth that fell from the sky's bright white light. Then she dreamt about a raiding party near the City of Devonport, and of course her best friend Freida, as she was escaping the palace in Gaza.

She awoke suddenly, and sat up with a start, at two am in the morning. Adah was sitting on the side of her bed, and started mopping her forehead, with a steamy towel.

"Bad dreams?" She asked. "I could see you moving frantically in your bed, and then you screamed out."

"Yes, the same recurring dreams. Nightmares in some ways."

"Well, there is nothing for you to worry about. You are safe here. Try to get yourself back to sleep."

Sarah, lay back down again, and fell asleep quickly. Only this time, she dreamt about the raiding party, being attacked in their port by drones, and a submarine below the waves.

She awoke refreshed. She had a plan, but wanted to be certain before she went to the Queen. She wanted to mull it all over first, maybe even run it past Freida first.

However, Sarah was torn between the advice of the Sophie-Smiths, and Boudicca. Boudicca had suggested using the Room of Prophecy to reflect. However; Adah and Benjamin were suggesting, she used the Devonport Synagogue near the base. In the end, she decided to go with the advice of the Sophie Smiths, and set off for the Temple, to try and "connect" again.

She was escorted by a security team, under the orders of Queen Boudicca.

Freida awoke half an hour later, to the news that Sarah needed her advice on a military idea, but would catch up with her later. Her parents took her to breakfast, (and stood close to her) while she ate. The children ate next to her. Freida knew that they were making sure that she was not tempted to go anorexic on them again. With her parents there, she was encouraged, and ate a good meal. She enjoyed the company. And for the first time in ages, she was starting to feel better.

Sarah had known of the temple for some time, but to this day had yet to visit it. The temple was located in the third left dome near the Devonport Base, and was hidden about one hundred and fifty metres below ground. It was originally set up for devotees of "The Whisper, and had become over time, one of the most famous temples in all Celtishia. It was an amazing site, and Sarah could see why Benjamin and Adah, had suggested it for reflection.

It was accessible via a huge glass elevator that took people underground. As they continued the descent, they could see the magnificent temple come into view. It was known to have ceilings over forty metres high, and yet Sarah could not have imagined the enormity of the building from images alone.

The synagogue was shaped like a half moon, with chairs around a central stage. The stage was surrounded by seven pillars, also in a half moon shape. This was just the first level, and it was reserved for the men only.

The second level was the balcony, which was reserved for the women. It was carpeted in green, and had chairs in a semi-circle also overlooking the stage, which was the reason why the temple was so well known.

One that stage was what looked like a giant fire pit, into which sacrifices of dead animals could be made. The meat could be smelled blending with herbs like lavender, and parsley, and most believed that it gave a pleasant aroma. Priests dressed in green and white robes, stirred the meat, and would then share some with the poor of the nearby communities.

In front of the fire pit, was a replica of the Ark of the Covenant. It was a beautiful large golden box, and measured about two metres long, by one metre wide and deep. On its side, it had two golden hoops, with golden poles for carrying. It had a golden lid, with two golden angels leaning across and touching their wings together.

Sarah sat in the right hand side of the balcony, and looked down on the stage. She stayed sitting in silence for about twenty minutes. To avoid distraction, she was saying a mantra to herself as suggested, and trying not to let her mind wander.

The truth was that she was not being very successful, and was about to give up for the day. Then her eye, was suddenly drawn to something else. A strange woman, whom she recognized as one of the people, who had insulted Freida in the Laundry room, had entered the balcony. She placed something down and then got up to leave rather sheepishly.

Sarah went to take a closer look. There below her hidden on the inside of the balcony was a painting of a crocodile headed human eating a lamb. The last thing she expected to see. So Sarah looked around, and beckoned over a female temple assistant.

"Excuse me, but what does that image have to do with this temple?"

The assistant looked horrified, and quickly confiscated the offending item, before replying, "oh. Nothing at all. It shouldn't even be here."

"So why is it?" asked Sarah.

The woman sighed, "well I guess somebody has placed it there. We remove three every day. Some people think that they are being diverse, (and showing tolerance,) by desecrating this place, with an image from another country, and by giving voice to a religion that hates us."

"Doesn't make sense to me," said Sarah. "What is it supposed to be anyway?"

"Well, it is a symbol of the supposed Egyptian Pharaoh's dominance over all other religions.

Among other gods the Egyptians worship the Crocodile God "Sobek," who is human, with the head of a crocodile. The lamb, of course, represents the Israelis who live here in Celtishia, and Europe. It is therefore an anti-Semitic symbol."

The assistant could tell that Sarah was not impressed, and wanted a bit more information. "That particular image is found on a miniature pyramid shrine that was put up on the Isle of Sark, in the Channel Islands. It has a crocodile pool in front of it, with a live crocodile in it. I believe that they feed it on rebels."

"When The Island of Sark was captured seven years ago, the Egyptians set up the shrine and the array. And ever since have used it for broadcasting their propaganda to these shores."

"Really?" Said Sarah. "Now do me a favor, and dispose of it for me will you."

"Of course," said the assistant. And with that she took the image, and handed it to a priest on the lower balcony. The priest placed it straight into the fire pit, along with some incense and more herbs.

"I believe that crocodile tastes like pork, but I don't eat that either." The assistant now turned to Sarah, and asked, "I don't suppose you know who left it here do you?"

Yes, and Sarah pointed to the other side of the balcony, where the same woman had now reappeared, and was doing exactly the same thing somewhere else. Another image, and another location, and a bag full of many more, could be seen in her possession.

The temple assistant was outraged, and blew a large whistle while pointing at the woman. The desecrator was immediately surrounded by other temple guards, (both male and female,) and placed under arrest for the crime of sacrilege.

The assistant looked at Sarah, and smiled approvingly, before explaining the incursion of male guards into the female area. "Oh yes, the male guards are allowed into the female part to make arrests only. And thank you for your help. Much appreciated." And with that the assistant left the room, to deal with the issue, leaving Sarah all alone in the balcony.

"You're welcome," replied Sarah quietly as the woman was leaving. And with that she tried to go back to her reflection, and it was here that the answer quietly came to her.

"The target for the counter strike is Sark, the Sobek Shrine, and the communications' array. It will prove to be a pivotal moment"

Sarah looked around in shock. The voice felt so real, even though it had been so quiet. She could literally hear it in her ear, and move through her entire body. Was she going mad, or was it real? She looked behind her, but could see nobody. Yet the voice seemed real.

The smell of the incense from the altar was getting stronger now, and the weird voice repeated itself from behind her.

"Hello, Sarah," it said.

"Hello. Do I know you?"

"No. But I The Whisper know you, and I pass on messages sometimes."

The voice continued now from her left. "I am found in "Ancient Wisdom", and in the conscience that eats away when things are wrong. I am always present, but rarely heard. But I always speak to those who listen."

This time the voice spoke into her right ear. "I am part of you. Within you. I am found in the building blocks of life called DNA, and I made the sand, sea, and sky. I am like your guide, and I will show you the way through, even when it seems there is no way forward."

"And what is your message?" asked a frightened Sarah. She was desperately looking around hoping to catch someone having a joke with her.

And the voice then spoke into both inner ears. "The target for the counter strike should be Sark, and the communications array. It will prove to be a pivotal moment"

"Why?"

"Because the array is being used to spread lies, via radio, to the people of Celtishia."

"Because the array is being used, to coordinate the raids, and the boats usually leave from the Channel Islands to do their raids."

"Because the very presence of the Sobek Shrine

challenges the Whisper! And I, The Whisper, have no rivals."

"But why are you telling me?" asked Sarah who was now face down on the ground in fear.

"Because you, the Great New Destroyer, have been selected to help."

"Ok. So why me? I am not a warrior." asked Sarah. For inside she felt that this was dangerous, scary and weird.

"Do you have to be?" The Whisper replied, "Besides, you are stronger than you think. You are an amazing leader, though you have yet to realize it. Your role is to motivate others, to think differently, to set an example, and to be seen to do so."

"So what do I do? What can I do?" Sarah was panicking now, and trying hard to get out of this.

"Go with all that is inside you, and give it your best effort. Appear with Boudicca on television, raise an army, and strengthen what remains. Take Freida, and work with her. Seek her advice, let her guide you. Free the people from their fears of the oppressors. Tell the truth, in whatever way you understand it. Go out with the intention to destroy all the false images, and fake shrines."

"But why? Why destroy the shrines? Isn't diversity and tolerance a good thing?"

The whisper came through quietly once more, and the voice cut like a knife into Sarah's argument, and reduced it to rubble.

"Yes it is, but sometimes diversity in practice means getting rid of evil for the greater good. When tolerance means putting up with the abuse of people, through slavery, intimidation and oppression, then it is not tolerance. It is wrong, pure and simple."

And Sarah didn't argue the point, or ask questions, but just sat there for two hours in silence. And eventually, the smell from the incense got lighter, and Sarah could sense through the mystery of the strange events that had occurred, that The Whisper was present, but silent.

11. THE PLAN

W hen Sarah left the temple, she knew what needed to be done. Furthermore, she had written it down on a beer mat. She had asked the assistant for paper, but that was the nearest thing to paper, she could find.

The first thing on the list was to go and speak with Freida. She found her at lunch, having her usual river snails, and green naan bread with green salsa dip.

"I don't know why you eat those things?" Sarah said focusing on the snails, and offering a kind of greeting in the process.

"Cause, I like them, full of vitamins, and they keep you regular."

"Well I can't argue with the last point. They look vile," she joked.

"Glad to see you too," replied Freida, responding to the banter.

So Sarah sat down next to Freida.

"We need to talk," she whispered to her. Now getting serious, she continued. "I have an idea, and I need your input, before I go to Boudicca."

"Of course, I will help anyway that I can. You

know that."

"Good, I want advice on a drone attack. Like how to do one"

"A drone attack? Why?" Freida was clearly mystified. "That is not a usual tactic for Celtishian forces, when we are boxed in, and very risky."

"I know. The stakes could be high, but it is important."

"Well, I know who to talk too," replied Sarah helpfully. She thought some more. "In fact the contact is on base at the moment. All we need to do really is plan a route and target for the drones."

"Well we already have the target. The idea came during a quiet time in the temple this morning."

"So, which port in France are we going after then?"

"That's the thing, you see. The target is the Egyptian communications array on Sark!"

"What are you serious? It is probably highly guarded."

"Perhaps not every day. We are aware from intelligence, are we not, that attacks come from Jersey every Wednesday. Well, when they are attacking us, the drones will attack Sark, from the other direction. From the French side."

Freida was bewildered now. "How are we going to get them there? To the French side? To attack Sark?"

"Well, that is where the submarine comes in, and I reckon that ten of your best drones could do the job."

Freida looked baffled, "A drone attack from a submarine. I admit they will never think of that. I certainly hadn't. So I guess that I had better introduce you to our contact then. His name is Judah by the way. Bit of a geek, but he knows his stuff."

They left the canteen and went to meet the contact on the other side of the HUB. He was in a large open room, with a sign on the door that read "N.S.T. - New System Trials." Inside there were many people in black uniforms, all playing around with electronical equipment.

"This whole building is where they design, create and trial some of the latest military technology, and our contact is one of many players," said Freida. "However, if you want somebody who is a bit crazy, and can commit to a solution, then he is the man. Most will just sit on the fence, and give non-committal answers, but this guy will take a risk. That's him over there."

Freida was pointing to a guy with green skin, and long hair. He wore the same uniform as the others, except his was notably scruffier, and un-ironed. On his shoulder was a Star of David crest, with a '6' in the middle, indicating his rank.

They looked through the window at what he was doing. At first glance, he seemed to improving a drone on the workbench. Although, he was clearly struggling to make the adjustments, and looked like he was getting stressed by the process."

"Are you sure that this is our guy? He looks like he is going to thump that machine next," Sarah pointed out.

"Its a good strategy. If in doubt; hit the thing. It will usually work then," replied Freida, and she knocked on the window, and signaled for him to open the door.

Judah looked up from his work. He seemed to gasp in horror, at the sight of Freida. Clearly he knew her, and did not like her. However, he got up to open the door, and let them both in.

"Oh I forgot to mention. We have some history. Haven't always seen eye to eye. You had better do the talking. Besides its your idea." And with that Freida entered, and Sarah followed.

"Hi, and welcome to the N.S.T. Division" Lawrence greeted them. "My name is Judah. I am the Rank Six in this department.

"So you are in charge then?" asked Sarah.

"That's right," he replied, "and you must be Miss Sarah Salter. Of course the whole Hub is talking about you. The girl from the Mist-Less Dimension. The girl with pink skin.

"Yes, but I wish people wouldn't mention it."

"I know Freida already, of course. She always comes to see me when she wants something crazy and possibly unrealistic. Anyway, I meant no offence to you Sarah." He paused. "So what can I do for you, Miss Salter?"

And for the next half an hour, they chatted.

Sarah explained all about the plan, and Judah occasionally interrupted to ask questions, and to say things like, "hmm, I see."

Finally, he summarized. "So let's get this straight, you want to attack a satellite communications array, from Sark itself. And you want to use about ten drones that can be launched from a small submarine, from underwater, on the French side. And you want the attack to happen and be over in thirty minutes?"

"Yes," said Sarah.

And at the same time, you want a drone to kill the crocodile? And you want to turn the pyramid shrine, (the one next to the array,) upside down, to cook it in? Are you two stark raving mad?"

"It appears so," said Freida smiling, and Judah grimaced like he knew he shouldn't have asked.

"The question is" said Sarah, interrupting the exchange of indifferent looks, "Can it be done?"

"Well. In theory. Yes!" And Judah, went on to explain. "But to do so, we will have to go full out timewise, to adapt a miniature submarine drone in time. And it will be a challenge to train drone flyers for the task of lifting the crocodile, and upending the pyramid. Maybe the local resistance can be contacted there to help? And we will need more than one type of flying drone. So I will need authorization from a high level?"

"Great, I'm seeing Boudicca next," Freida casually mentioned, as if taunting him somehow.

Judah's eyes noticeably lit up at the mention of the Queen's name, but he tried not to show it. Eventually he responded to them. "I'll get started then. I have never known her say no to Freida."

The meeting with Boudicca was not going to be easy. Freida know of course that the idea had to be well thought out, and presented formally to her. And she also knew that there would be military advisors with her. However, Freida already served in the armed forces, and knew many of those that would be present. Most of them were sympathetic towards her, as of course was the Queen.

But Freida and Judah also knew that she would have to have worked out the details, and be prepared for any emergency that could arise on the day. There would have to be a back-up plan in place in case something went wrong. This would probably mean self-destructing drones, to avoid them being seized, and backwards engineered by their enemies.

With this in mind, they requested a meeting with Boudicca, and her staff, at 7pm. Even with three hands going flat out, the preparation took all afternoon, but was just finished in time.

When the three of them arrived at the meeting, they were starting to feel the pressure. Being told to, "wait outside until you are called," did not help matters much. After five minutes, they were invited in, but the time seemed longer to them.

There was Boudicca sitting in the center of the room, behind a circular table. Her advisors sat on either side of her. Sarah guessed on there being twelve other people in total. They included Chief Airman Boaz, who was drinking from a hip flask, and telling jokes in a jovial manner.

Sarah studied the face of Boudicca for support, hoping for some encouragement for her and Freida. However, it appeared that the Queen had her eye on Judah. Sarah suspected that she pitied him, for having put up with the Freida and herself all afternoon.

The lights went off, except for the projector that was shining onto a white wall. An image of the target array came up. Freida took two steps forward, paused, drew in some breath, and began the presentation.

"My learned Queen. Let me take this opportunity to thank you, and your advisors for your time. My colleagues Sarah, and Judah have been putting together a strategy for fighting back against Egyptian aggression. Our objective is not just to weaken their propaganda potential, but send a message that our islands will not be messed with anymore. It is our hope that the humiliation that this raid will cause, will encourage them to withdraw from our region as soon as possible."

And over the next ten minutes, Freida explained the strategy in full, then Judah answered their questions.

By the time that they had left the meeting, Boudicca was smiling positively, and they had the go ahead to proceed. The raid was set for four weeks later.

The first two weeks were a very stressful time, as the requirements of the raid got discussed at length in the N.S.T, and not everybody was as enthusiastic about the ideas. There were arguments over specifications, and whether getting the drones to lift weights was a good idea. But eventually thirty drones were up to the required standard, and then the three leaders Sarah, Freida and Judah moved to another room in the hub, to work with the drone flyers.

This room had been set up as a sort of mission control. The military drones meanwhile were over one hundred miles south, being controlled over a long distance. The room was fitted out with state of the art technology, including radar and satellite imaging. Admittance was by security clearance only, as it was from here that the drone controlling would take place on the night. Sarah preferred the second group much more. They were positive people, who would try anything with their flying drones. The drones themselves resembled round flying saucers, and their specifications had them at seventy-five center-meters in diameter, and capable of lifting half a ton each. The controllers had started to develop rapport with individual drones, and the plan started to take shape. They practiced almost continuously, with simulations of what was required. Eventually they were ready with two days to spare.

The two days were ideal for the drones had to be loaded onboard a mini submarine, and that had to make its way across to Sark, from the South of Celtishia. This was a journey of about eighty kilometres.

However, because of technology, she could view the action, one hundred kilometres south of her. There was a marina, and a sloping jetty going into the sea. The sea itself looked crystal clear, and the green mist was hovering above it as Sarah came to realize was usual. There were small waves coming in and going out continuously, and lapping gently on the jetty.

But yet again, Sarah had not quite expected the shock that was in store for her, when she saw the sea drone. It was about two metres wide, with two bulging eyes, two pincers, and six legs. It was painted in a red and black camouflage pattern. It looked like a giant crab.

"What is it?" Sarah asked.

"A submarine drone. Designed to travel from here to Sark, without a driver," replied Judah.

"So why does it look like a crab?" she asked.

"Because, it is a crab submarine drone. State of the art. Talks and shoots flames from its eyes when its above water. And to keep the look, it even goes sideways."

"I can see that! But why in the name of The Whisper, would you want it to?"

"So it can travel underwater. Cut cables, carry stuff, and avoid radar detection. Its advanced scanners fool other technology, into thinking it is smaller than it is. They think it is a crab, when they see it. Not the fastest machine, as it only goes six kilometres per hour below water, but it should totally fool the Egyptian surveillance systems."

This was one of those moments when Sarah was stopped dead in her tracks, and couldn't think of anything to say. She had to admit, there was genius in the stupidity.

Judah continued. "If it is launched now, it will carry the drones hidden in its shell, and make the journey to the Beach at Sark, in time for the raid. Its shell opens, and the air drones fly out and take over. Finally, it can help use its pincers to help lift the pyramid and start cooking the crocodile."

"Then it returns to the water, where it will cut some fibre-optic cables on the way back to here. This means that re-establishing communications afterwards from underwater cables will be next to impossible."

"And what could possibly go wrong?" asked

Sarah, with a sense of humour in her voice.

"Well. I believe that we have thought of every eventuality," said a random techie, who clearly didn't get her humour.

And with that the sea drone was placed on the ground. launched, by walking itself into the sea, and submerging until it was out of sight.

From a screen, Sarah could see that a map of the area, she had just seen. There was now a flashing red light, where the crab drone was.

"We will monitor its progress from here, and steer it, if necessary, to avoid obstacles. It is following a safe route through the sea bed, that our satellites in orbit have tracked for it."

"How long will it take to reach the target?" asked Freida.

"About twenty hours. Now go, and get some sleep," said Judah, looking pleased with himself. "And, by the way, Boudicca is joining us to watch, when the raid starts." He looked very pleased at this.

The first ten hours passed quite quickly, but neither Sarah nor Freida could sleep. They talked, and joked, and watched films in their room. Then they finally gave up on the sleep. Instead they returned to the operation room. There was another six hours to spare.

The room was full of techies sitting at desks. They were monitoring a variety of screens. There were maps, and statistics everywhere.

And most of it made no sense to Sarah. Freida, however, looked a bit more interested and knowledgeable. In fact, Sarah thought that she had returned to being the confident and no nonsense Freida she first met.

Sarah saw her ask questions, query the results, give disapproving looks, and motivate others. And this pleased Sarah, because it was the first time in weeks, Freida had shown any real confidence.

Finally, Freida came over to Sarah, and offered an explanation.

"The most important screen is the big one on the wall," she said, and pointed at it. "It shows a map, and where our key forces are. They are in green. If enemy forces move from their current locations, they will show in red. The techies to the left will then try and get a closer look, through satellite and other visual technology."

We then instruct our forces on what to do, and the map responds accordingly. However, please remember that we are not just dealing with images on a screen, but people, drones, and warships. Real lives are affected by what happens today."

"Sounds simple, yet dangerous," said Sarah, feeling humbled by the enormity of it all.

Freida realized her concern, and spoke kindly to her. "I know, there is a lot at stake here. War is rarely a pleasant business. People die, and the consequences are real. But the plan is set, and if it goes well, a difference will be made. Lives could be saved in the long run. But let's also hope that the long-distance signals work ok, as it seems the mist if particularly strong today, and it affects the signals, both theirs and ours."

"That could be a problem?"

"Yes, but the local militia, are being primed to initiate self-destruct on the drones, if necessary. We are communicating securely by an adapted Morse Code as we speak."

"So what now?" Sarah asked.

"We wait, until the Egyptians start their raid from Jersey. Our spies in Jersey have told us that a major attack is on today, and at least half their stationed forces are involved. The target is Devonport again. But this time, we are waiting in numbers, and planning to destroy most, if not all their forces."

Sarah looked a little worried, because the stakes had just been raised. But Freida continued with her explanation. "This will also allow us to do our counter raid. It will send our message to The Mega Pyramid in Luxor, and to everyone in Europe. Pharaoh will not be pleased, but who cares."

"Indeed", agreed Sarah.

And so, for the next six hours, they waited and watched the screens. Sarah particularly studied the big screen. She utilized the time to familiarize herself with what each symbol meant.

Eventually, she came to understand that the

techies were taking constant detailed looks at Jersey, and monitoring the positions of their enemy. In effect, studying the screens for any sign of movement, to indicate when the attack had got under way.

Sarah was worried for the City of Devonport. She knew that it might have to receive damage, to make her plan work. Sure, it was well defended, and used to military activity. But it was suntil felt it was her home, even though she was from another dimension.

"How many buildings will be destroyed" she wondered. "How many lives will be lost, and are we just sacrificing people for a greater good. Could I be sacrificing my own family here, my other self perhaps." But these were the questions, that she dared not voice out loud.

And the questions continued, and ate into her making her feel queasy. But this was waiting time, and there was nothing she could do to change things.

It was six o'clock in the morning when things began to change.

"Over there," said a techie called Steve. He was pointing at a blip on his monitor. Immediately a supervisor approached him, and suddenly looked very alarmed.

"Position 16," he exclaimed. "Something is clearly happening. Check your monitors." And sure enough, nearly every monitor was now tracking position sixteen. And there it was, the first of the Egyptian raiding boats. Slowly advancing menacingly through the water.

He looked at Steve. "Good work," he said, "now give me a close up." He stopped and turned to Judah, "and please inform Boudicca what is going on."

"Already on it," he replied holding a "Tech-Tab" to his ear.

The close-up, revealed a large boat, about twenty metres long, by six metres wide. It was armed at the front with a cannon, and a man behind it ready to fire. He was wearing a yellow uniform, and some sort of plastic body armour. His dark black helmet was emblazoned with a yellow snake symbol to represent Egypt.

There were six other people sitting down inside the boat, all wearing similar uniforms, but it was not clear what they were doing. They were however, carrying sickle swords, which were about two feet long, made of steel, and curved. Their presence was clearly menacing.

"They like to get up close and personal, to slash their opponents and intimidate people to obey them," whispered Freida into Sarah's ear.

On the back of the boat was a long flag, that blew in the wind like a wriggling snake. It even had a snake design on it. As she looked Sarah could see other boats starting to emerge behind it.

"Where exactly are they coming from," asked the supervisor.

It was Judah who spoke first. "From that long building there! You see" He was pointing at a new metal structure that stood out from the rest because it was not dome like. "The one with the blue roof. Looks like they erected in for the very purpose of hiding their sea craft. Now we know, we can destroy it later."

"Good idea," said Boudicca as she entered the room, clearly exhausted from running.

Everybody in the room was flabbergasted at her arrival, for it had been so prompt. Her quarters were more than ten minutes away. And yet, here she was standing next to Judah.

"How did you get here so quickly?" asked Freida. "I was sleeping close by. Judah leant me his room, while he was working here. So, I could be nearby, you understand..." She turned to him, blushed, and said, "Thank you for that Judah. And, it was nice of you to change the sheets for me. And to make the room smell nice. I really appreciated it."

Judah also blushed. "You are welcome, your majesty. I was happy to give up my room for my queen."

And after a few puzzled expressions, everybody got back to work. And the next hour was spent with continuous surveillance and progress reports, as the number of boats grew in number, and continued to get closer.

Suddenly, the screens started to flash red.

"What on earth?" asked Sarah.

"About time," said Freida. "That's just the monitors alerting us to the presence of Egyptian planes."

"How many?" asked Boudicca.

"Forty," said Judah. "More than usual, and they are escorting some one hundred raiding boats. Suntil. We prepared for about three hundred, so things are looking good."

"Yes," replied Boudicca. "But remember everyone, the objective is not necessarily defeating their forces today. But delaying them to allow our counter strike on the Sark Array."

At seven thirty am, the planes were arriving in Celtishian airspace. They were intercepted by the Royal Air force and the aerial fighting began. Chief Airman Boaz could be heard yelling directions, and getting excited as this happened.

The Egyptian boats were intercepted by the Royal Boudiccan Navy, five minutes later.

As the battle progressed, Sarah could see some of the images were vanishing from the screen. Each of these was indicating that a plane, a drone, or a ship was no more, and either sunk or exploded into possibly a thousand pieces.

It was clear from the screen, that both sides were taking casualties. However, most of the casualties were clearly Egyptian.

"Looks like they weren't expecting this today," Judah pointed out to Boudicca, while standing next to her.

"Well, the Egyptian planes are slower, and unreliable," argued Freida. "Too much show, and not enough fire power. And their boats are primitive raiding boats, taking on purpose built fighting craft. And these are our waters, so it is on our terms."

"Yes. We seem to have the upper hand now," said Boudicca eventually. "The officers on the ground will handle it from here. So. Let the attack on Sark begin."

And with that the screens began to switch to maps and images of the Channel Islands, especially Sark. And Boudicca quietly took the hand of Judah, and held it tight, as if looking for reassurance.

12. COUNTER RAID

S arah could see clearly that they were looking at the beach on Sark. It was made of fine
sand, with cliffs going up around the sides. The
sun was starting in its usual bright red hue, and
reflected both the water and the green mist.

Eventually Sarah could see two giant crabs
emerge from the water. Sarah recognized these
as the drones she had seen earlier. Yet here they
were in Sark. Two metres tall, and walking sideways onto the beach.

And it was clear that they weren't the only ones
aware of their presence, as there was a lot of
screaming going on in the background. One of
the monitors turned to face a screaming green
child,

"I'd scream too if I saw a crab that size," com-
mented Freida. And Sarah nodded in agreement.

And with that the techie manning it, took some
initiative, and spoke into a microphone.

"Fear not young child," he said. "We are here on
the business of Celtishia. We mean you no harm.

Go tell the village elder, we are here." And with that the other crab started to raise its pincers.

"There is no need," came a voice, "I am already here, as promised. Welcome, and how can we help?" Sarah could tell that the man thought it was strange, to be talking to a huge robotic crab. "For now, stay out of the way, then join us at the array, in ten minutes, when the guards are dealt with" replied the techie through the crab.

And with that the crabs walked sideways up the beach to a level spot, where they stopped.

"Please stand clear," both crabs instructed.

The local people, who were now starting to gather, got out of the way, as quickly they could. And the crabs began to open their shells.

Back in the base, the relief in the room was visible for Sarah to see, as there had been fears of the signal not working. Yet those fears were proved groundless. Instead the other drones, now started one by one, to emerge, flying from inside the crabs. They hovered in the sky, formed into a "V formation," and set off on their mission.

The crabs closed their shells, and started walking the route to the array. They were guided by the locals, who were gathering sticks, stones, and any form of crude weapon they could find. Clearly, they did not like their Egyptian oppressors, and spurred on by the drones, were ready to fight in any way they could.

The target was just five to ten minutes away, and

positioned on the top of the cliff. Overlooking the sea, it had the height to send signals all over Europe. As a menacing feature, it overlooked everything else in the area.

The drones had already arrived and taken out the guards, with green laser lights. The stunned guards were then tied up, by the locals, but left otherwise unharmed. The presence of drones and crabs ensured that there was no attempt to enact reprisal for previous harms.

Then the drones circled the dome at speed. They fired their weapons, and dropped explosives around the legs of the array, until the array collapsed through lack of support. And it lay there, as just a mess of steel on the ground.

Now they were hovering above the pyramid shrine, and checking out the crocodile tank, that lay in front. The tank was largely made of glass, but attempts had been made to blend it in with its surroundings. There were reeds, and trees, and it even had a small island for the creature inside to sunbathe. At first glance, it even partially resembled a pond.

The pyramid towered above the pond. Six metres high, and looking out of place. There was a sign saying, "In honour of Sobek – the crocodile God. Please give generously, and you will be blessed."

Underneath another sign read,

"Judge Of All People, Upholder of Egypt, Enjoys

human flesh."

The crocodile was hiding underwater in the reeds. And the local people were trying to draw the crocodile from the water, for a clean shot by the drones. However, it wasn't coming. But the local resistance, had thought ahead, and brought a large piece of lamb.

"Here you go boy," said the lead resistance woman, and with that she chucked the lamb onto the island.

Slowly and steadily, the creature began to surface, until its head could be seen above the water. Its big red eyes clear for all to see, and now surveying the area around it. The drones were now hovering silently. Waiting. And avoiding sudden movements. Then, very slowly it began to emerge from the water, until its whole body was visible. And finally, after what seemed like ages, it could be seen walking slowly up to the meat, with its great tail swishing. It picked up the lamb, moved back a little into the water, and started to eat by the side of the island in the pond.

Back in the Hub everyone held their breath. And the people there in Sark remained quiet, while the drones silently positioned themselves. Eventually that shot was taken.

There was one loud bang. Then silence, and a small pause. The crocodile lay injured only. Another shot rang out, followed by several laser blasts from other drones. And the crocodile now floated on top of the water. Nobody knew which drone had performed the killer shot.

Once again, the local resistance sprang into action. They scaled the wall of the pond, and made loops that attached to the crocodile's legs using ropes. They then attached cables to the drones, and connected the cables to the loops. The drones rose vertically, and the dead creature was lifted high in the air.

Meanwhile the crab drones used their pincers to get below the pyramid, and turned it upside down, so that it looked like a giant cauldron. The Resistance wedged it in shape using wooded poles, and then dropped sticks and charcoal in. Finally; the drones dropped the crocodile on top.

"Stand back," yelled one of the crabs, and people fled out of the way.

After a pause, the crab spoke again. "Good people of Sark, and Europe, we light this crocodile as a sacrifice to The Whisper, and for the honour of Celtishia, and all who serve them."

And with that, the second crab shot a large flame from its mouth at the pyre. It caught fire immediately. The flames rose high, and the dead crocodile started to cook.

"I bet it tastes like chicken," a small boy could be heard saying.

And of course, all this was beamed via satellite and cable to the whole world, via the Hub in

Celtishia. The details of the counter raid, and the news that Celtishia had completely destroyed a raiding party. And finally; the great news that The Channel was now effectively free from Egyptian influence, as most of their boats in the region were destroyed.

Furthermore, the resistance in the Channel Islands were now starting to take over the troop bases, as the insurrection against Egypt grew. Most Egyptian bases surrendered as they had lost the majority of their troops in the raids.

And for the first time in ages, there was much celebrating in Celtishia. The news that the Egyptian menace was defeated, for a while, lifted their spirits. Reports were coming in of parties in the tunnels, and above ground in the trees.

In the Hub, they started to bring in sparkling wine, and food, and everybody started to enjoy themselves. Even Chief Airman Boaz was telling jokes. However, in the media room the tone was soon to change.

The Egyptian Pharaoh in Cairo, was furious, and went on the television, saying that "a raid has caused some temporary damage, but more boats are on the way to take their place. Order will be restored within a few days. And 'the illegal squatters' of the Channel Islands will pay with their lives.

13. SEA RESCUE

P anic broke out back in the Hub, as the celebrating stopped almost instantly. Had they really just heard that?

"Surely," they all thought, "nobody had actually died in the counter raid. Did they rteally view, the occupants of an entire island as no more than squatters? Could the entire islands be made to pay for the attack? Was the Pharaoh really that vindictive and evil?"

"Does he mean that?" asked Sarah eventually, "or is he just blowing hot air?"

"No, I'm pretty sure that he means it," said Boudicca, with an expression of concern.

There was silence and fear in the Hub, until Judah spoke up.

"Then we must help them! But what we desperately need is 'A Plan C.' Any ideas?"

There was a small silence.

"Well maybe," said Sarah in a low, almost unheard voice.

"Speak up!" yelled Boudicca at her. "This is no time for mumbling. Any idea, no matter how bizarre," and she looked at Freida, "will be considered."

"Well in our dimension," she said, "there was a time when Great Britain rescued its entire remaining army from the shores of Normandy. I learnt about it in school. It is known as the "Dunkirk Evacuation." Thousands of troops were saved, and the war effort continued. I can't remember all the details, but roughly just over three hundred thousand troops were evacuated in a period of eight days."

"Well we have about nine days, by my calculations," said Judah, trying to be positive.

Every eye in the Hub was now focused on Sarah. And she started to realize why The Whisper had brought her to this place. To save lives and save those who couldn't speak up for themselves. And the stakes were high. The people of the Channel Islands were going to die, unless she relayed the story as best she could, but she was frozen in silence, almost scared to speak.

Boudicca could see she was in distress. So, she signaled to Freida to bring her a chair, and position it behind her.

"Now take a seat, Miss Salter, and tell me. Just me," said Boudicca. "How did they do that?"

Sarah sat down, and took a deep breath. "Well, the government appealed to every British citizen with a boat capable of crossing the Channel, to rendezvous at a certain point, called Dunkirk. They managed to raise about eight hundred craft, and they made several journeys each.

Eventually the beaches were cleared of troops".
Boudicca smiled, and looked at Judah.

"Judah. You are a person with a head full of facts, and that is why I care so much for you. So please; do you know how many boats there are, that are capable of reaching the Channel Islands?"

"Yes," Judah replied. "There are about four thousand. And just under two hundred thousand people live in the Channel Islands. I reckon we could evacuate the place in five days, if we can motivate the nation."

"In that case, contact the media," ordered Boudicca. "Sarah and I are going on television tonight. Freida contact the resistance in Sark and Jersey and tell them their people must be ready to move, if they want to live. And Judah, I know you are tired, but get working on some suitable rendezvous points in the Channel Islands, and tell the Navy they are going to be busy."

Everyone in the room stood to attention. As one, they looked to Boudicca, as their leader, wanting to obey and serve.

"Well don't just stand there everyone," she yelled, "we have work to do." And with that, Sarah, and Boudicca left the room. Both determined to win the cooperation of a nation.

The television studio was a short helicopter flight away, and located in the City of Ringham, which Sarah had previously passed over. When she consulted the map, Sarah noticed that Ringham was located where Birmingham was in her world. It was considered a central location for broadcasting purposes. Using the helicopter, it would take them about one hour to get them there.

The television station was built like a giant dome, but made of white fibreglass. Sarah thought, it resembled half a giant golf ball. A big red neon sign outside read "CBC – Celtishian Broadcasting Centre." It was considered to have the most up to date television technology, and to be at the cutting edge of media innovation.

In addition, it was in a large natural park, with trees everywhere around it. In the center, there was a helicopter landing pad for their convenience. The ground crew waved them in.

As soon as the chopper landed, they were greeted by an official delegation and a Royal Guard for their protection. Boudicca disembarked from the chopper first to meet and greet them

"Welcome your Majesty," they said. "we are honoured to have you here, of course." Then they saw Sarah.

"What! So the rumours are true. Miss Salter. The girl from the Mist-Less Dimension, or is this some kind of hoax?" asked a key official

"No, she is the real thing," Boudicca responded, "and her name is Sarah. Now do you know why we are here?"

"To appeal to the nation. Live on television. Which we are happy to oblige with, but why?"

"Because the time demands it."

"OK, let's get started then."

They were live within the hour, and a fresh young green faced presenter called Esther was introducing them, in a northern accent.

"Good evening everybody, and welcome to this special broadcast from Her Majesty. We have two key guests here in the studio. The Queen herself and her advisor. And no your eyes do not deceive you." The cameras focused on Sarah, who was sat next to the queen. To the viewers, she was human in every way accept for the fact she wasn't green.

"So your majesty, we are delighted to have you here, of course," the presenter continued. "But what is going on, and what do you have to say?"

"Well," Boudicca started, "this is my friend Miss Sarah Salter, who has crossed over from the Mist-Less Dimension, as my relatives did many years ago. And ultimately, we are here to ask for help. But first Sarah will tell us about herself and how she got here."

And so Sarah told the nation the story. How she took a bus ride, stopped in Central Park, got caught in the rain, and saw the planets merge.

"In my dimension," she continued, "this land is called Great Britain, and people usually have pink skin. But I am here now, and there is mist and green skin, And Celtishia is in danger, and I believe that I am here to help, although I do not yet know all the details of how."

"What we do know, however," interrupted Boudicca, "is that right now, we are at war with Egypt. We have passed the point of diplomacy and reasoning, to stop the raids. Starting today, we are fighting back."

"By defeating their raid on Devonport, we also sent a warning to Egypt to stay away from the area, as they have no place here. Our warning is simple. These are our waters, in our territory, and we will defend them. We are armed, and can outdo all you can throw at us. Turn your forces around while there is time."

"Furthermore, under Sarah's advice, we destroyed the communications array in Sark, immediately after the raid. This was to limit the Egyptian Empire from communicating their threats to us, and coordinating future attacks. In doing so, we confirmed our ownership on the Channel Islands. However, their Pharaoh, says his 'honour is offended,' and has responded with a death threat towards two hundred thousand people."

"We are going to take this threat seriously, by rescuing the entire population of the islands. Therefore, we call on everybody who owns a boat, to set sail for the Channel Islands, and collect as many people there as you can. Everyone from the Channel Islands is welcome on the Celtishian mainland, and can stay here until Egypt is driven back to Cairo."

"Nobody is to be left behind. If they are not safe, then neither is anyone. And let Pharaoh remember that the woman crushes the snake's head, while the snake only strikes weakly at her heel."

The next few hours seemed crazy to Sarah. The message was well received. The response was astounding, as it seemed to unify the country around a common goal, of saving lives. Of course seeing a white person was a shock to them. But they accepted it as an important 'sign'. Within the day, the boats had set sail from every port on the South and East coast.

Sarah wanted to be seen to practice what she advised, so she herself hitched a ride to Guernsey on a boat, that was owned and driven by Adah Sophia-Smith, (Freida's adopted mother.) Adah's boat was old and made of a dark wood. It was covered in a kind of gluey glaze to protect it from warping in the water. At first glance it resembled something from a bye-gone era. There were two sails, which were made from canvas, both had a Star of David logo on them. At the front, the boat was emblazoned with the name. "The Reliable Freida".

"I named it after my daughter," Adah volunteered.

"It is beautiful."

"It is also a very slow, but traditional boat, and it is the only big thing I own," Adah volunteered on the journey over.

"Do you sail a lot?" asked Sarah.

"Not very often, as I am too busy with farm business. But I always wanted to learn how to fish, after returning from Palestine, and I bought the boat to allow me some time to do so. Didn't quite pan out that way though."

"How come?"

"Child issues. My daughter, the other Freida could be a handful. Extremely damaged, you see. Was forced to become an adult far too early, when some would say she was suntil only a child herself."

"I don't understand?"

"Well the age of consent here is eighteen, but you become a full adult only at twenty-one here. Up to then you suntil attend school, studying vocationally, and learning about life. Well Freida, had come from another country. She had been deprived of a childhood, and missed out on so many things. Therefore, she didn't fit in easily, and was behind in her studies."

Sarah had never imagined it had been that hard for Adah, supporting Freida as she matured into adulthood. "But you kept loving her anyway?"

"Yes, but it wasn't easy at times. She had seen things she should not have seen, and experienced the unspeakable."

"Boudicca helped, I hear."

"Yes, she used a lot of discretion, and gave us some land. And we needed it, because by this stage, there were the twins. It is ironic, you wait ages for one child, then three come along at once. So anyway, I was kept busy, sorting things out, and navigating hurdle after hurdle."

"Was it worth it, though?" asked Sarah.

"Of course," said Adah with great patience in her voice. "I wouldn't have missed it for the world. And Freida has turned out really good." And they sailed on together in silence, pointing out anything they saw to each other.

Within the hour, they were passing military ships, that had positioned themselves to form two blockades on the Channel. One was to resist the Egyptians from the South, and the smaller one at the north to resist Scandinavia. Every so often they would also pass the wooden debris from the previous sea battle with the Egyptians.

"Is that an aircraft carrier?" asked Sarah, looking up at a huge ship with a runway on the front.

"Yes, but most of the craft it carries are probably drones. You can get more of them in that space."

"But the aircraft, do the bigger damage, is that right? "

"Probably. But you would need to ask Freida about that, I'm afraid. I am out of touch these days. Unless of course, you want to talk nappies and children?"

"Not today," she laughed. And they sailed on.

The journey was smooth sailing until they were about mid-way across, when the breeze started to become a force four wind, and the boat was leaning heavily on the sea, to compensate for the weight of its keel. Sarah was not used to sailing, and was a bit freaked out by being on the bottom side of the leaning boat. She felt closer to the water and worried about capsizing.

Adah of course was used to this, and was enjoying herself and the journey. "Isn't this fun," she would say over and over, as Sarah looked in disbelief. It was shortly after this that Sarah started to feel sick.

"You will need this," Adah said, and handed her a bucket, just in time. "Wow! You have gone green! And all it took was a bit of vomit."

"Thanks" said a sick and sarcastic Sarah, as she emptied the bucket over the side of the boat. But when she turned around she noticed that Adah had been looking at her oddly.

"Something wrong?" asked Sarah.

"No. Its just that!" She paused. "Well. I can't help noticing, but, you seem to be actually changing colour."

"That's the sea sickness."

"No! I mean really changing colour. The back of your ears are starting to turn green, like mine!"

"Oh." And Sarah went silent. "Well Vincent said that are skin colour is mostly influenced by melanin, but diet can have an effect too. And I have been eating a lot of green things recently. So I guess..."

'Even so, when we get back, you are getting checked out by a medic."

The rest of the way over was quiet by comparison, as Sarah now had something else to worry about. However, the boat pushed on, and they arrived on the beach in Guernsey, a few hours later.

The sea by the beach was cold, and the wind was until blowing. But the mist provided extra cover for the people getting on board the boat. This was viewed as a good thing, as drones could be heard battling it away overhead, and it was obvious that the beach was under constant threat.

They were able to take ten people in addition to themselves on board the boat. These included two children. But there were many more waiting, either in the sea or on the beach. The Marshall in charge thanked them for coming, and told the others to wait. Sarah quickly handed out blankets to the refugees, as they boarded.

And of course the Channel Islands news was there recording Sarah "doing her bit," as they saw it. "The white girl getting her hands dirty in the refugee rescue." And the refugees, for their part sat down quietly, and just looked numb. This media stunt disappointed and annoyed Sarah at the same time. For she felt she had genuinely wanted to be there, and to help. But instead, her kindness was being used as a public relations exercise.

Shortly afterwards they turned the boat around, passengers and all, and got on their way. It was to be a six hour journey back to The City of Devonport.

It was only when they were as good hour out to sea, that the refugees started to talk.

"Are you Sarah Salter? Because we saw you on TV?" asked the refugee nearest to Sarah.

"Yes," Sarah replied.

"I just knew it, I recognized your earring."

"Her earring?" questioned another passenger in a voice that suggested exasperation at an insane comment. For whilst her earring were unusual for Celtishia, it was obvious that her skin colour was her most unusual feature.

"Well I was being tactful."

"So why are you not green?" asked one of the children.

"Cause, she is not from here Dumbo," replied the first woman.

"Only asking," said the child.

"Why are you asking," asked Sarah"

"Because you is a pinky-whitey type of colour."

"Well, don't you watch the news?" asked another woman.

"Yes, I watch it."

"So then, Jimmy, you know the answer. She is from another dimension. And it is really winding Pharaoh up. Mind you, her plan of attacking the array in Sark didn't help much either."

This conversation was starting to offend Sarah, because she didn't like being talked about by people who didn't know her, "I am here you know," said Sarah

"Yes, we know, and don't mind us. We are just sitting here quietly, you know. Just minding our own business" said Jimmy.

And Sarah could think of nothing else to say, all the way back to Devonport. Although the passengers talked almost constantly about the attack on the array, what they were going to do next, what it would be like in Devonport, and why Sarah was not green like them.

They were a third of the way back, when Sarah was sick into the bucket again. The passengers all laughed, and said she would "need to get her sea legs." And it was at this point, she decided not to cross the Channel again in such a small craft.

Finally, they arrived back in port. The passengers all disembarked, and Sarah joined them, somewhat relieved not to be using an excuse to avoid another journey across the Channel.

Now Adah took Jimmy and his father to one side. "Do me a favour now Jimmy, will you?"

"Yes, of course, but what is it?"

"Make sure Sarah goes to see a medic, and don't let her take the transport back tonight. I would do it myself, but I need to turn around, and get back to Guernsey again."

"Will do, my lady. I would be honoured, so I would."

"And go easy on her, we don't all enjoy sailing. It has been a bit of an ordeal for her, I'm afraid."

And so, Jimmy turned to Sarah. "Well follow me." And off they went, following the signs until they got to a make shift medical bay in the harbor.

The medical bay was a large white dome, within the processing Centre. It had large clear round windows, resembling port-holes on a spaceship. At the reception, Jimmy and his father both departed, back to the 'arrivals section' of the Processing Centre. Sarah watched them go, and hoped they would be okay.

Sarah was not sure of the protocol in reception, so she asked Vincent to check her in, by speaking into her Tech-Tab. Almost instantly the Medical Bay's screen told her to sit in the waiting room. This was the next room. When she had sat down in the waiting room, there was great excitement, as everybody was looking in her direction.

"I am sorry," she said sarcastically, "have you not seen earrings like this before?" And the atmosphere started to get lighter.

Whilst this was going on, Vincent was linked in to the Medical Bay's systems. Initially he was told that there would be a wait, as the staff were busy 'providing care for refugee arrivals.' However, five minutes later, Vincent was able to inform her, that her name was being bumped up the list, due to her 'Royal Advisory Status and Security Reasons.' Another five minutes later, a female doctor approached her.

"Sarah Salter, I assume?"

"That's right."

"Nice to meet you. My name is Doctor Martha Zing. Please follow me, and we will talk in private."

Doctor Zing was a very tall and slim girl. She was eight feet tall, and without a doubt the biggest girl that Sarah had ever seen in her life. She had long brown straight hair, and the usual pale green face. However, her eyes were slightly slanted, and she wore bright red lipstick.

Her uniform consisted of a white coat, over green leggings. Her legs of course were long, and stopped at Sarah's breast. Around her neck was a Tech-Tab on a lanyard made from beads.

Now she led Sarah to a quiet room, in the complex. As she entered she could see a brass plaque, with the words, "Doctor Martha Zing – Military Field Medic."

"Take a seat," said Doctor Zing, and she pointed to a giant bean bag in the corner of the room. As soon as she was seated, Doctor Zing began her consultation. "I am glad to meet you. I saw you on TV with Queen Boudicca the other day. So I know a little about your background. And I won't lie, I am fascinated to meet you, as I have never met a person with pink skin before. In this dimension, I am amused to say, that you are a medical anomaly."

"Great," said Sarah, "that's all I need. A medical anomaly to a giant."

"No, please, don't get me wrong, I meant no offense. Ultimately we are both human beings. I am tallish, and you are pink skinned. But I have no reason to assume that our plumbing is any different, so to speak."

"Good to hear," said Sarah.

"So. What can I do for you?"

"Well, its my ears? I was told to get them checked out by a friend. She reckons that they are starting to turn green."

"Oh really," replied Doctor Zing with a small laugh. "You do realize that green is the usual colour here?"

"I know. But as we know, I am not green."

"Ah. But neither was the original Boudicca when she arrived. Her skin changed colour over time. It is well documented. I even took the liberty of calling up copies of those files, when you arrived." She held up a very tiny round disc, and continued. "And interestingly, it was her ears that changed first. This was also true in all other recorded cases of people from the Mist-Less Dimension."

"So I will change colour?"

"Probably. But for now, let's get you totally checked out. I will leave the room, for you to get undressed. When I return with a nurse, we will do a series of tests." And with that Doctor Zing handed Sarah a dark green uniform to change into, and left the room.

Sarah had always wondered why so many of the

uniforms here were green in colour, and why no-body thought this odd. For to Sarah it was obvious that green skin, against the greenness of the uniforms made people look like they weren't wearing much. However, for the first time, she could also now see that her ears turning green made them almost invisible and enabled her to blend more into the background.

The nurse and doctor returned about five minutes later. And they escorted her to very large medical scanning room. The tests took an hour, and confirmed that Sarah was in good health. In fact, Sarah acknowledged, that she "had never felt so good," and "was busting with energy." Doctor Zing advised her that it may be because of "a higher level of oxygen on their Green Earth." Sarah could not comment on this as she had no idea, how much oxygen her usual atmosphere would have.

They talked for about an hour regarding any inter-dimensional differences she was experiencing, including the green mist. Doctor Zing advised her that the extra chloroplasts in the atmosphere would probably help her keep healthy as well. They also discussed the recent change in her diet, and Sarah realized just how much green food she was eating.

By the end of the consultation, Sarah had warmed to Doctor Zing. She was efficient, and friendly, forgiving but thorough. Her knowledge was exceptional, and she had a good way of communicating things.

"Of course, I will refer your details to the Devonport Base, and ask the chief medic there to keep monitoring you, if that is ok?" asked Doctor Zing eventually. Sarah nodded.

"Ok then, so what now?"

"Well, its up to you. I am confident that you are in good mental and physical shape considering all that is happening. But if it was me, I would head back to the HUB, where decisions are being made. Boudicca has, I believe, made a transport available to you should you need it. Just ask for Sue at reception, as she knows all about it."

And so Sarah left the room, and went back to reception. She asked for Sue, as advised, who arranged the trip back to the base.

The military helicopter was much smaller than the previous ones that Sarah had travelled in. It was guarded by two members of Boudicca's security. They took off within the hour, surrounded by drones and three other aircraft. This time however she was the only passenger, and was able to use her Tech-Tab to speak to Vincent about the stuff she was not sure about. This included information about the chloroplasts Doctor Zing had mentioned. Vincent was able to inform her that these were harmless little green algae that live in the lower layers of the hemisphere. Together with the extra oxygen, they were giving Sarah more energy than she was used too.

"One other question," asked Sarah. "Why is Doctor Zing so tall?"

"Doctor Martha Zing – Medical Consultant, eight feet two inches tall," repeated Vincent in a robotic way. "Looking up her data, and checking your clearance levels. Yes, it appears you have been granted access to that information."

"Just a simple answer would do," Sarah pointed out.

"Well, basically she has what is called 'gigantism,' or an excess of growth hormones in childhood. This is multiplied by the extra oxygen and chloroplasts found in the mist. It is not uncommon, and affects about one in every six hundred women in some countries."

"It is unusual in Celtishia, however in Japan where Doctor Zing originates from, it is more common. There some women are known to grow even bigger, and reach heights of nine and a half feet. When the condition remains untreated women have been recorded as reaching over eleven feet in height."

"Ok thanks for the information"

"Is there anything else you wish to know?"

"Not for now."

"Ok, then I will turn myself off then."

And with that Vincent vanished.

Sarah was left all alone now with her thoughts. But it wasn't to remain that way for long. Five minutes later, the TV screen came on, and Boudicca was making an announcement, surrounded by some of her elected officials.

"My loyal people. As you know, we have already announced that we are at war with Egypt, and this shows no sign of change. However, our forces now have a strong block on The Channel, and already half the people of the Channel Islands are on the Main Land. We are confident of a full evacuation, within two days. So I would like to personally thank everyone involved for their efforts in this monumental task."

"However, this year is my seventh year in office. So following on with the theme of freedom, the elected cabinet and I have decided to celebrate it as a special 'Year of Jubilee."

"This means that student debts are cancelled. Grade two business debts are cancelled. Grade two, three or four prisoners will be released to their previous holds and families under supervision orders. Grade one offenders will have their records wiped clean."

Boudicca paused, for what was clearly dramatic effect. "And most importantly of all, our country releases less developed countries, from loans used correctly on the developments they were given for."

"I believe that this is well overdue, and will help us as a nation to move forward. Thank you for your time. Remain strong, and willing to serve."

The announcement ended. And Sarah was confused. There was lots she didn't understand in that, but she knew who to ask.

"Vincent," said Sarah into her tech tab. "I need to ask you something."

Vincent appeared, "Hello Sarah, how can I help you?"

"Well, Boudicca has announced a jubilee?"

"I know. And about time too. It is a few years overdue though. That's politicians for you. Always dragging their feet."

"Yeah, ok, but what is a jubilee?"

"An anniversary. It happens every seven years, or should do. They release some prisoners, and give people a fresh start. Debts can be cancelled. A sort of levelling of the playing field, so to speak. It is a time of celebration. But in this case, convictions for serious offenses like murder suntil stand."

"Why?"

"Well, some offenses need paying for, and you don't want to endanger others by releasing the most dangerous people, who might reoffend."

"No. I meant, why release people anyway? Shouldn't they do their time?"

"In one word, mercy. It can break a cycle of bad behaviour in some cases."

"So, it doesn't always work then?" Sarah asked Vincent.

"No, because people can be people. Some don't want to change. Others relish the chance of a fresh start. There is often a party within the communities, as free people return home, or join the military."

"So when was the last Jubilee?"

"Twenty-seven years ago, just before Boudicca's mum came to the throne. But then she was too busy drinking, to get around to administration."

"Boudicca's mum was a bad queen then?"

"Well, more like unfocussed, and ineffective against the politicians. Easily manipulated. And the government didn't want to risk the country's finances. They would regard Boudicca as naïve in this respect. But she is a tougher Queen, and they act in her name. What she says is kind of meant to happen, subject to the will of the people of course."

"Anyway, Vincent continued, it will begin on the Day of Atonement, after a national ceremony. The country recommits to helping the released. The released prisoners are given a set of conditions to adhere too, and a fresh start."

"So when is this day of atonement?"

"It is just a few weeks away. Gives everyone a chance to prepare."

Sarah sat there and reflected on this for a bit. Although not convinced, she could see the merit in the process. Eventually, she spoke into the tech tab. "Thank you Vincent, that will be all for now." And Vincent vanished.

Of course not everyone agreed with Vincent. The business community was upset at having lost the option of interest repayments on some debts, and having to write off others. However, they tried to put a brave spin on things, saying things like how "it was welcomed with reservations."

Elsewhere in the World, the reaction was mixed. Some countries even thanked Celtishia for the cancellation of their aid debts. However, Egypt was raging. Pharaoh in Egypt was already fuming over having his plans to commit genocide on the Channel Islands thwarted. Now he had the announcement of the jubilee to deal with.

In his country, people were asking questions like, "if they can have this, why can't we?" It was making him seem like an oppressor, and a dictator, and he didn't like this. (Even though it was true).

Knowing that he was losing the PR battle connected to the war, Pharaoh appeared on TV. His aim was to appear strong, and limit the damage to his reputation and pride.

The Pharaoh stood there in a mask, surrounded in a semi-circle by a selection of about twelve officials. He was easily recognized by the mask he was wearing, for it looked like a cat. It was made of pure shiny gold, and covered his entire face. He also held a scepter of gold, with what looked like a giant ruby on top. The officials were also wearing masks, that were white in color and more suitable for a masquerade ball, as they covered only their eyes.

There was one other noticeable key person in

the delegation. The Egyptian interpreter, who was standing next to the Pharaoh. He wore an expensive black suit, and a white mask. In his hand was a microphone for him to be heard. His role, Sarah had been previously told, was to speak for Pharaoh who would maybe hiss his desires, for he thought it made him sound mysterious. And besides he considered himself above "*speaking to mere humans*," as he saw everyone else.

"It has come to my attention," said the Pharaoh, through his near identical interpreter, "that the small insignificant country called Celtishia," (he laughed), "has declared war on us. That is myself, Pharaoh."

"Well, this will never do. How dare they even think they could stand up to us. The sheer audacity of that small nation will be their undoing."

"Well. once again they have thwarted my plans, by rescuing the people of the Channel Islands. But this is just a temporary set-back. Now my main forces will move up through Malta, into Spain. Then we advance through France, until we can attack and take the Celtishian Isles. Boudicca can expect no mercy from me then, and their best officials can expect to become my lowest slaves. If we let them live."

"We say to Celtishia, that we have the bigger army, and you should be afraid. Enjoy your Jubilee when you can. Right now, we will start negotiations in Europe to enlist the help of our allies.

As the leader of the alliance, we unfortunately have procedures to follow before we can send troops through other countries. However, we hope to have many armies united against you, and we will be there in three months, whether you are ready or not."

Sarah, however, was laughing. "It is the same in our dimension, people using fear to intimidate others into surrender. Meanwhile Europe is all talk and no action. But led by a minority of people, they make crazy decisions affecting everybody."

14.
PREPARATION

An hour later, Sarah was looking at the TV screen with bemusement. So far, the Pharaoh's plans were not amounting too much. But they were worrying just the same. Things had escalated. This was no longer a game of tactical espionage. It was now war, as far as both sides, were concerned. An evil army was on the move against them. It was time to prepare.

It was as she was starting to think about these things that her Tech-Tab rang. Immediately Vincent's voice spoke into her ear.

"Sarah, Queen Boudicca is calling you, do you accept the call?"

"Yes, put her through. This should be interesting."

There was a click, and Boudicca spoke into her ear from elsewhere.

"Hi Sarah, are you still on the helicopter?"

"Yes, but I am returning to the HUB."

"Good. I need your counsel?"

"Thought you might."

"You saw the news then?"

"Yes, I expect the whole country did. I am sorry, is there anything I can do now?"

"No just get back here asap. I assume that we can rely on you?"

"Of course, I think I know what needs to be done next."

"That's good, but what is it? Any hints?" asked Boudicca.

"The Whisper told us to raise an army! Basically, we are to go on the offensive."

Boudicca was shocked, for she was expecting a more defensive strategy. "Are you serious?"

"Yes," Sarah replied, and there was silence, as Boudicca thought through the next step.

"Then we need to get you on television again. I can divert your helicopter to Ringham, if you like. I will meet you there. With our top military leaders, and top elected cabinet officials."

"And bring Freida" Sarah requested. "I don't know why. But she is somehow a major part of this."

"Ok, but are you sure. I like the girl, you know that, but she is technically in recovery," Boudicca gently pointed out, with a real concern in her voice.

"That is true. But we also know that she doesn't think like others. Crazy as it sounds, she could be our edge."

"Ok, I will send for her now. I am also bringing Judah, by the way." Sarah could not help notice the casual way that this had been dropped into the conversation. She decided to ask about it.

"You two are getting serious then?"

"Yes. Is that ok? Not that it should matter," Boudicca pointed out. She was starting to blush a little.

"Well, I think it is great. He is a decent guy. Handsome. Committed. He almost worships you."

"Glad you think so. It may not go down well with certain people that he is not nobility though?"

It was clear that Boudicca was concerned about this, but Sarah thought she was being ridiculous. "You should date, and even marry who you like. And most people will like the idea that you are open to ordinary people. It says that you are one with them. The opposite of the Pharaoh."

"Glad you think so," Boudicca acknowledged. "Anyway I will see you in a couple of hours, but take care now." And the call ended.

Within a minute, the helicopter changed course, clearly under Boudicca's orders. The pilot announced the course change over the speaker system. And Sarah tried to relax, as the chopper started to learn towards the right. The drones also started to lean and change direction. It was clear that they were in part doubling back the way they had come.

Looking down she could see Celtishia below her. The tallest of the trees rising above the green mist. And it made a beautiful sight. Through a pair of binoculars, she could see more tree houses, and the occasional white dome.

Sarah was unsure about what to do next. So she just sat there silently in reflection. Until a voice spoke to her from seemingly nowhere.

"Be brave. Lead the offensive"

"What?" Sarah looked around, and realized nobody was there.

"Lead the offensive!"

That was it? No details of how. Just the command, that struck the heart in her soul, and challenged her to the core. Once again, Sarah looked around in shock. The voice had been so quiet, but that was clearly meant to be obeyed. There was the same smell of incense, even though she was on a helicopter at least a mile in the air.

Sarah took her small round tech tab in her hand, pressed the centre screen, and said, "Vincent I need your help."

Vincent appeared in holographic form in front of her, wearing a sharp black suit, over green skin.

"So what do you need he asked?"

"I need help planning a speech."

"Really, and who are you speaking to?"

"Everyone in the country. Via Television. Both men and women. Anyone willing to take up a gun, a knife or any weapon, and move against Egypt."

"Okay. Is it a presentation, or an appeal you are

doing?"

"An appeal, I guess."

"Well, let's get started," and a projected image of a power point appeared on the wall. The word "greeting" appeared as a red header.

"This is a template," said Vincent. "It contains three sections, greeting, what you need and motivations. Now how would you like to greet your audience?"

And for the next hour, Sarah and Vincent, (her holographic helper,) worked through the template together, until the speech was complete. They then spent time practicing it on the helicopter, Vincent focusing on helping Sarah with the projection of voice, and learning the script.

Finally, after what had been a few hours in the air, the chopper pilot spoke into the speaker system.

"Hello Sarah. This is the captain speaking, we are now approaching the CBC. The weather is sunny, and the mist is thinner than usual. We will be landing in approximately thirty minutes, and security will meet you at the gate. Please fasten your seat belt, and we will start our descent process"

"And may I say, good luck with your speech!" the pilot continued. "I was listening to your practice and it is starting to sound good."

The descent and landing were uneventful. And the guards ushered her through corridors and into a room, where Boudicca stood.

Sarah immediately noticed that Boudicca once again had her back to her, and was staring out of the window. Boudicca's guards stood silently to attention, and Judah sat quietly in a nearby armchair, clearly focused only on work.

"These are worrying times, Sarah!" she said after a while. "But I am glad you are here."

And Boudicca turned around, approached, and hugged Sarah warmly. This was not what Sarah had expected. She returned the hug, and then gently withdrew to give herself space. Sarah then recommenced the conversation. "I am glad to be here."

"Good! But we have some serious work to do. There is something we need to discuss first."

"I am ready to do my part. I can speak to the nation tonight."

"I know Sarah. But there is more to it than you think." Boudicca was building up to ask her something.

"How so?" enquired Sarah.

Sarah could see Boudicca take a deep breath, before progressing her request. "Well it is one thing to raise the army, but we need people to lead them into battle, and you may have to be that person. So are you sure you are ready to do this?"

"Lead them?"

"Yes, as in actually fight alongside the troops. To lead by example. Otherwise, why would they put themselves on the line."

"I had not planned on that. The front line, you

mean?"

"Yes. Lots of people are volunteering to go with you. They all want to keep you safe. But don't kid yourself. It will be dangerous."

"I guess," said a slightly worried Sarah, because she had not considered that she would actually be put in danger.

"Well? Do you need time to think about it?" asked the Queen.

However, Sarah had quickly made her decision. Sarah paused and took a deep breath. "Yes," she said, "I will go with them. But I will need help."

"And I know just the person," said Boudicca, who touched the screen on her Tech-Tab. She can get you trained up, and up to the correct standard."

Freida arrived on Boudicca's demand five minutes later, dressed in her usual green and brown military uniform. She had clearly been running, and was out of breath. But Sarah was glad to see her, because she knew that Freida was a capable fighter, and valued her friendship.

"You called for me, Bou?" And she stopped to correct herself, "your Majesty?"

"Yes. I have decided to accept your offer to train, and accompany Sarah on the front line. Listen to her ideas. And when the time comes, do as she advises," Boudicca instructed her, "and you are tasked with keeping her safe."

Freida looked delighted. "Yes, your Majesty," she replied.

"And train her well. Teach her to use weapons, climb and use nature as camouflage. Improve her combat skills. Start tonight after her address. And help her formulate a strategy. Can you do it?"

"Yes your Majesty. And I will make sure she is ready."

"Then go now, take her to the studio. Look after her, and take the pressure off." Boudicca was now looking at her directly. Studying her every movement.

"Yes your Majesty."

Sarah was slightly amused to see Freida being so obedient. Especially as Boudicca was her friend.

"And one other thing," Boudicca continued, "you are to keep me updated on all progress. Whether good or bad?"

"Yes, Of course, your Majesty."

And Boudicca, nodded at them both with approval.

"Off you go then, with my blessing. Both of you. I believe you have a broadcast to make."

And Sarah and Freida turned as one and left the room, leaving Boudicca behind them. They did not know then it would be some time until they returned to the Hub, or how tough things were going to get.

The broadcast and appeal for help was to take place in the main studio. In front of an audience. They were both briefed by the presenter (miss

Denise La-Rooche), who Sarah thought seemed a bit snobbish, and forceful. They disagreed at first on the interview format, but eventually it was decided that Sarah and Freida would appear together as a show of unity.

"Boudicca will go on air, immediately after you," the presenter said. "She will be there with just her partner - Judah. She will firstly confirm her backing of you both, and then wants to do something else I am informed. Boudicca spent some time talking to Judah's parents, last night I believe." The presenter was holding a hockey stick, and twiddling it.

And Freida smiled knowingly at the presenter, and Sarah. Sarah was not entirely sure what she meant by it. Freida smiled again and addressed the issue.

"We will watch what she has to say, and do after us, if that is ok? It sounds entertaining."

"I agree, and have arranged for a TV in your dressing room."

When they were out of earshot of the presenter, Sarah asked Freida what she wanted to know.

"What's with the presenter?"

"You mean Miss La-Rooche?"

"Yes, she seems a bit rude?"

"Well. Her dad owns the station. Wealthy man. Gave his daughter a job on air."

"And the comments about Queen Boudicca?"

"What about them?"

"What exactly was she implying?"

"You don't know?" asked Freida, who was starting to realize that she didn't. "I guess things are done differently in the Mist-Less."

"Don't be coy, what is going on Freida? What is Boudicca doing?"

And Freida looked temporarily amused at Sarah's naivety. "Nothing bad," she replied. "But The Queen has spoken to Judah's parents."

"Yes? Why?"

"To ask for his body in marriage, I guess. You know, a union!"

Now, things were starting to click into place for Sarah. "Well, she said she liked him. And they make a nice couple, but why the hockey stick?"

"Honestly, you don't know?" And Freida realized that she didn't. "Well I guess you will find out later."

Sarah wanted to know more, for there was lots she didn't understand. There were lots of unanswered questions, like "why was she asking him? And where did a hockey stick come into it?"

However, the conversation could not continue, because it was at this point, that their Tech-Tabs flashed with an incoming call. Freida touched her Tech-Tab, and took the call. It was from the presenter. They spoke briefly, then Freida ended the call and updated Sarah.

It was time. The studio audience was in place. The cameras were ready to roll. Now the presenter was calling them to the studio, to give the live broadcast. And this was where their attention was focused. And so they walked together into the studio, and took their seats.

15.
COMMITMENT

They were sitting on two different sofas in a studio. Across from them both was an interviewer, and a speaker's podium. The lights came on, and beamed down on the presenter and the podium.

The audience was visible behind the presenter, and facing them in a semi-circle. The rows of chairs then arched upwards, making the studio look like a theatre. Sarah could only estimate the number present, and guessed at around two hundred, with every chair filled.

"Good Evening," said the presenter from behind the podium. "My name is Denise La-Rooche, and welcome to "News As It Happens," the show where history happens live before your eyes." And the pre-selected audience burst into their usual prompted applause.

"And we have an interesting program for you to-night. In the moment we are going to be joined by Queen Boudicca herself." There was more even louder applause. A bit more spontaneous this time. "And she is always welcome on this program. But first we have an extra visit from two of her advisors."

A light beamed down on Freida, and Denise continued. "First of all we have Captain Freida Sophie Smith, spokeswoman for the Specialist Services." The applause was muted. "Welcome to you Freida. We understand you have been busy lately."

"Yes," said Freida. "Confidential stuff, in dangerous times. Can't discuss it all I'm afraid."

"We understand," said Denise, "and we gather you have been working with Boudicca herself, and our next guest. Must be stressful?"

"Can be, but I like to be kept busy. I find it helps to keep your mind off things."

"And how is your state of mind? We know you have suffered from mental illness and social problems in the past?"

Sarah gasped, but the audience was quiet. Did the whole country know this previously, before Denise told them? It certainly seemed a very aggressive line of questioning. She looked over at Freida, but Freida looked composed, even unbothered, and in charge.

"I am fine, thank you for asking. Of course, having great friends in Boudicca and Sarah does help. And my parents. Well. Where would I be without them?"

"Where indeed?" asked Denise, in a disapproving voice. She was continuing the aggressive questioning, and soon got to the point. "You are adopted aren't you? Originally from Palestine? Is that right?"

"Yes. I was adopted at the age of seventeen, when I came over here. From Palestine. I was fleeing slavery and the murderers of my parents. My other parents, that is."

"And you now have a top role, thanks to Boudicca?" The sarcasm in her question was unmistakable, and hinting at favouritism.

Freida countered, like she had been expecting this. "Thanks to hard work you mean. I did well in the military. I worked hard and succeeded in mission after mission. The great thing about Celtishia is that everybody has a chance to move forward."

"And is it true that Boudicca kept you out of jail?"

"I suppose it is. She heard my case."

"I thought so," interrupted Denise, in a smug way.

Again Freida defended herself verbally against the questioning. "But it was to give me a second chance, which I took and used to change my life around. Slavery had traumatized me, and I had issues. I was told it was my last chance though."

"Just two more questions, and I am sure the audience would like to know your opinion. How do you feel about the prisoner releases that are coming? Is it safe to let people out of prison?"

"Well. Firstly, as you are already aware Denise,

the prisoners that are being given early release are certain categories only! They are not considered dangerous. The prisoners that are being released are being released under a license. They have conditions to comply with, and will be put back inside if they fail to meet them," Freida pointed out. "By placing them back into their communities, at least those willing to take them that is, they will receive support and be given a chance to make amends. This kind of worked for me."

"So what is your role exactly, Freida? Our audience would like to know, where you fit in. How your reform is benefitting society? What you actually do now."

"Mostly security, and making things happen. I am a kind of go to person, and strategist. I liaise with different factions of the military, and coordinate missions between them. And I keep her majesty, and top military officials, informed of the details as they happen. I have a top security clearance, and a high rank, that I have earned by outperforming my colleagues at every turn. I believe in working harder, and being better at every turn."

Denise didn't look very impressed, at being fobbed off by Freida like that. But it was obvious that the audience was starting to get alongside Freida.

"Anyway," Denise continued trying to hide her embarrassment, "let's move on now to greet our second guest." She nodded to Freida. "Your friend from the Mist-Less Dimension, I believe."

And another beam of light fell on Sarah, and the audience erupted in applause.

"This is, of course, Miss Sarah Salter, now Royal Advisor."

The audience applauded louder. Some even stood up. And Denise turned to speak to her.

"So! Sarah Salter... Royal Advisor!" She was faking being impressed. "From another dimension. And I thought that they were works of fiction?"

"Well, here I am," Sarah said. 'In the flesh, so to speak."

"Yes, indeed, and it is mostly pink. I see however that your ears are turning green though?"

"To be expected apparently. Something to do with diet. Too many green naan breads, and kiwi smoothies I'm afraid."

The audience laughed, but Denise did not look amused. She continued questioning. "And you are here today to do what exactly?"

"To appeal to your viewers, as they are mostly the right demographic. Our target audience, so to speak."

"Well. Now is your chance. We have about twenty million viewers at present."

Sarah knew that this was the moment, and took a deep breath. But it was like a fear had griped her, and she just sat there in silence, unable to speak. Overwhelmed by the audience and the idea of twenty million people.

Sarah was staring at the floor now, and in a panic, when Denise spoke.

"Come now, have you lost your voice? You lead us into a war, and have nothing to say? You advise people to tear down shrines, and demonstrate it to the nation, and yet now you sit in silence?"

And at that moment, another hand touched hers. Freida had come to support her, and was now sitting next to her on the sofa.

"Perhaps the Israeli has something to say?" Denise sneered.

"Well technically," Freida responded, "the coming war was started by Egypt by invading the Channel Islands. Pharaoh threatened to kill the people of the Channel Islands. He has also ordered the raids on the City of Devonport, and nearly every port in the country."

The audience started to cheer and applaud.

"Is that so?" retorted Denise. "They were just raids, we could have ignored them. And avoided war."

And Sarah started to find her voice.

"I think you'll find it is impossible to avoid conflict, when the other side keep attacking you. Every effort was made to appease them, but the demands kept coming, and the forced slavery suntil continues. By rescuing the people of the Channel Islands, they will live free to fight another day. Alongside us."

"We? You are from somewhere else! You both

are?" The argument was now getting heated.

"Actually I am from Plymouth, you prejudiced idiot" said Sarah, and the audience cheered. "I admit, it is another dimension's Devonport, but it is on this island. "Besides," Sarah continued, "I was brought here by The Whisper, and I have a job to do."

And now, Sarah felt inspired. Angry even. So she took another breath, and spoke out.

"Right here, and right now, I appeal to the nation. We need volunteers to fight. If you are aged twenty-one to Forty, then your country needs you. Get yourself to a base, and bring your weapons. We have the drones. and we have the ships. We even have the guns, but we need the manpower. We need you!"

"Make no mistake! The enemy is on their way. But they move slowly. They will be here in force, and organized in about three months. But we can send them back home again. We can prepare for their arrival. We can defeat them. And we can win this war.!"

"Are you serious?" asked Denise.

"Yes," said Sarah. "We will be fighting an enemy that is all hot air. Look how easily we defeated their forces off the coast of Devonport, because we stood up to them. Now imagine what an entire army could do."

For the first time in the conversation, Denise was silent. And Freida spoke.

"My friend Boudicca, our Queen; and her government, would never have sanctioned this, if she didn't believe that we can win it. Why should we keep paying appeasement money to a country that keeps demanding more? Do we not all know that the demands will increase in frequency, and amount, until we can't pay them anyway? Surely it is better to make the stand now, before they bleed us dry, and we cannot?"

"But what about peace?" asked Denise.

And Freida retorted, "sometimes we have to forego peace in the short term, to achieve a greater peace in the long term. Otherwise the tensions just simmer along below the surface. And one side in effect holds the other to ransom."

"We all know," said Sarah, "that the Egyptians have already taken what they call "peace payments" from us. I call it 'tax.' And we get nothing in return, except not invaded. The time has come to say 'no more', and that time is now."

Sarah continued, "I repeat what I said before. Let all volunteers between the age of twenty-one and forty, enroll into the forces. We need their assistance. We need them to defend our freedoms."

"Well!" said Denise La-Rooche, in a patronizing voice. "I guess this interview is finished as well then? Let us now move shortly onto our third guest. I am of course talking about Queen Boudicca herself, speaking live in the studio. First however, we have a musical break. Please welcome the chart-tipping "Juno Sisters'."

The lights over Sarah's, and Freida's sofas, both went off. The band started to play their song. It was about some "hazy idea of love."

"Chart-tipping?" asked a mystified Sarah.

"Yes, top forty songs. They are number forty!"

By the time the song ended, Sarah and Freida were backstage. They were looking at a giant screen, in their dressing room, as they had been promised. The sofa where they had previously been, was now empty, but Judah could be seen sat on a stool nearby. He was drinking hot chocolate.

"Like a lamb to the slaughter," joked Freida.

A light beamed on Miss La-Rooche. Then onto a door, through which Boudicca herself could be seen entering. She looked amazing with her long ginger hair tied back into a bun, and wearing a gorgeous body hugging black dress, with two diagonal yellow stripes. It stretched to just above the knee.

"Good evening, Boudicca, and welcome to the show." And the audience clapped.

"That will be 'your majesty' to you, Miss La-Rooche."

There was a gasp from the audience. Queen Boudicca had spoken in her harshest voice, and did not look pleased. The presenter, Miss Denise La-Rooche looked both taken aback, and embarrassed. There was a small silent pause, while the presenter held her ear. It was clear that she was getting directions yelled at her, from off the set.

Also off the screen, Freida had nudged Sarah, and was smirking at the sudden and unexpected discomfort of Denise La-Rooche.

"I apologize unreservedly, Your Majesty. But all the same, welcome to the show," said Miss La-Rooche in a groveling tone. There was another pause.

"Well," Denise continued. "Freida and Sarah have indicated.."

"Do you mean Captain Sophia-Smith, and Chief Advisor Salter, by any chance?"

"Yes of course. Your majesty." Miss La-Rooche now looked very flustered, and was seen to be pulling her ear piece from her ear, to avoid being yelled at further, from off the set. After a pause she continued in a now tactful and respectful low tone. "They have bluntly said that you have sanctioned military action, and agree to the raising of an army? Surely that isn't correct?"

'Yes! It is correct. It is time we stood up to Egypt. I agree that we can win this war, and send them back to their homeland. I believe that we should."

"And you don't think that that is risky?"

"Of course. We don't expect Egypt to go without a fight. They have far too much arrogance for that!"

"And you trust your advisors?"

"Yes. A lot more than I would trust you! They are knowledgeable, and guided by the most reliable sources. Not the latest liberal, and fashionable nonsense."

And with that Boudicca spoke clearly for all the viewers to hear. "So I repeat their request for people to come forward and join our forces. And to do so now."

The spotlight went back onto an embarrassed Miss La-Rooche, who now knew what she had to do. So, she spoke into the camera. "Well! You heard it here first. If you are aged between twenty-one and forty, enlist now for training and action. This is your duty, and I for one support it, and encourage it."

Boudicca was now smiling. "Thank you Miss La-Rooche. I knew you would agree. And of course, seeing that you are aged twenty-five, you will be joining the volunteers I trust? You are keen to set an example, are you not?" And this time, Sarah smirked at Freida, while Boudicca asked another rather hinting question. "So I understand you have something of a more personal nature to ask me as well? Is that correct?"

"Yes, that's right, I almost forgot. How serious is your current relationship to Mister Judah Shalom. I understand, he is a member of your staff at the HUB, and you are very close."

And Judah who was sitting on the stool near to Boudicca, choked on his hot chocolate.

And Boudicca responded, "Good question. Can I

borrow you a moment, Judah, my love?" And she beckoned him over to join her.

Judah had clearly been taken by surprise, and was mystified by the request. He clearly had no idea what was going on. But like an obedient puppy dog, he rose and sat down next to Boudicca. She reached out her hand, and he took it.

"Well," said Boudicca directly to Judah. "We have been going out for three months now. We often spend time together, and it is true to say that we are boyfriend and girlfriend."

"Really?" Denise was finding her feet again, and clearly starting to hint. As one the audience leant forward on their seats.

"Yes. And I am very fond of Bou," interjected Judah defensively.

"Yes, I am sure you are. But is her majesty fond of you?"

"More than you will ever know," Boudicca retorted. "But it is difficult. You see Judah here feels that he is unworthy of me, as I am a Royal and he is not."

The audience gave a sound of sympathy.

"Well we have talked about it. Including last night when." But he was unable to finish the sentence.

There was an awkward pause, but Boudicca was clearly claiming the moment.

"Yes Jude, and I hope you will forgive me, but after that moment; I called your parents. I spoke to them about us." The audience gave an excited clap, like they were catching onto something. And Boudicca continued. "They told me that your feelings for me were genuine. And very deep. They were the ones, who told me that you felt you could not propose, or take things further. So I asked for permission to advance things."

"But how can you do that?" asked Judah, who clearly was not keeping up with the conversation.

"Well," and she smiled for the first time at Denise, and then at Judah. A C.B.C. servant had come in bringing a clean hockey stick on a very large silver plate. Sarah noticed that its hook end, had been wrapped in a kind of protective padding.

Sarah was shocked, but the audience instead gasped with a kind of excitement, when paramedics with healing scanners appeared on stage. Sarah instantly realized that they were there in case something went wrong.

Freida, meanwhile nudged Sarah, and said, "blooming health and safety. Always take the fun out of things." Sarah chose to ignore this comment, as she had never seen anything like it, and was wondering what would happen next.

Everyone was quiet, as Boudicca thanked the servant. She then took the hockey stick, and placed it on her knee. She looked knowingly at Judah, took his hand, and placed it on the padding that covered the hook end. The end Sarah knew was usually used for hitting a ball.

Boudicca leant forward and touched her forehead to Judah's. She looked him in the eyes, and spoke for all to hear. There was silence in the studio, as everybody wanted to hear this moment, and what she was saying.

"If you let me, I will make it official! You are the man I love. I want to be with you permanently Judah. But it is also your choice! And I will respect what you decide."

"I may be Queen, but I am also a woman. I have desires I have reserved for you, and I hope you feel the same way about me, as I do about you?" Her voice changed to a plea. "And Judah Shalom, my love. I am asking you here and now. Please; if you feel the same way, take this opportunity. Please stand up, look over there, and close your eyes. And I will do what our custom allows. And when you awake, we will be engaged."

And Judah gave a nervous smile, for he had now twigged what was happening. He paused, clearly shocked, but continued to look into Boudicca's eyes.

Only five seconds passed, but they seemed like an eternity to everyone. It was clear, he was deciding under pressure. But he smiled again, and said "Yes Please, I would be honored to be unified to you, Bou. You are everything to me."

The audience cheered, but Boudicca was already on her feet. The hockey stick in her right hand. Her left hand was helping a nervous Judah up. They hugged momentarily and smiled at each other, before resting foreheads against each other once more. Looking into each other's eyes, Boudicca was starting to cry, and so was Judah.

Then in happiness, they kissed each other passionately on the lips for about a minute, while the audience cooed approval. And then slowly Judah withdrew from her gently. He then turned around in the direction of the wall. He walked forward two paces, stopped and stood motionless, but for a bit of shaking. He then closed his eyes, and took deep breaths.

Boudicca paused, took three deliberate short breaths, and spoke.

"I want everybody present, and watching; to know that I, Boudicca, Queen of Celtishia, claim Judah Shalom for my own. His parents have consented, so there is no known reason why I cannot take his body in marriage. Judah Shalom and I, will soon wed, and be a couple for all eternity. And may the Whisper grant us many children."

Sarah could tell that Judah was moved by these words. But Sarah could also see he was shaking at what was coming. However, he tried to hide it bravely, as his eyes remained firmly closed.

Boudicca stepped forward, but slightly to Judah's side. She now grasped the hockey stick firmly, at the mid-way point of the stick, using both hands. She then lined it up carefully, before taking one more breath.

"Yes or No?" she asked Judah one last time.

"Yes, do it!"

And with that phrase of consent, Boudicca swung the stick. It struck Judah's head, with a gentle thud. And Judah fell to the ground, in a state of mild unconsciousness. The silence was interrupted only by the paramedics, who were already moving to check out Judah, and make sure he was ok. The audience, however, erupted into a standing ovation, and even Freida could be seen giving a "yes" with a clenched fist.

Boudicca dropped the stick, and in excitement virtually throw herself on Judah, while the paramedics continued to check him out.

"He's coming around," an unknown voice said. And Boudicca held him in her arms, cuddling him for all to see. Meanwhile, Denise's voice spoke out over the airways.

"The C.B.C sends its congratulations to Queen Boudicca, and to Judah Shalom, on their engagement. You both have the nation's blessing, and support."

16. REALITY BITES

Immediately after the broadcast, Boudicca came running to meet with Freida. She was so excited that she grabbed Freida and hugged her affectionately, before dragging her away to talk in private.

Sarah could not make out what they were saying, but could tell that Boudicca was giving orders. Freida was listening attentively, ready to do as she was told.

When they returned, Sarah guessed that Boudicca clearly felt she had given Freida every last instruction she could. And so Boudicca now turned her attention from Freida to Sarah.

"Now listen carefully, you," she said.

"Of course."

"Firstly, I am unlikely to see you again on a face to face basis, until this is over. My security is putting pressure on me to take my safety seriously. But you can speak face to face with me at any time. You can also go directly to all my military chiefs, and any senior politician you choose. Judah will also be with me, and you can talk to him as well."

"I understand," replied Sarah

"Good. Because I need you to look after yourself. I want you to lead the charge against Egypt, but I also need you to come back safely. So listen to Freida, follow all the training she puts you through. And it will be hard. She is most driven. Don't expect it to be easy."

"Of course."

"But I also need you to be willing to stand up to her, and give orders at the right time. But until then, and you will know when, I am sure of it. Never settle for what is acceptable. Instead aim for excellence."

"I will try," Sarah promised her.

"Good to hear," Boudicca pointed out, "because this is where it gets real. War is serious. It is not like a computer game, where you can try again. If you get hit with a bullet, you could die. Simple as that."

"I know," said Sarah sounding almost scared. And they all paused and looked at each other.

"Well then," Boudicca continued, "I will give you both personal access to the very best armour, and any equipment you choose. Use what suits you, but remember it is not about fashion, but to be able to do what needs to be done."

There was another pause, and Boudicca spoke once more to Sarah. "I also need you to do something else for me?"

"If I can?"

"I need you to look after each other, mentally as well as physically. This is a testing time for us all, and will require us to draw on our best inner strength. I believe that you can both help each other here, and will certainly need to do so."

And with that Boudicca left the room, to be with her new fiancé; and make decisions affecting her country.

The news that evening was mostly repeats. First the appeal for help, and then the proposal. For Sarah, however, things were getting both interesting and intense.

Firstly, Freida had decided there was no time for resting, and ordered Sarah onto a flying craft, (which resembled the flying saucers of science fiction), to set out for the "Mossad training center" in Devonport. She was to participate on a three months intensive course in all she would need to know. Freida was to be her trainer, and drill sergeant. And Sarah knew, that for the next few weeks, Freida was going to drive her hard physically, and mentally.

The second shock that night was that Denise La-Rooche was being ordered to join them. She had after all agreed to enlist live on air, and Freida was keen to capitalize on that, with Boudicca's consent. Denise La-Roche now joined them looking shell shocked, in her smart silver coloured clothes and gold necklace.

And so the "Saucer" took off with Freida's conscripts on board, flying to Devonport, and its Jewish Quarter.

The flying saucer was very silent in the air. It was designed to carry people in bulk, and hovered at about fifty miles an hour over the countryside.

Freida showed Denise and Sarah into a room, marked virtual reality.

"Right, listen carefully now. Both of you," she started to explain. "This next bit is about fun, efficiency and practicality. There are two booths here, one each. Take off your clothes, and stand in one. You will be scanned, all over, to check your health. It will also measure you for your clothing size."

"It is a private and painless process, and nobody will see your details, as it is all electronic. The data is saved, and you will then have a choice of how loose, or body hugging you want your clothing to be. I prefer body hugging myself, as it is better for movement."

"When this is done, you can get dressed again and try out a Virtual Reality fighting game. You can try various styles, and decide for example your weapons, and whether you want to fight with a modern shield or not. Now get to it."

Sarah and Denise just did as they were told. Sarah took the right cubicle, and was scanned. She opted for the body hugging design of uniform.

And then as asked they spent their time in virtual reality, fighting together and trying out different styles of fighting. Both girls decided that they hated the use of the see-through shields, as they just got in the way of their guns. They made very few hits, but learned to hide in virtual bushes, and keep their heads down.

Meanwhile, the Saucer continued its journey, and they finally arrived at the Mossad Training Centre after three hours. On arrival, they were registered very quickly, and then fast marched by Freida into their barracks, where a changing room awaited them.

"You two! Sit," Freida commanded, and pointed to a wooden bench.

Sarah and Denise sat where they were told.

"Right! Here is how it is. From now on I am in charge, until the Egyptians are in place and ready to attack. By the time negotiate access to key areas, that will be about three months away. Then and only then Sarah, will I take orders from you. Until then, I am your boss! Understand?"

"Yes Boss"

Freida leant over Sarah and yelled. "I think you will find the correct response is 'Yes Captain'."

"Yes Captain!" Sarah responded, with more humility.

Freida now rounded on Denise.

"And you, spoiled little daddy's girl. This is no joy ride. But you will have a great military media role, after this advanced training. After all, you do have the experience. But for now, you do as you are told, when you are told, and by me. Do you understand?"

"Yes Captain!"

"Good. "And Freida walked to a locker, and produced two uniforms. She gave one each to Sarah and Denise.

"Right you two. Get showered. Get rid of all make up, and necklaces, except Tech-Tabs, and torcs. Place all unauthorized possessions into your lockers and hand me the keys."

The girls looked shocked. But slowly removed their earrings, necklaces and other accessories. But Freida was not letting up.

"It is important you both learn to survive with what you need, and nothing else. If it is not issued, then it is not needed. Starting now, you have five minutes to undress and shower." And Freida turned on the showers, and turned to leave the room.

"I will be back in that time, and you had better be wearing these. They are your uniforms for the next three months. There are three sets, one for now, one for the wash, and one spare. Understand?"

"Yes Captain," they responded.

"Good. You will wear your uniform continuously. You will train in them, and sleep in them. You will fight, swim, climb, and even wash in them. They are breathable and extremely hard wearing. Knickers you must change daily, and place in the wash. Now hurry up. Five minutes only."

Freida left the room, and Sarah and Denise, just did as they were told. They showered quickly, and put on their uniforms.

There was a full-body suit, and a separate jacket. The body suits looked a bit like the wet suits, she knew from the Mist-Less World. However, they were lighter, and mostly of a green, black and brown camouflaged design. This was ok to Sarah, but harder for Denise as they made her look extremely 'natural.' Sarah's pink skin, stood out against the green.

The jackets were black and green only, but had camouflaged hoods. Where normally she was used to pockets, there was a large knife hanging downwards.

There was a belt, and a hand gun in a holster. Denise was disgusted that there was "no ammunition."

"These are climbing helmets?" Denise pointed out after the next bit of kit arrived, looking equally disappointed.

Finally, there were the shoes. They resembled running shoes, and were made of a kind of plastic, with zips. They were also a green and brown military design, but fitted exceptionally well, down to the advanced scanning process.

Freida reentered the room after the five minutes

were up. She fast marched in two other recruits. They were both female, already dressed and in uniform.

"Right you two," she said looking at Sarah and Denise. "This is Louise and Charlotte. I have already told them, about you two. The four of you will make up my squad for the first part of the training. Now follow me!"

Sarah checked out her two new colleagues. Both could be regarded as very good looking, in their own way.

Louise was as thin as a stick insect, with long blonde curly hair. She wore her uniform skin tight, and was carrying her helmet in her hand. She wore a bronze torc around her neck. On her back was a backpack, and a rectangular shield the same size as her.

Charlotte on the other hand was curvy, and could be seen wearing a tattoo of a dagger on her neck. Her uniform fitted her perfectly, and complimented her enormous chest. She also carried a shield on her backpack. On her left leg, and thighs, were two daggers in their scabbards. Charlotte looked the keener of the two, as she was already wearing her helmet, with the face visor up, revealing a set of trendy blue glasses, and the fact she had shaved off her hair.

Freida now led her squad to a small round dormitory. Inside there were five single hammocks, suspended to a centre point and stretching out to different parts of the room. The only furniture was a table with some food on it.

"It is now eleven pm," Freida pointed out. "Talk and get to know each other if you must. But eat well, and get yourselves rested. We start tomorrow at six am."

They talked and chatted for an hour. Whilst they ate and shared the food, Sarah discovered that Charlotte and Louise both came from Devonport, and had enrolled prior to the appeal. Both girls were keen to get started, and delighted to be in Freida's training squad.

In Charlotte case, however, it was part of her jubilee release from prison deal. She explained that she had welcomed service as a chance to start afresh. She never said what she had been in prison for, and nobody asked.

Later on that night, when the others slept, Sarah took out her 'Tech-Tab,' and spoke to Vincent about the proposal.

"Vincent. I still don't get it? What just happened between Boudicca and Judah?"

"Well. Basically, when a man is unable to propose, the woman of higher status, takes the lead. And with the permission from the lad's parents, she asks the man for a union. To marry him. If he says yes, she hits him with the hockey stick and knocks him out. Assuming he is basically okay, when he regains consciousness, she gets to call a priest, and they are engaged."

"Really, and this is usual? Isn't it dangerous?"

"Not really. Not nowadays anyway. You saw the paramedics, with scanners. They can heal nearly all immediate damage through a vacuum technology. And the hockey stick is padded as well you know."

"But this was, you know live? On TV? A woman proposing to a man? And hitting him with a hockey stick."

"Yes. Of Course. Boudicca is a Queen you know." Vincent computed that he would still need to elaborate, so he continued. "A man of Judah's rank couldn't propose to a Queen. He would feel overpowered by it. Understandably scared probably. No! In this case, it had to be the other way around. And Boudicca really wanted to unify with him. So, she took the initiative, as per Celtishian custom. Judah had the right to say no, even on TV."

'But I feel this could have gone wrong, and it would have been my fault. I advised her to basically follow her heart. Was that wrong?"

"No. It was inspired. Those two have been dragging their feet for ages. The people thought that it was getting tiring to watch."

"Will people accept this union? The Queen, and a commoner."

"Why on the Green-Earth wouldn't they? They are both young, and in love. Besides, these are tough times, and there are others, like Prince Mustapha Sword, who are after a union with Boudicca, for political reasons. And the people hate him. No. This is much better. And settles the issue."

"By the way," Vincent said "there are reactions coming in from all over the world to the engagement. And it seems to be escalating things."

"Then you had better show me."

The first reaction was from America, and the President congratulating Boudicca on the news. Ghana's reaction was very positive, saying it was great news but a little unexpected.

Sweden's comment was that it was great she was marrying for love. Germany said they would "endorse the engagement.

Egypt on the other hand, was furious, saying that "Mustapha Sword would have made a better partner, and how dare she a woman think she should choose for herself." But things took a bad turn, when Egypt said "it was unlawful, by their rules, and was yet another insult. They were appealing to other nations to join them in war against us."

America responded to this by saying Celtishia should make "its own decisions," and was moving its ships towards the area to assist Celtishia in any aggressive assault. Now it seems that we are not fighting on our own.

The reactions in "VR News" had stopped. And Sarah lay on her bed somewhat stunned, and asked herself? "How could an act of love result in so much disagreement?"

Now a voice spoke into the darkness. But it was

definitely not the voice of the Whisper.

"You were watching that too?" asked Denise. "The World Reactions?"

"Yes, and I find it baffling," Sarah responded, and stopped to think. "Wait a minute, you used to work in media, you might know. Surely Boudicca can choose her own partner?"

"Of course she can. Under Celtishian law, that is. However, the Egyptians don't think that way. They are not bad people, they just view things differently, and believe that that only their laws matter"

"But shouldn't different opinions be respected?"

"Yes, and I am disappointed by the turn of events."

Sarah was surprised, and asked Denise, "why is that?"

"Look, don't get me wrong, please? I am loyal to Celtishia. And I hate the way Egypt functions. You know, the slavery, and oppression of other countries? I just hate conflicts and wars. I just want everyone to live together in peace."

"But is that always possible?"

Denise gave a look of resignation, and responded. "Sadly no. So when called upon to do so, I will do my bit, and am proud to do so."

"Good to know," said Sarah. "Good night, Miss La-Rooche," and she turned over and went to sleep.

And that night, Sarah slept well, because she knew then that Denise La-Rooche might be naïve, but she could also be trusted. Truth was, she meant well, but had had a sheltered upbringing. This training time would change them all.

17.
DEVELOPMENT

T hey were woken up at six am by Freida entering the room. She was holding a dustbin lid, and was banging it like a drum.

"Really?" asked Denise. She spoke in a slumbering voice, that really said "go away, and don't wake me up."

That one word was probably not considered wise in the circumstances, as Freida had clearly picked up on the undertone. And within a second, Freida was straight over to her, and yelling in her ear.

"Get your backsides out of bed, and get dressed. Now!"

The women in the dormitory started to rise obediently. Denise looked embarrassed, and the rest didn't dare argue. They just got dressed as quickly and quietly as they could.

Finally, Freida broke the silence again. "Breakfast is in five minutes in the canteen. Eat well, for you have a tough three months ahead of you. And don't forget to check the board, it will tell you where your individual meetings are."

Freida had warned all the recruits the night before, that they would have a one to one session, at seven am, to assess their fitness, combat knowledge and general experience. The idea was to work out a series of personal plans, guaranteeing that all recruits were up to a set standard.

And so Sarah set off with the others for breakfast, checking the board on the way.

"Damn," said Louise, "I have Freida. I hear she is a right slave driver. Efficient and ruthless."

"I have Training Captain Jones," said Charlotte.

"Sarah, you have Captain Milkos? Bad luck," said Denise. "I hear he trained Freida. So he must be tough."

"Who do you have, Denise?"

"Captain Tersia Rainey. That's good, I have the only lady, from a respectable family." Denise was starting to brag a little. "I have seen her around during press conferences, and she seems very nice. And classy too."

And with that they continued to breakfast.

Breakfast was simple. Toasted green soda bread, turkey rashers, and eggs. There was also the usual green smoothie.

"How common," said Denise. "I had hoped that there would, at least, be a buffet. You know. Better choice."

"Is that so?" said a voice behind them. And they all turned to look, to see one of their superiors, and she did not look amused. Sarah, Charlotte and Louise instinctively took a step backwards, to distance themselves from the situation.

"Well its like this Captain Rainey," continued Denise with an heir of familiarity. "I expected that there would be some beans, and cereals to choose from at least. Perhaps a yoghurt to help with the.."

But she was not able to finish the sentence, because the superior officer had grabbed her by the ear, and was yelling into it.

"Are you for real?!" hollered Captain Rainey, at a stunned Denise. "Firstly. It is "Yes Captain" to you. Learn some respect! You are not working for your daddy now! On the ground, and give me one hundred and fifty press ups, and you can forget the idea of breakfast, Recruit. Your one on one assessment is starting right now, as it seems you have more than most to learn."

And a shell shocked Denise La-Rooche started her press ups, while the others started to eat. And from this moment onwards, none of them dared to make comments about their trainers. However, out of the corner of her eye, Sarah could see Freida had seen the whole incident, and had not been amused by it. She knew that the whole group could expect some sort of extra training, but decided to not tell her fellow recruits this just now.

After breakfast, Sarah walked quickly downstairs and below ground, to find the room where she was to meet her trainer. She arrived on time, but only just, for the training base was a bit like a maze to navigate around.

She knocked tentatively on the door of the room. Almost immediately, she heard a rough voice. "Come in Recruit Salter." And Sarah entered not knowing quite what to expect.

Captain Peter Milkos sat at his desk, and motioned for Sarah to sit down. Her first impressions of him were positive. His hair had all been shaved off, and he wore a pair of expensive glasses. For a man in his forties, he looked very attractive to her.

The room itself resembled the inside of half a giant football. It had even been constructed using a design of hexagonal panels. A door and a window behind him, indicated the gym where the assessment would take place.

Sarah sat down in the spare seat, and tried to remain calm. Meanwhile Captain Milkos studied her interest, observing the difference in her skin colour, and to try and engage her state of mind.

"That silly La-Rooche girl was right about the green ears then?"

That was it, thought a miffed Sarah. His opening line? About her ears.

"What?" she asked.

"That silly La-Rooche girl was right about the green ears then?" he repeated, and smirked.

"What is wrong with my ears now." She was

trying to sound puzzled, but she knew what he meant.

"Nothing, but she was right when she said they are changing colour. They even seem darker than the other day, and you are getting some green, on your face as well."

"And?"

"And so the Earth will make a Celtishian out of you yet," he laughed out loud.

"Right." Sarah was laughing too.

He now proceeded to get the meeting properly under way. "Well down to business. My name as you are aware is Captain Peter Milkos, and my role here create and monitor a personalized plan for your training, based on your current abilities. Do you understand things so far?"

"Yes Captain."

"Good," replied a pleased Captain Milkos. "You on the other hand are Sarah Salter. Recruit on a specialized program. Advisor to the Queen. You grew up in a country called 'England,' and you are I suspect, someone who needs a lot of training in certain key areas."

"That is correct."

"Your reputation of course, exceeds you. And it is mostly positive. I was assigned you by Freida, who feared she would go easy on you, due to your existing friendship. She thought, I could for the most part, train you the same way that I trained her. By correcting you whenever needed, but allowing you to develop a style of your own."

"Sounds good."

"Good? No!" he corrected her, "but necessary! It will help to keep you alive."

"Captain Sophia Smith will, however, continue to teach the whole group for close combat, hand to hand fighting, and for climbing."

Sarah nodded approvingly.

"Anyway, let's get you assessed, and develop your plan. I can see you are dressed appropriately, so let's head to the gym." And with that he opened the door behind him, and ushered her through.

"Welcome to our smallest, and basic level gym," said Captain Milkos, once they were inside.

It didn't take long for Sarah to realize that the gym was absolutely enormous, especially for a room underground. Sarah guessed that it was the size of three soccer pitches, and about thirty metres high. It was so large, that it even had a running track, and an enormous swimming pool in the centre.

Everywhere she looked there were recruits being put through their paces. They were climbing walls, and practicing sprinting with their gear on. In the swimming pool, she could see that Denise was being given a swimming assessment. However, she and Captain Milkos were not heading in that direction, but were going instead; towards the weight and exercise room.

The exercise room itself contained every form

of training gear imaginable, some of which she had not even conceived of before.

"Ok," said her assessor pointing at some weights, "let's start with these. I want to see how much strength you have."

And so for the next few hours Sarah was assessed on everything in the room. It included climbing, weightlifting, swimming, and target accuracy with both handgun and bow. Her results were recorded on a Tech-Tab. Finally, when the morning was over, she was taken back to the office of Captain Milkos, for some feedback.

Tired and exhausted, she sat down on the spare chair, glad to get the weight off her feet. She was dreading the results, and was worried about potential consequences of her performance. Captain Milkos paced the room a little, studying his Tech-Tab. Eventually, he took the seat facing her.

"Well," said Captain Milkos after a while. "You actually did quite well. I am very pleased."

Sarah was so relieved, that she felt like a huge weight, had been lifted from her. Now being lost for words, all she could say was "Oh?"

"Yes," continued the Captain, in a matter of fact way. "You certainly did better than Freida did in her first assessment, but don't tell her I told you that."

They both laughed. And the Captain handed her his own Tech-Tab screen to show her the results, in more detail.

"Basically, as you can see. You performed very well in areas of basic fitness. I guess that was a result of the martial-art training you have done. Some of our recruits can hardly even do press ups, when they join. You can run fast, and have some real athletic skills."

"Your swimming skills were also very good. You could swim a great distance without breaking sweat, and I am sure you will cope well with tides. But I am concerned that you are swimming a bit noisily."

"Noisily?"

"Yes. You need to understand, that there are times in war when stealth is essential. Like if you are trying to surprise people via the water. And you do unfortunately swim loudly. I will put you down for some lessons in swimming with elegance. Quite standard really. I hope that it is ok with you?"

"Yes. Thank you Captain." But Sarah wasn't really sure about that one.

"Your hand to hand fighting skills are good. But I am concerned that you lack killer instinct. There are times when you seem uncertain, and that could get you killed on mission. I will make sure that you get plenty of sparring practice. You can expect to get lots of bruises while you learn."

"Yes Captain. To be honest, I had always avoided the sparring side of martial arts."

Her assessor did not look surprised at this. "Well

now it is vital you learn, and improve at it."

"Of course Captain," said Sarah trying to convince him she understood.

Captain Milkos, now stared at her over his glasses. It was clear he had something serious to talk about. "Now tell me honestly, Sarah. Have you ever used a gun or bow before?"

"Not really. Freida took me to the range one evening. You know? For fun? She could shoot a pimple off a man's bum, but I could not even hit the target."

Captain Milkos looked amused by Sarah's tone of phrase, and responded. "Good, because I originally trained her. And I will train you as well. In three weeks you will have the potential to be as good as she is. Your results were awful here. In fact, you missed everything. So that means extra lessons teaching you from scratch. The positive here, is you don't have bad habits to unlearn. You start bow training this afternoon after climbing. Gun practice is tomorrow. The times are now on your personal plan."

Sarah had not expected that her plan's changing would be so instant. "Thank you Captain," she replied sounding surprised.

"Don't thank me, just don't let me down. Keep to the plan. Continue to accept instruction and keep learning. Then practice and practice, until you get it right. Now go, and get some lunch."

Lunch was basic rations that most of the squad

seemed to enjoy. Denise of course, was not impressed, but said nothing. It looked like she was simply too exhausted. Sarah herself, had seen her being really put through her paces, by her assessor due to her indiscretion earlier. Most of the squad felt she deserved it, but Sarah couldn't feel a little sympathy towards her.

The conversation over the table was over how the morning had been. Nearly all had performed badly with the bow and arrow. Charlotte had also been lousy with the gun, but had at least hit the target once.

It was at this stage that they noticed that Denise was sporting a black eye. She explained it had happened during the sparing assessment, with Captain Jones. He had a particularly strong hook. Denise, it seemed was not used to sparing, and had let her guard down.

"I won't be doing that again," she said, and the group laughed.

Louise, on the other hand, was fairly upbeat. Whilst she had been assessed as average in most things, she had performed better than she had expected at climbing. In fact, she had got a "distinction" for this. Now she was looking forward to the afternoon session which was a group climbing exercise, with her personal tutor "Freida," who she was starting to bond with. This made Sarah jealous.

After lunch the group set off for the climbing

exercise, with Freida. When they arrived Freida was sitting down looking over their reports.

Freida motioned them to some stools next to her desk. They sat there in silence while she finished. Eventually, she looked up.

"First of all, well done all of you for getting through such a tough morning. Your assessment results were approximately what I expected, with no real surprises. Recruit Charlotte, you will join Recruit Sarah, immediately after the climbing session for archery basics. I trust you will both work at this."

"Yes, Captain," they replied as one.

"Now listen Recruits, I want you all in the boxing ring at every opportunity. Work on kicking and punching. And develop your respective crafts, as much as you can."

"Yes Captain," they replied, but Denise looked uncertain. It was clear her eye was hurting her, but she was trying to cover it up.

'Now I know that eye hurts Denise, but next time keep your guard up. I watched your sparring on playback, and could see that hand to hand fighting is not your strongest point," and Denise was taken aback. However, to the group's surprise, Freida then changed her approach towards her. "In the meantime, I have arranged a series of extra training sessions on sparring to assist you. I will be taking them in person, because I can see exactly where you are going wrong. It is mostly bad positioning, and can be corrected easily."

"But be assured Denise, I was pleased with how you did this morning, despite getting off to a bad start with your assessor. Your results were the best of the group, in most areas, and showed great promise."

"And talking of focus," Freida continued, getting serious again. "You were mostly considered 'satisfactory' at climbing the easy stuff this morning. So let's get over to 'The Wall'."

And so they set off to climb 'the wall' in question.

When they got there Sarah could see why it was called 'the wall.' It had a variety of hand holds, and places that stuck out. There was also a series of timed challenges.

Not only did it cover most of the end of the gym, but they could then see what they hadn't previously. The ceiling of this end of the gym was held up by pillars. Furthermore, so were the levels above. All ten of them. This made the wall an eleven story climb, and a total of about three hundred meters from bottom to top.

"Welcome to the basic climbing," said Freida. "Put your helmets on, because this is where you will learn to really climb. You will learn both safety and speed. Now follow me, but take only those handholds marked out." And with that she pushed her Tech-Tab, and a selection of the hand holds turned a bright red.

"The good news is," Freida continued, "is that this is still an easy level. But should you be tempted to cheat, and use other handholds: you will receive a buzzing sound in your ears, and an electric shock for multiple offenses. That happens automatically and hurts by the way."

"Now, Louise you can go first." And Louise started to climb. "Charlotte you follow, Sarah next, then you Denise. And remember, keep to the red handholds."

Sarah was now on the wall, looking up at the backsides of Louise and Charlotte, who she thought had nice figures. They also seemed to be better climbers than her, because they had practiced most of their life.

They kept climbing straight upwards together, until they reached the second level. Then the handholds started to take them sideways.

"Keep up Sarah," yelled Freida, as Charlotte was getting further away. So Sarah dug deeper mentally, and tried to speed up her climbing. Denise remained on her heels.

They reached the end of the sideways climb on level two, and then continued to climb upwards for another two levels. It was here that they started to hear some jeering.

"Oh I forgot to mention this," said Freida, into their earpieces. "There is a bar on this level, and the boys? Well they will be boys."

"Nice bum on number four," came a male voice from behind them.

"Sexist pigs," yelled Denise who had attempted to turn around, and yell abuse back at them. Next minute there was a spark heard.

"Ow," yelled Denise, and the group knew who had received it. They could see that Denise was now suspended from her safety wire, dangling in mid-air.

"Do you need rescuing Miss La-Rooche?" came the laughing voices from behind. "Who's a fallen woman then?" For everybody below had recognized her from the TV.

Denise was being a good sport about this though, and started to laugh.

"Ignore the boys, and focus," yelled Freida, into all their ear pieces. "And try swinging back to the wall, Denise."

"Damn" said Louise a minute later. "I got a shock too." But she was at least still connected to the wall. Five minutes later, Sarah got her first buzz in her ear, warning her to pay attention to where she was placing her hands. They continued to climb another level.

"Please stop. and climb on board the platform for a rest," instructed Freida.

And one by one, the all-girl recruits, reached the platform. They climbed on board, and with their feet dangling over, faced down at the boys.

"Thought you'd never make it," yelled one, clearly aiming his jibe at Denise.

When Freida, reached the platform, all the boys became silent, and were now curiously looking up at the girls. Checking them out.

Freida came alongside her squad. "The one who caused you to lose grip, is third on the left, Denise," Freida informed her, and pointed him out. "Comment about liking the look of your backside, if I remember?" The boy realized he was being pointed out and looked embarrassed.

"Really?" Denise La-Rooche looked the boy over approvingly. "He's quite cute really."

The other girls giggled.

"In that case, I might as well tell you. He is called Peter. The son of a wealthy farmer."

"Sweet," said Denise, "does he like sparring, I could do with a practice partner."

"Any excuse, eh," joked Louise.

"Oi, Peter," Charlotte suddenly called out to the man. "What are you doing this evening? Our celebrity wants a date."

"I'm in here most of the night," he yelled back, blushing a little.

"Good! Then she will see you after ten o'clock. And you are buying the drinks."

"Ok, I'll see her then."

Another man had started to speak in Peter's ear. After about ten seconds, Peter stepped forward. "Is the other one coming too?"

"Which other one? "

"The hot blond one!"

"You mean Louise?" asked Charlotte.

"Yeah, my mate, Tim, wants to know if Louise is joining us."

Charlotte looked at Louise. Louise was nodding uncertainly. "Well," Charlotte asked, "are you joining them?"

"Yeah, why not. Tim looks ok," she replied.

And Charlotte yelled down to give the answer. "She says she is. So she will see you then?"

Another slightly older man whispered in Peter's ear. But before he could ask, Charlotte yelled back, "he can forget it, I am already spoken for. Sarah is single though."

Sarah looked alarmed, but another young man stepped forward, and made his move.

"Then forgive me for asking, is there any way we can make this a six-date, Sarah?" he appealed, "because I think you look awesome. My name is Simon, by the way."

Sarah, was flattered by the complement, and impressed by his boldness. She wanted to say no, but perhaps due to the nerves, found herself saying, "yeah, looking forward to it."

There was a cheer from the boys below, and a few "get in there my sons," which the girls thought quite amusing.

Now, Sarah was already thinking, that the conversation was taking place rather too openly, for her liking, and was feeling embarrassed. She looked at their Captain for help, but Freida seemed to be amused by it. And so she just went along with it.

However, she was relieved when Freida interrupted this conversation with the boys, to focus on what was in hand.

"Time to get climbing again, this time to the very top. All the remaining floors," she said. "I will reset all buzzers to zero. Remember to follow the red lights. Denise you go first this time. Louise you go second, Sarah third, and Charlotte last."

They all looked at her. "Did she really expect them to climb eight more floors?" they thought.

"Well don't just sit there gawking, get climbing," said Freida. "To the next rest point, which is five levels up!"

And obediently, they started to climb. And the boys looked up, and checked out the girls from below. But this time, the girls were more focused on their task, to even notice. Although during the afternoon, all the girls, (except Freida;) got a shock, and fell off at least once on the way up to the top.

When that session was over the girls were exhausted.

"What have you got now Sarah?" asked Denise.

"Archery with Charlotte! What about you?"

Denise was looking at her tech tab with worry. "Sparring practice! With Captain Sophie-Smith."

"Ooh. Double Freida," joked Sarah mischievously.

"I know," said a worried Denise. "That last session was a killer."

"Well I have an advanced camouflage session,"

said Louise, whilst instinctively stroking her blond hair.

"Do you mean make up?" joked Sarah. And the group looked at her oddly. Clearly not understanding the joke.

"What I mean is... green make up, on green skin... To go into green woods, and green mist, under a twilight sun. Is it really necessary?"

"Yes" they all said in unison.

And Denise explained. "If they can't see you, they can't kill you. Camouflage has often been Celtishia's biggest strength against Egypt."

And Louise continued, "it is also about being able to spot people in camouflage. You know to get them before they can get you."

Sarah was taken aback, by their strange way of looking at things. And with that thought, Sarah and Charlotte went off to their class.

"I meant to ask? Is that how relationship things are done in this dimension?" Sarah asked Charlotte on route. Charlotte looked baffled by the question.

"I mean," said Sarah, "are people always so direct in approaching each other? And so loud?"

"Of course, why wouldn't we be? We only have so many years together if we don't pair off quickly. I want to love the person I marry, for at least seventy years. There is no time to wait around."

The dates went well.

"What's with the coins, you know, around the

edge of your head scarf?" Sarah asked Denise, who decided to dress traditionally.

"They represent wealth! We use them to highlight social status."

"Really, is that a lot?"

"Yes, in my case, each coin on my head, represents a thousand more. You can tell by the markings."

So Sarah studied them. But her eyes were drawn to one particular coin. It was placed in the middle of her scarf, and then she realized. "I have thirty like this one in a locker in Plymouth," she exclaimed. "But how is this possible?"

Charlotte looked stunned, and jealous. "I don't know, but they are extremely valuable. I wish I had thirty of them."

"Perhaps," interjected Denise, "they belonged to someone who crossed over secretly. You may even have some wealth in a bank here. I would look into it, if I was you."

Louise, then entered the room. She had just had a shower, and now her blonde hair was injected with some green highlights, and extensions, made from vines. She also looked stunning, although very different with a polished torc around her neck.

Sarah was to realize over the next few weeks, just how different relationships were. For one thing, there didn't seem to be much hanging about. If they liked each other, they just tended to pair off as a couple. However, there was no real casualness about it, as pairing seemed to be a lot more permanent. And Sarah learnt a lot from them, and was encouraged to rethink her own millennial view point.

Meanwhile her own relationship with Simon, started to flourish. And they would spend at least part of every evening together, after training.

Over the next few weeks, the group started to learn all combat scenarios. They even had simulations set up with other squads, and through virtual reality. During this time, their skills improved immensely, and they learned to work together as a team. Freida being constantly on top of their every mistake with advice.

At the end of the training, Sarah had become one with her gun and the bow. Instead of missing shots, she now made the target every time. Her instructor looked dead pleased that she had become so good.

She got to know her team well, and learned to accept their little quirks. For example, when it came to relationships, Charlotte remained a mystery. She habitually refused all advances by men. Whenever asked, she just kept saying that she was "already spoken for." Charlotte was less brazen, and more relaxed with the others. It seemed that she was enjoying the time with Denise. This had surprised the others at first, for they seemed polar opposites. However, they both remained focused for the most part on their training. Charlotte especially also had made some tremendous strides, especially in the use of her shield and weapon skills.

The biggest improvement in the training unit was experienced by Denise in her sparring, for Freida had taught her well. With new found confidence, and a desire to impress her mentor, she was now entering competitions in the base, and beating more experienced opponents. She had also gone from being initially hostile, to spending most of her spare time with Charlotte helping her with studying and rule learning.

Sarah was continuing to change colour. Her face and body had turned from a pink to a grey, and her face was now almost the same green as theirs. But this was just accepted by the group. This was especially true after, Doctor Martha Zing was officially enlisted to their squad, and joined the recruits for room sharing. She was apparently undertaking a refresher course on combat and field mission skills. But Sarah felt it was odd, that this one doctor whom she had met, had been assigned to their specific training unit. At first this caused concern in the base, until it was openly revealed she had been relocated under the orders of Boudicca, specifically due to her consultation with Sarah Salter. In private she told Sarah, that she felt it was best to be close to supervise the situation, in case of issues. This made sense to everyone, in the base.

For most of this time, the girls were kept very busy. The training was constant. But in the late evening, they normally managed to listen to the news with the other recruits. Mostly it focused on diplomatic discussions on the continent as Egypt tried to provoke the others into joining the war. In other sections, they would talk about the building up of troops following the appeal they made on Denise's show.

One day, towards the end of the training, the presenter announced that there was now a build-up of enemy ships just outside the Spanish Port of Cadiz. A spokesperson for the African Alliance, was boasting that "most of these had been assembled on the cheap, using wood for speed purposes, as their main purpose was to transport troops across the Channel, and would be making their way up to Brittany in the near future."

These were followed up by images of the Pharaoh announcing that after the diplomatic delays, their attack was imminent. "Celtishia," Pharaoh said, "can surrender now, or die."

This was met with a series of boos from the assembled troops, which had grown considerably in number since their appeal.

The feature however then continued with something everyone thought strange. It was a series of interviews with the locals. It was clear that they were not happy with Egypt's interference in their affairs.

"I have moored my boat here all my life, but now it is grounded to make way for this make shift fleet," said a fisherman. "What about my livelihood? I complain, but they just say that; 'Pharaoh doesn't care about little things like that, when there is a war on'."

"And what about the local export business," said another Spanish local. "Nothing can leave port at the moment, and the number of small channel craft just keeps growing. It is not like this is our conflict, so why are we losing out."

"Then there is the safety of our women," came another background voice. "We are seen as conquerors' spoils. Many have been attacked."

And then something inside Sarah suddenly clicked into place. "Oi Freida," she yelled out loud so everybody stopped listening and focused on her. Freida was sitting at the front, and looked around annoyed.

"How many more times, must I tell you?" She yelled in a rage. "That will be Captain Sophie-Smith to you..."

But Sarah interrupted her. "Ok, I apologize, Captain Sophie Smith. But did she just say 'Cadiz?'"

And everybody, including Freida, looked at her with interest. "Yes. They did say 'Cadiz'. Why?"

"And did they say, mostly wooden craft. Make shift boats. Made on the cheap? To cut costs?"

Freida stared hard at her, secretly hoping this

was the lightbulb moment they all hoped for. "Yes they did. What is it, Sarah?"

"Well, Captain Sophie-Smith," said Sarah, "there is something, we may need to discuss in private."

18. EMERGENCE

Much later that evening, after their final session of the day, Freida summoned Sarah to her office. Sarah went quickly in case she was in trouble.

"Well?" she asked. "What is the issue with Cadiz?"

Sarah stopped, and thought how best to answer the question, before she responded.

"Did you ever have a Francis Drake in this dimension?"

"Yes, a former Queen Elizabeth had him hanged for treason, and piracy. A well-known incident. What of it?"

"Oh?" She was taken aback by this information, but continued anyway. "Well in my dimension, he is viewed as an historical hero. Basically he led the English Fleet into battle against the Spanish, which was the larger navy. And he won."

"And this was at Cadiz, off Spain."

"Don't be daft, Cadiz was earlier." But as soon as she said this, Sarah realized that there was no way Freida could have known that. And it was that sort of comment that could damage their friendship.

"So what happened?" asked an exasperated Freida.

"Well, it was two years earlier. He mounted an attack on the Port of Cadiz, when the Spanish were stationed there in force. Virtually the whole navy was in port. The attack wiped out nearly all their navy. The Armada had to be rebuilt from scratch, virtually bankrupting the Spanish economy"

"And he defeated that navy too?"

"Yes."

"So," said Freida pulling herself forward to look Sarah straight in the eye, "tell me everything you remember, from the beginning. And let's start with Francis Drake."

The discussion that followed lasted about an hour, and Freida recorded everything on her Tech-Tab. Finally, Freida decided to report back immediately to Boudicca, regarding what they had just discussed. She asked Sarah to stay with her.

Freida dialed up Boudicca, using her Tech-Tab, and a link to her projector. The phone rang for a minute before The Queen answered. The technology linked and Boudicca was there in front of her on the giant screen.

"Hello Freida. I assume it must be important for you to ring me on a private line?" said Boudicca, noticing Freida and Sarah. "Oh, and hello Sarah, good to see you again."

"Hello your Majesty," said Sarah.

"I was getting worried, as I hadn't heard from you in a few days. Most unlike you Freida?"

"Sorry Bou, I have just been busy," continued Freida, "you know recruit training."

"I know. How is that going? I assume that Miss Charlotte is behaving herself?"

"Of course, but why do you give me the hard cases."

"They remind me of you, Freida! A right hard case in your time, if I recall."

"Fair enough. But she is talking about meeting up with someone called 'Leslie' after her training?"

"That was to be expected," Boudicca replied, indicating she was in full knowledge of whatever the situation was. Sarah was still in the dark. Although Freida had clearly hinted at something.

Boudicca continued with the informal questioning, "now, what about Miss La-Rooche? How is she getting on?"

"Very well, and exceeding expectations in everything. She is easily the most helpful of the team, and a very different person."

"Really?"

"Yes. She started as a right stuck up madam, but has changed and gained focus. She is in a steady relationship as well."

"Now that does surprise us."

"Us?" asked Sarah.

"Yes, us. Judah is here with me too," Boudicca pointed to off screen.

"That's good it will save us some time." Freida stopped before adding, "Hi Judah, by the way."

"Hello Freida and Sarah," replied the familiar voice from off screen. "Is everything ok there?"

"Yes especially considering what Sarah has just told me. It is probably best if I send the details over. I think we have an opportunity to turn the tables and start winning this war. I suspect this is the break we have been waiting for."

"And you are giving us a heads up?" asked Judah from off screen. Boudicca was looking curiously in that direction, like she was trying to read a note.

"Forward whatever you have, and I'll read it immediately. Judah and I, are both curious. We will call you back within the hour. Meanwhile both of you, any ideas, keep them coming. Bye for now."

"Bye Bou," said Freida taking the hint.

And with that Boudicca rang off. Her face was replaced with a message from the HUB, "Boudicca thanks you for your personal call."

Sarah looked at Freida, trying to guess what she was thinking.

"I hope she likes it," said Freida, "because I am recommending a precision attack on Cadiz, while their ships are there. This will stop the Egyptian movement North, allowing us to enter the continent, form alliances on the ground and prepare for battle. It is the best chance to gain a competitive advantage, at an early stage."

"We will know soon enough, I guess," said Freida trying to reassure her.

Freida looked resigned to the wait. "You may as well get back to your room. I suspect the unit will be waiting for your return there. Be careful what you say to them at this stage. I will come and get you if there is any news." And with that she hugged Sarah, for the first time since the advanced training began.

Back in the dorm, the other squad members were all wondering what was going on. They knew of course that Sarah was in discussion with Freida, and that neither had been seen for some time.

There was an excitement in the base. So much so that, even though it was a break from protocol, their partners, and members of other squads all kept coming into their room asking if they heard anything yet. The question that Sarah had asked had caused some discussion, and everybody was desperate to know more. But naturally the girls knew nothing, and were worried for their colleague.

When Sarah finally showed her face, there was chaos in the room, because so many people were there. Everybody wanted to ask their questions at once.

Charlotte, as the oldest of the women, however,

knew what to do.

"Right," she yelled. "I don't care who you are. If you ain't part of this squad. Get out!" She looked around again. Sarah's boyfriend Simon was looking hurt. "Simon of course, you can stay. But everybody else, out!"

And everybody in the room looked at her, except Sarah who just crashed into her hammock, and put a blanket over herself, as if trying to hide.

"You heard our colleague," yelled Denise. "Get out." And she turned around fiercely to her boyfriend. "And that includes you Peter! No exceptions, out all of you!" And with that she drove them all from the room.

When they had gone, Charlotte got Sarah a drink of water, and Denise got her some biscuits. Louise gave her another blanket.

Then Charlotte sat down next to Sarah, took her hand and said, "rest here now, and tell us only when you are ready."

"That might not be tonight, Charlotte," said an exhausted Sarah. "And, it will probably be Freida, I mean Captain Sophie-Smith, who fills you in, if it is needed."

"That's ok with us. Now get yourself some rest," said Simon as he took her hand and stayed beside her hammock.

And with that, Sarah closed her eyes and slept for about two hours. Simon and the girls kept watch on her from their hammocks. None of them saying anything out of worry about what could be going on.

She was woken by a stressed, but determined looking Freida' entering the room, and shaking her gently to wake her, without speaking to the others. Speaking quietly in Sarah's ear, Captain Sophie-Smith was heard to say, "I am glad you got some sleep. I have just heard back from Boudicca, and Judah. It was a multi-way call, and her godfather, Chief Airman Boaz, was also in on the conversation. This is serious, it is really happening."

The team was gathering around, in both interest, and alarm. So Freida grabbed the opportunity and announced, "the plan is a go, recruits. I have the instructions here in my hand." And with that she waved her Tech-Tab in the air for them all to see.

"They are also downloading personal detailed instructions to the Tech-Tabs, of all fully trained recruits in this section. Details should arrive within the hour." Freida paused for them to take this in, before continuing. "Get ready to ship out, we have a journey ahead of us, and an important mission."

"Do we get a briefing? You know, some more details in the meantime?" asked Denise, who looked far more serious than Sarah had ever seen her before.

"Yes," said Freida, "in my office in ten minutes.

Pack your bags, and meet me there. All of you."

"Can we call our loved ones? Let them know?" asked Charlotte, a little naively perhaps.

Freida gave her a look that could only be reserved for stupid questions, and replied, "not in the ten minutes, no. You must pack uniforms, spare knickers, and essentials only. No luxuries." There was a stunned silence from the recruits, as the order sank in. Then Freida elaborated about the phone calls, with sympathy in her voice.

"Look, tell you what. You can make a call from the transport craft, if you like. But right now, get packed, and be in my office in ten minutes, starting now."

"Yes Captain!" they all replied. Then as quickly and thoroughly as they could, they all packed what they needed, and set off for Freida's office.

The base was in turmoil, as instructions to meet in the main 'Assembly Room," were coming through on Tec-Tabs. Sarah and the squad however, headed to Freida's office in the opposite direction. As they passed the others, they were getting funny looks from everyone, but when asked could shed no more information, because they didn't know what was happening either.

When they arrived at Freida's office, her door was open. Out of courtesy, they started to wait outside, but soon heard her yell, "in here now, close the door, and take a seat."

The girls sat down, while Martha closed the

door.

"Well done for being so prompt," Freida began. "And well done for getting through your training early. I have just signed you all off as successful."

The girls looked stunned at this; as they thought they had another week to go, and a few assessments. But before they could raise this, Freida continued speaking, "So here's the plan," Freida continued. And everybody leant forward in interest, while a map of Europe lit up the giant screen on her wall. A big red arrow on the screen pointed at Cadiz, in Spain."

"Why there?" asked Louise.

Charlotte responded with irritation. "Because that is where their fleet is, of course," as if to say "you are a complete idiot." However, before things could escalate, Sarah motioned for them to stop bickering and listen to Freida at this point. And with that Freida continued her briefing.

"Basically it is very simple," she said pointing at the board. "We attack Cadiz, and destroy as many ships as we can, with explosives. They won't be expecting us, so we have the advantage of surprise."

The unit all nodded that they had understood, so Freida continued. "First we fly to a cliff top and land. Next we mount a coordinated attack via land and sea, utilizing stealth technology. Basically we come up through the sea weeds, while they sleep and party nearby. Its festival time in Spain, you see? Then we get out as quickly as possible, without upsetting the locals. Sounds easy right?"

"How many troops are involved in this," asked Denise.

"All two hundred of our company," Freida responded. "And our first stop is back to the main Devonport Base, where we will rendezvous with them. Assistant Captain Jones will hand back his temporary command of the company. And you will all get new uniforms, weapons and combat-armour. And by the way, your "unit of five" is about to join another unit that is missing a few people"

And with this she turned to Charlotte, and said, "you can call your friend then, if you wish, using my personal phone."

"Thank you," said Charlotte sounding relieved.

Then Freida turned back to the rest of the unit, and said, "I regret that we will all be spending the night at my parent's sub-holding, with no last night boozing. We need to be up early next day."

"But why?," asked Louise.

"It is Boudicca's orders I'm afraid," she said. "Apparently. she suspected that this group, (including myself,) would get into trouble. Something about going out on the lash just before our mission. She wants a top performance tomorrow."

Everybody knew that Boudicca was right about this, of course. But it was also obvious that the majority of the unit was disappointed. Furthermore, Louise and Charlotte came from Devonport, and know all the best pubs. Together they had been planning "a unit night" out, before being shipped away.

Sarah realized that Freida would also go wild in this situation. She clearly needed to let her hair down, and would probably join the girls, and lead them astray, if it got quiet.

So the ban on going out was viewed as great news to Sarah. But in order to not offend the rest of them, she made out, that it was because she did not recognize the Devonport of the Twilight Dimension. It just wasn't "the Plymouth, she knew in England, with its "Union Street,' and "Mutley Plain" areas." In fact, she preferred the idea of just spending time with them and Adah, and getting some last minute advice.

The girls did not buy into this, and planned to drink 'a few beers' at the sub holding instead.

The journey to Devonport was to take about three minutes onboard another flying saucer. This one, however, was much larger than the previous one, and painted in green, and blue colours. It had four levels, and port hole windows, and it was the most impressive air craft that Sarah had ever seen. Freida could tell that she was impressed.

"It is the property of the special forces, and can transport our whole company," Freida informed them. "It is a top secret craft and unknown to Egyptian intelligence. It will take us to Spain, to arrive within a twenty-four hour period. It has advanced stealth systems and should remain undetected in the air. It is also armed to fight of enemy craft. We call it 'The Dragon,' because it can swallow a lot of people!"

They entered the Dragon, into a central room, that served food, and had a series of pool tables. Once onboard, Sarah observed that it had a series of eighteen compartments, on three floors arranged in a circular pattern, like on a protractor. Each room was accessed via its own door from the central room.

Freida pushed a button to the side of one of the doors, and it slid open. They went inside, and discovered that it had ten hammocks for sleeping in, and shower facilities. When the door shut, it doubled up as a screen for virtual reality projectors. The unit felt at home.

"You may not enter the three doors with the large red circles, especially the central one," Freida warned them. "That room is the cockpit of the craft, and the other two doors are the crew apartments. They like their privacy."

The unit nodded to indicate that they understood, and agreed.

"You will also find a scanner in each shower room," Freida informed them. "You know the score. Take of your clothes, and stand in one. This will determine you get the right size clothing on arrival at the base. And just like before, nobody will see your details. When you are finished you get your shower."

"Are the other showers available to use or do we have to wait in line?" asked Denise. "You know seeing that most of the other rooms will be empty? Until Devonport."

"Use whatever shower you like, but remember to do the scan, I want you all ready to change into your uniform on arrival."

"Yes Captain," they chorused.

"Ah that reminds me," said Freida. "There is something I need to do. Please stand to attention."

And they did, enabling Freida to continue.

"I am in charge of the company of two hundred troops, as you know. But we need one person to lead this unit". And with that, she put a hand in one of her pockets, and drew out a pin badge. "This badge is for Denise," orders from Boudicca, for being the best in training. "It comes with the rank of Sargeant." And she pinned it to Denise's lapel, and everybody clapped, knowing it to be a good choice. "Be proud, you started slow, but have grown in character, and skill. And you have won your colleagues' respect, and mine."

"Well done, Sargeant Denise La-Rooche," Freida congratulated her, with a supportive hug. "I am so proud of what you have become, and will allow our friend here to guide you." And she looked at Sarah, "but you must obey Sargeant

La-Rooche, and let her protect you in the field. Contribute your wisdom and support to her as you do to me."

And she turned to the team, "now go shower, and familiarize yourselves with the plans." I have to talk to the crew of the Dragon. We need to make sure it is battle ready, as it has been released early, and remains untested."

19. AN ENEMY RETURNS

T he arrival at the base was a simple routine affair, as the flying saucer touched down quietly and without incident. Within ten minutes, the unit had all showered, changed into new uniforms, and were ready for whatever came next.

The unit left the craft via some stairs that descended from the Central Room. They then walked out onto the grass in front of the base, to be ushered into the main building.

The hangar building was a giant metal dome with glass portholes. It was the size of a soccer stadium. A sign over the main door said, "The Devonport Regiment, Home of the Loyal." However, the word 'Loyal' had been graffitied out and replaced by the words, 'nut jobs.'

"And to think, they haven't even met us yet," joked Charlotte.

The inside of the building was laid out into three sections. The largest section took up half the building, and consisted of offices and indoor facilities, like gyms. They were spread out over three levels, which were unusually above ground. The all-girl unit was led into one of these offices, by Freida, who clearly knew where she was going. As she passed, ordinary soldiers saluted her, and greeted her as "Captain."

They soon reached their destination, which was a room on the second floor, entitled "Supplies." The unit entered as one, and were greeted to a view of the other sectors of the hangar. Sarah's first thought was that they were very different, and provided the feeling of being outdoors, despite being under a dome.

The first area was a grass area for sports. It included a hockey pitch, and a running track. The final area was a leisure facility, made from a mixture of wooden floor tiles with trees at various spots for aesthetic reasons.

Five more soldiers entered the room, looking a little lost.

"Oh good, you're here," Freida said to them, as if to put them at ease. Most of the unit looked surprised by their arrival, except Charlotte, who seemed suddenly pleased by something.

"Well gather round all of you," she said to them all. "For those who don't know, my name is Captain Freida Sophie-Smith. You will address me by my title 'Captain,' unless I give you specific permission to do otherwise."

"Yes Captain," they all replied.

Welcome to our newest recruits. I hope you will enjoy being part of this unit. For reference to the others, they are called Nigella, Amber, Donna, Leslie, and Morwenna.

There were a few murmurs of "welcome," towards the new arrivals. Then Freida continued, "For the benefit of the newcomers, you will be aware that two of the team are very well known," and she pointed out Denise and Sarah. "The team are all recent recruits like yourselves, and you may use first name terms with them." And the newcomers murmured consent to this.

Freida now drew Nigella out of the newcomers, and directly addressed Denise. "Denise this is your second, of course, is Sarah."

"Finally, Freida continued, "I hope that you will all have the chance to get to know each other better, after you receive your kit. Although I am also aware that, Leslie you asked to be stationed to this unit, because of an unofficial coupling with Charlotte, is that correct?"

"Yes," replied one of the younger recruits, who had approached and was hugging Charlotte very close.

"And would you like to explain for the benefit of the group, the exact nature of this unofficial coupling? To save any misunderstandings down the line."

"Of course Captain." And Leslie addressed everybody else whilst holding Charlottes hand. "Basically, we are a couple. Prison married."

"Prison married?" asked Louise, who was not always the quickest on the uptake.

"Yes," said Leslie in a slightly irritated voice, "Prison married. Not officially recognized, but real to us."

Charlotte put her arm around Leslie, and elaborated further. "We shared a cell together, and became close to each other whilst in correction. We accepted our punishments by society for medium grade crimes, and found we could be honest with each other. We then accepted temporary separation to enlist, and ensure the option of early release, and a second chance. We share everything, including the same hammock."

"I hope this is ok with everyone?" asked Leslie, "you know us being together in the same team? It could cause issues."

And Sarah was the first to reply, "if its ok with you, then its okay with us", and everybody kind of agreed.

"Good," said Freida at last, "and we are all glad to see you together again. And you will both be granted a fair second chance. You have my support if you need it."

And with that Freida, turned and rang a bell on the wall. There was a small chime, and within seconds a hatch had opened in the wall, and an officer appeared with a clip board. He acknowledged Freida, and started to address the unit directly.

"Good Morning all. My name is Officer Davide, and it is my role to issue you all your kit."

He looked at them slowly, and deliberately, as if making some sort of point. "Now when I call your name, you step forward and I will give you what you are to receive. Any questions?"

But before they could answer, he said "No! Good!"

He looked at his clip board again, and called out the first name, "Nigella."

Nigella, stepped forward and collected all her gear, which was put in a large rucksack which was also supplied. In front of the team, she was made to sign for her kit, and then pointed towards another door to change.

"Louise next," yelled Officer Davide. And Louise also stepped forward to receive her kit, sign and change. The process lasted about half one hour.

Sarah was the second to last to receive her kit, after Denise. But she changed quickly, and joined the rest of the unit. But by this time, the rest of the unit was messing about with their uniforms, and exploring how to use the gadgets. Freida was joining in the fun, and helping them figure things out.

The key change in the kit was that the base suit, which was a mixture of camouflaged green and blue.

"To help you stay hidden underwater," Freida explained. In addition, the had a seam, that glowed fluorescent green on voice request. There were the usual knives to attach onto her left thigh, and left ankle.

"Go easy on the batteries though," advised Freida, referring to the glowing seam. "You will need to use these in the field."

Sarah, however, was more concerned with the body armour, and was trying to work out how to put it on. Whilst made of a light plastic like material she didn't recognize, it was bulky and awkward. There was a belt attached that was made of blue leather, but went diagonally from left shoulder to right thigh, where it attached and fastened the armour in place. The whole contraption confused Sarah, who was looking at it blankly.

"Try putting it over your head, and slide into it like a dress," advised Leslie, who was wearing one. Sarah looked around and took a small moment to study Leslie. Leslie looked athletic, and had long and braided hair, with green cords.

"Thanks," Sarah replied. "Is it bulletproof?"

"It deflects most things, but you are suntil at risk if you are hit. Best to keep your head down anyway," Leslie replied, "and don't forget to secure the belt at your thigh," as Charlotte started to assist Leslie with the same thing.

In the holster was a gun, made of some very light plastic. It was strong in structure, and virtually weightless. Sarah was convinced that it had been weighted to her hand, courtesy of the scanning process. It had sights for targeting, and fired lasers up to fifty times before reloading. She was glad they did not exist in her dimension.

The helmets issued to the unit were all blue and green. They were clearly designed for movement in the water, as well as deflecting bullets. They came with a visor, and Sarah's helmet fitted her head perfectly.

Sarah was delighted with her new compound bow, made to assist in drawing her arrows fast and with deadly accuracy. The weighting was perfect, and it was a cool balance of pink and green. It came with ready to use arrows, that were ideally suited for the journey underwater, and made from some kind of metal alloy.

The team was bonding well, as they discussed differences in their kit. And it was clear to all that they had been selected to perform as a group, using a variety of skills to complement each other. For example, not all the team, including Sarah, had been issued shields as they had different fighting styles. However, the bonding session was to be cut short, and the enjoyment short lived, for without warning, a news update was suddenly projected onto the wall.

"Good Evening," said the presenter, "and welcome to 'News As It Happens.' On this show, we show the news as key moments occur, and discuss them with our guests. Tonight we have a live interview with the Pharaoh of Egypt, to present an alternative viewpoint. But first an update."

Sarah looked at Denise, wondering how she would feel about a new presenter on her old show. To her surprise, Denise didn't look bothered at all. In fact, she had cringed at the words "alternative viewpoint," as if disgusted with herself, for what she may have said just three months ago.

The update continued.

"Just in. and breaking News. In his capacity as Regional President, The Pharaoh has promoted Princess Phillipa of Lebanon, to ruler of Palestine. Our correspondent, 'John,' is on the scene."

And the screen, switched to another person, with the palace in Palestine behind her.

"Yes, thank you, Juniper. As you can see, I am speaking live from Palestine, and the palace, which as off two am this morning, has become once more the official home of Princess Phillipa. However, she is not here today to celebrate as you would expect."

"Palace sources here, say that Egypt has decided to allow her coronation in the near future, so that she becomes the Chief Princess of Palestine. They say that the delays have gone on long enough, and as there are no alternative heirs, she should be made Chief Princess, as soon as the upcoming war is over."

"Palace Sources here also confirm that the Palestinian State is satisfied that Princess Phillipa has no involvement in the death of her father in law, ten years ago. They believe his death was caused by overexertion."

Sarah chuckled to herself, thinking "that's one way of putting it."

"Palace Sources also say that Princess Phillipa is desperate for things to progress. And it is to this end, that she has opted to go to Cadiz, to fight alongside the Egyptian forces in Spain, and assist in the attack of Celtishia."

"Of course, at the moment we are waiting for confirmation from Cairo, that this is the case. But we can confirm that there has been an application submitted for her to regain her status with the league of nations, and to claim the throne with international support."

"Ok, John, but why now? A good ten years have passed? And the country has been under a supervision order?"

"Well, it would appear that many officials have been campaigning for her promotion saying she is the logical heir. We can also confirm that Lebanon has pledged a lot of money to the Egyptian campaign in recent days, although this is co-incidental."

The reporter John continued his narration. "Most concerning however, is the fact that Princess Phillipa's brother is now ill, with food poisoning, gained while visiting this palace, just last week. She is next in line to the throne of

Lebanon as well. Naturally, our prayers go out to him, and wish him a quick recovery."

"Turn that off, now!" yelled Freida as she left the room in a rage.

"What's up with her?" asked Denise, as she switched the channel off.

Sarah walked over to Denise, and whispered in her ear, "I think we should just give her some space to calm down. That message would be quite a shock for her. She grew up in the area, you see. And there are things you would not know."

"She needs space to calm down," repeated Sarah to Denise. And Denise knew from her time in the media, that something was up.

"Right then," yelled Denise, "Get yourselves ready, we will be leaving for the home of the So-phie-Smiths very soon."

"I'll go and quickly speak to her," whispered Sarah, when everybody started to move, and she popped off to find her friend. Sarah eventually found Freida sitting alone on a bench, cussing loudly to herself.

"Is it okay to join you?"

"Yes, of course. I was just angry you know."

"Not surprising. Your worst enemy prospers, and still evades justice. And who knows what the im-plications are. Looked political though."

"And she will be in Spain," said Freida, now start-ing to brighten up, as if realizing another oppor-tunity. "She will be in the same city, at the same time as us."

Sarah was concerned about this, as she realized that it could be a distraction to the mission. "Yes, she will be, and we should call Boudicca and tell her."

And as they said this, their Tech-Tabs started to ring. Boudicca was calling them.

Freida answered, and Sarah connected into the call.

Boudicca's voice could be heard clearly as if she was speaking from the next room. "I take it you both heard the news tonight?" It was one of those funny questions that people ask, when they already know the answer.

"We heard all right," said Sarah, "we didn't have much choice."

"How are you Freida? How do you feel about the coronation of Princess Phillipa?"

She abruptly replied, with just one word which summed up totally how she felt. "Angry."

"I figured you would be," Boudicca responded, with some sympathy. "But now is not the time for revenge? In fact, there may never be the time to go after her. It is important that you remain professional, and do what needs to be done."

"But, that woman? You know what she did?"

"I do know what she did to you, Freida. And I know the effect it has had on you. And I know you are more than the person you were then. This is testing, I admit, but vengeance is not yours to take," Boudicca reminded her, in a way that suggested, she had never been more serious.

"Going after her will put everybody in danger. I need your reassurance that you are focused on the mission only?"

"Yes, of course. I promise to focus on destroying the ships and port." She paused before saying the next bit down into Tech-Tab. "And nothing else. The bitch can wait, besides if this is her first time in charge, success would put her in good stead with Pharaoh. If she messes up, then the effects for her will be monumental."

"That's the spirit," and Boudicca turned her attention towards Sarah. "Now Sarah, make sure you keep an eye on her."

"Yes, your majesty, I have it on my radar, so to speak." But as she said this, she realized that trying to stop Freida doing something daft would take some doing. Yet as a friend, maybe she was the only one who could?

"Ok, then I will ring off, but remember, I am trusting you both."

"Bye then, speak to you soon," said Freida, as Boudicca rang off.

20.
REFLECTIONS

N ow alone with Sarah, Freida turned to her and said, "I guess, it is a good job, that we are staying with my parents tonight."

Sarah could not agree more, for they were the people that Boudicca had subtly called when she last went down-hill. Their presence as parents was able to calm her, and help her refocus. Sarah understood, that they clearly knew Freida better than she did, and understood what motivated. In these circumstances, Sarah knew that it wasn't just Freida, who would need their advice. But then it occurred to her. Was Boudicca, somehow, aware that this was coming? And was she previously already aware that Phillipa would be released? And if so, perhaps the real reason the night out was banned, was that she wanted Freida at home with her parents tonight being comforted.

"Yes, they will be helpful at a time like this," Sarah replied.

"You mean the attack? I assume?" Freida didn't

look too pleased with Sarah over the vague response.

"Of course, what else? Your parents know what it is like to be behind enemy lines."

"True, perhaps they will have some advice for us?"

"That would be good, for all of us."

They arrived at the farm, within the hour. The unit was still upset at being denied a night on the town, but were resigned to the idea of getting ready for the morning. Besides they had all enjoyed the journey on the Military PTMs, as it gave them the chance to get used to using them as a team. It even enabled them to practice some battle formations on the way there.

Adah and Benjamin had clearly been expecting the unit, and were waiting at the door when they arrived.

The excitement of seeing them both had overwhelmed her, and Adah called out. "Freida! Sarah!" And Adah came running, and tried to hug them both, only Freida was unusually withdrawn towards her adopted mother, and just put out her hand to shake. Sarah hugged her anyway. "I am glad to see you both," Adah said, and looking at Freida said, "so this must be the latest unit of yours. I am glad to meet you all." The unit murmured back that they were glad to meet her as well, and Adah made a point of speaking to everyone in the unit. When she had finished meeting everyone, she announced "supper will be in ten minutes, and help yourself to the beers from the fridge."

The group sat around a very large table for the supper. Adah, Benjamin and the twins Ruth and Enoch, joined them at the table. But for some funny reason, the tenseness between the mother and Freida continued. Even during the meal whilst everyone continued to talk. They were all very relaxed, and drinking their beer, and yet there was a tension in the air. Although everybody was ignoring it, they all felt it.

Eventually, Adah got up to organize the dessert.

"Freida can you help me please?" she asked.

"One of the squaddies will," she replied, trying to pass the buck.

"No," said Adah as she left the room, "you will, and you will do so now! We need to talk."

And to everybody's surprise, Freida quietly rose from the table, and did as she was told.

"Busted" said Enoch and Ruth, towards Freida. Sarah had often noticed that The two young twins would often talk simultaneously, which she found quite amusing. Ignoring them, however, Freida walked past and didn't say a word.

"She is definitely in trouble," said Ruth, to her brother Enoch, but loud enough for everyone to hear.

Freida and Adah had both left the room, and Adah had shut the door, when the yelling could be heard coming from the room.

"Freida Sophie-Smith? Are you taking the mick or something?"

"Don't be ridiculous," Freida was trying to protest. But Adah it seemed, was just warming up.

"They might be your unit, but this is my house! They are here as guests, not servants, and you of all people should know the difference. And you can stop with that look."

"But you don't understand what has.."

"Don't I?" yelled Adah interrupting her. "I know about the release of Princess Phillipa, and I am as annoyed as you are. I saw what she did to you, and have been trying to put it right ever since!"

"I know it is tough, but you are a Sophie-Smith now. We adopted you, and that means you are expected to be social at all times. Now get out there, and be polite as you should be. And remember lead by example, not by criticism."

"Yes mum. I'm sorry mum," they heard her reply from the other room. They could tell that she was remorseful.

"Now come here and give me that hug," Adah could be heard to say.

Then there was an awkward silence. It was broken eventually by Benjamin asking Denise the question, "so my dear, do you prefer the media or the armed forces?"

"Funny enough the armed forces," Denise replied, "because I feel I belong, and enjoy the companionship."

It was obvious from her tone, that she had

not expected to feel like this. And everybody was wondering what could have changed in her. However, nobody got to find that out, because Freida entered the room with a crate of small beer bottles, and a bottle opener. They were placed on the table, and one by one, Freida opened them and handed them out to each unit member in person.

"Thanks" said Sarah, as she received hers, "and cheers everybody."

"Cheers," they replied, holding up their bottles.

The rest of the evening was much nicer, and coupled with the beer Adah supplied, they enjoyed a lot of conversation, until they all went to bed. Although of course, Leslie and Charlotte had actually sneaked off to their room earlier, when nobody was looking.

Sarah and Freida were still sitting up later with Adah, drinking another beer, after nearly everyone had gone to bed.

"Are you two ok?" Adah asked.

"Yeah, just nervous."

"That is not what I asked. I know you are nervous, who wouldn't be. It is the day before a deployment," Adah politely corrected her daughter. "I am asking, if you two are ok, as friends?"

"I hope so," said Freida, looking at Sarah for an answer. "I drove her hard at the training base, these last few months?"

"Yeah, we are cool."

"Good. I am glad you both have that settled." And Adah took another sip from her beer bottle. "I will be worried for both of you tomorrow."

"You needn't," Freida said.

"Of yeah, I must. You are my daughter, and things do not always go according to plan with you." Adah now took hold of Freida's arm, as only a worried mother could. "Now promise me you will do everything you can to come back safe. Keep your head down, and don't let your emotions cloud your judgement."

"I promise," said Freida, as she gave her a hug.

"Then I am off to bed," said Adah. And she turned and left the room, leaving Freida and Sarah alone.

"I am going to bed too," said Freida five minutes later, "before this beer goes down the wrong way."

"Ok, I'll just stay here with my thoughts."

"Good night then, Sarah."

"Good night, Freida. Sleep well."

When Freida had gone to bed, Sarah was, at last, left all alone, with her thoughts. And she wasn't sure that she liked them much.

Sitting on a sofa, she was worried about the possibility of deadly violence, and maybe seeing someone she knew killed. She worried that she might have to kill somebody herself. She was also worried about the possibility of being captured, tortured or worse.

Now on her own, Sarah stared up at the night sky, with its continuous twilight. The forest was the same as she remembered it the first time she had arrived. Only it was quieter, and the green mist looked very eerie, like this was the lull before the storm.

The trees were motionless, and glowed in the light, and the mist seemed to reach higher than usual. She saw this as some kind of sign. Looking down from the tree house, and into that same green mist; she could see that most of the compartments had their lights out. Most had clearly settled down to sleep. Even the compartment with Charlotte and Leslie was quiet, suggesting that all was well there.

Looking left, Sarah noticed that there were some fire-flies nearby. Sarah sat quietly and watched them for a while, as they hovered and moved in and out of the mist. They were glowing a fluorescent orange, and stood as little moving lights. They looked amazing, and provided a soothing presence to her.

It was then that Sarah thought she heard a voice address her. It was clear and seemed to come from behind her. "Stop worrying Sarah, the mission will succeed. Your worries will mostly not happen, and I am with you."

"Who said that?" she asked, and turned around, only to find out that nobody was there. And she asked herself, if she was imagining it? But then like before she heard the same clear voice, speak directly to her, and it penetrated her very being leaving her feeling both warm and alive.

"I spoke," replied the voice. And again nobody could be seen. "And you know who I am, am I right?"

"The Whisper?" Sarah had returned the question very quietly, and now awaited another reply with bated breath.

"Yes, and I will be with you in Spain, as I have been in Celtishia, since you arrived. Even though at times you had no idea that I was there."

"Good, because I am scared... of everything that will come."

"That is natural. There is much that can go wrong, yet won't."

"So how can I get rid of these fears?"

"You can't, because you are meant to have them. Fears are designed to keep you safe. However, sleep is often the best way of reducing them. You will feel better in the morning."

And with that, she felt overwhelmed in drowsiness.

Whether it caused by the mist? Or by the effect of the alcohol? Sarah couldn't tell. But soon fell asleep where she was, right there on the sofa, despite being fully clothed. And she slept soundly.

"Wake up, sleepy head," came a voice, "we are being shipped out soon." It was Freida, with a cup of hot chocolate. "Now get this inside you, as you must be cold."

Sarah realized that the rest of the team was there and looking at her, partly out of concern and partly with amusement. The clock said ten am.

"Too much beer eh," said Charlotte, now gently mocking her. "You total lightweight you!"

Sarah rolled over where she was and fell off the sofa. The girls' laughed and cheered, and this embarrassed her. But to make matters worse, it was now that she discovered that somebody had placed a blanket over her, and the fall had caused it to wrap itself around her.

Denise came over to help. "That beer was strong," she said with sympathy, "but it was what we all needed. I hope you haven't got a hangover?"

"No I will be fine," said Sarah, still trying to wake up. "I'll get dressed shall I?"

"That would be good! And get yourself a shower," Denise added. "You stink of sweat."

Sarah didn't feel it was a helpful comment. "Thanks," she said, before smelling herself and realizing that Denise was right. But what was odd to her was that she rarely sweated at night, and yet the time she heard The Whisper and fell asleep, she woke up covered.

"And by the way, your bag is on the truck already," Denise continued, and then reflected. "I took the liberty of removing a fresh uniform for you to change into. I hope that is ok?"

"Yes. That's great. Thanks again."

"You're welcome. We are part of the same team aren't we. And this time is hard for all of us. It must be very hard for you?"

"Yes. But I believe, it is all going to be ok," said Sarah confidently.

"Good to know," said Denise.

Sarah recalled the previous conversation in the room, the night they arrived for training. And she realized just how much Denise had developed, and how different she was to the naïve girl she knew then.

And with that thought Sarah quickly got showered and put a clean uniform on. Then, they headed out to catch the transport to the base. She was glad to see that there were PTMs present, as it gave her the chance to gain some much needed fresh air whilst she rode.

From the moment they arrived at the base, it was clear that they were not alone, as there were about twenty other units present. All dressed in uniform, fully helmeted, and ready for action.

Their unit stood out as being the predominantly girl unit, as most were mixed sexes. However, they were clearly war ready, for they carried shields, and a variety of guns. Some of the units were also on Military PTMs, but most were on foot. Their officers were loudly giving final advice and instructions.

They pulled up in their Military PTMs, and stopped, as one. They were behind Freida in front of the waiting units, who were positioned in formation, and standing to attention.

"Captain present," shouted one of the officers. This officer then marched over to Freida, and presented her with a large shining sword, using both his hands. "Welcome back, Captain Sophie Smith," he said loudly for everybody to hear. "May I present the sword of the company, which you entrusted to me whilst you went on assignment. I have kept the standards of the company high, and return the command of the company back to you in top condition."

"Thank you, John. I have read your full report, and am glad to be back in command," said Freida, who took the sword from him, and placed it diagonally on her back, before addressing her company. "As you are all aware, my name is Captain Freida Sophie-Smith, your commanding officer. And I have been on assignments, for the last four months. I return today with an extra newly and specially trained unit, led by Sargent Denise La-Rooche."

She paused and laughed. "Yes I did say Denise La-Rooche, the same girl you all know from the television." And she paused. "I did not think she would make that grade either, but despite my initial reservations, she proved by far the best recruit I have seen in ages, with additional useful media skills." And she looked in Denise's direction. "So she will now lead Unit Twenty-One. And I trust she will have your support?"

There was a loud "Yes Captain" from the company.

"I will not introduce all the new team to you, but would also like to point out Miss Sarah Salter, whom you have also seen on television. She will be going with all of you into the front line. I trust you will keep her safe and assist her whenever it is needed?"

And there was another loud "Yes Captain" from the company.

"Good," said Freida, "Now I am very pleased that all is well, and look forward to catching up with everybody in transit."

The troops looked amused at this., and Freida gave a final command. "Right now it is time to get your kit and get into action, because our time of fun and training is over. The mission is a Go," and she pointed at the flying saucer. "Please enter the Dragon, and get ready for action in the field."

"Our mission will take us to a major strategic location. It is dangerous, but vital to the over-all scheme of things. If successful, we will gain a major military advantage in the longer campaign.

What is more, as we perform this attack, most of our other troops will cross the Channel. In doing so, our country will begin the offensive in France. So troops, follow me, and let's get this done."

And with that last command, Freida rode her military PTM up the ramp on the saucer, and the unit followed. They in turn, were followed by other units, each looking a little worried, yet determined to go ahead.

Once inside "The Dragon", each unit went to their assigned rooms where Freida ordered them to get as much rest as possible. Unit twenty-one's room was on the upper floor, and reaching it via the rigging was a most unusual touch. It took them only five minutes to climb.

Sarah noticed that there were only nine beds in this room, and yet their squad consisted of ten. Denise was obviously ahead on this, and pointed to the top bunk.

"Charlotte and Leslie, would you like to share that bunk there? There is an extra big locker there for you both"

"Thanks Sargeant," they replied, and climbed to the top bunk.

"Everybody else, put your kit in the lockers. And try and rest! Take off time is in ten minutes. I am informed the Dragon will go straight up towards the edge of space, where it will hover for many hours avoiding radar, until the right moment to enter Spanish air space. At that point, things will happen very quickly."

"I should probably mention we are working as one part of a three-unit team, led overall by Adah, who is ex-special forces, and trusted by Freida as her mother."

This was a shock to the unit, as Adah had made

a point of waving them good bye and wishing them "good luck." It was Charlotte who started to voice their feelings, although she only got as far as the word "but?"

"I know what you are all thinking," said Denise, cutting her short, "but it was essential it looked like this is just a minor raid. Spies are everywhere, watching us constantly. And the presence of Special Forces, will alert opposing forces, and motivate their defenses."

"To this end, Captain Sophie-Smith has played down the importance of what is going to happen, and fed some false information. We are hoping that they think that Adah has retired, and has no intention of being involved anymore. This is not the case. She can't wait to get back into action."

"She is mission experienced, and good at thinking on her feet. Her battle experience means that Adah is the right person to lead the three most essential units, and that is why she bought us beer. Basically, she was bonding with us, getting us to relax, and also to see how prepared we were."

Things started to fall into place for Sarah. Like why she had been so keen to tell Freida off, and it wasn't just for being rude, but for accidently making her look weak in front of the unit. Clearly the rest of the team had similar thoughts. But Denise used the opportunity to ground them back in reality.

"Now! As well as resting, take the chance to familiarize yourselves with your tasks that are downloaded to your Tech-Tabs." Then Sargeant La-Rooche stopped talking, and after a moment of quiet transparency addressed the unit again. "And from now on, I would like you all to start calling me Denise again. When we are in action, it will be easier to distinguish mine from other officers' orders."

"Yes Denise," came the reply.

"Thank you," she said relieved. "Now if you need me, I will be in the third bunk on the left."

Sarah spent the next hour looking over the plans for the attack. It was clear to her that the strategists had been very busy with this one. They had called it "Operation Firework."

The plans were simply laid out, telling her exactly what needed to be done by herself, and how to know when to do it. It also included details of what the other units were going to be doing. Adah would be leading her unit and three others in the assault via the seaweed. Their objective was to open the gate, and place explosives, before activating the other units.

Other troops were looking at their Tech-Tabs, and familiarizing themselves with the details. Some were even discussing them. Of course, most of the locational details were obscured and deleted, but Sarah knew they were talking about Cadiz, in Spain. However, this was brought to an end by an announcement, that came over a live stream into every room.

"Good Morning everyone, this is your Flight-Captain speaking. My name is Flight Captain Abraham Beer, 8th rank. I am the officer in charge of the Dragon for the duration of the mission. It is ten am in the morning, and the weather outside is misty and pleasant. The signs for a smooth flight are good. Please buckle up the seat belts, in your hammocks. And don't forget to keep your helmets on. Their headphones will help with the rise in cabin pressure."

Sarah had of course never heard of hammocks with seat belts before. But here they were, attached to the hammocks, and providing an excellent safety feature. Sarah fastened herself in, and put her helmet back on, when the Flight Captain spoke again,

"We will be taking off for the outskirts of the biosphere. There we will hover until it is time to move to our destination. Make yourselves comfortable, and try and relax. Captain Sophie Smith wishes to remind you that you will need your energy later."

Sarah looked at the man on the screen, he was wearing a blue uniform, not unlike most pilots she knew, and gave the impression of a conservative style of man.

"Cute isn't he," whispered Louise from the opposite bunk.

"In the mean-time," Flight Captain Beer continued, "the communications network is restricted to this ship only, and you will have no more contact with outside until we return."

"You will need to take one of these, when we take off," said Denise offering Sarah a sweat from a packet. "They help with the pressure."

"No thanks," said Sarah politely, "I am not a fan of spearmint flavour."

The craft took off from the ground within half an hour, rising vertically upwards at quite a rate. Initially it reminded Sarah of riding in a very tall lift, and her ears started to hurt as she rose. Denise offered her some sweets again to help with the rise in pressure, and this time Sarah took one, saying a "thank you" under her breath.

The sweet was round in shape, but it came in a paper wrapper. In every other respect however, it resembled the boiled sweets she was used to back home. However, once it was in her mouth, and being sucked, the effect was almost instant, as the pressure building in her ears started to reduce and her ears popped.

The first thing left behind was the green mist that rose to a kilometre above the surface. After this they were soon among some green clouds, and looking down. The rising continued for another five minutes.

Looking out of the porthole windows, they could make out some features, like islands, and were starting to see the Earth as a round green planet. In excitement they pointed things out to each other, but Sarah was left with a sense of smallness. For the first time since she crossed over, she realized her basic insignificance in the great scheme of things, and it was the guidance of the Whisper that was making the difference.

At last, they reached 'The Karman Line' of the atmosphere. The screens indicated that they were now located 80.2 kilometres above the earth's surface.

"Hello again," came the Captain. "We are now on the edge of space. In days gone by, rich tourists paid a fortune to see what you are now seeing. Most people still never will. This prototype ship is the first giant military ship to reach this altitude, and we hope that you enjoy the view, while up here."

Sarah looked out off one of the crafts portholes, and did just that.

"Now feel free to take of your seat belts, and move about if you wish. And by the way, expect zero gravity and weightlessness here. So happy flights everyone."

There was a cheer of excitement from the whole unit, and others around them.

"Your oxygen level is fine of course. Just be ready to get back into your hammocks when asked."

And everywhere she looked, the other soldiers had undone their seat belts in excitement, and were starting to fly across the room. Some were doing various swimming strokes, and summersaults in mid-air. Only a few stayed behind to gawp at the view.

For Sarah, the fascination with zero gravity didn't last very long. After she had done a few circuits of the spacecraft, she returned to her bunk, and belted herself in again. She then, placed her head on the pillow and went to sleep for a few hours.

The dragon hovered in space for about four hours. During which time, Freida monitored the military broadcasts from below. She was attempting to find out whether they had been spotted, or retained the element of surprise.

There was no mention of the ship over Spanish air space. And most of the attention was on the build-up of Celtishian troops pointing towards the beaches of France.

For all intents and purposes, they had kept out of the range of the radar defense system. And no warnings were being sent form the ground operatives.

After she had spent those hours asleep, Freida invited Sarah to join her in the cockpit, and meet the flight captain. And Sarah was delighted to go and spend time with her friend.

But her thoughts were with Simon, now probably getting ready to cross the Channel in a major advancement of troops. It had been a case of waiting, and Sarah was relieved when she had discovered, he would go in the third wave. Clearly her thoughts for his safety were very strong, and growing daily, and now she worried about him more than herself.

Over the past three months, they often chatted together for hours on end, although to Sarah this always seemed shorter. The truth was she enjoyed his company, and was always stimulated by his conversation.

However, the worrying was to be cut short, when Freida made her announcement.

"Attention all hands, this is Captain Sophie-Smith. Get yourselves kitted up, and belted in. We start descending to Spain in about ten minutes, and the mission starts as soon as we land. Be ready, because this is where it gets serious."

There was movement everywhere, as the troops rushed to get their equipment, get dressed, and get back into their seatbelts. Sarah grabbed her equipment, and moved quickly to her place, before most of the others. But somehow, they all got ready in time, for the next announcement.

'Good evening, this is Flight Captain Beer. We will now start our descent. We can expect some offensive fire, and resistance, but nothing we need to worry about. This is all calculated into the plan. The most important thing to do, is remain seated until we land, and good luck."

The silence was broken for Sarah by Denise, offering her some boiled sweets.

"For the descent, and your ears," she explained. "I hope you like strawberry?"

The journey down was quick and jerky, as The Dragon entered the atmosphere and rode up and down between clouds for about half an hour. Sometimes turning on its side, and rocking as it sped through the air. Gradually they were getting lower and lower, until the green mist below became evident from above.

"Please keep your seat belts on," instructed the flight captain, "and brace yourselves, we are about to meet some enemy craft."

There was a very brief exchange of fire between them and some helicopters. But it was obvious they were far superior in fire power, and had taken them by surprise. The resistance did not last long, and the enemy helicopters were seen exploding into two giant fireballs.

"Those poor people," Louise was heard to say.

"Don't worry" came the flight captain through the speaker addressing the whole ship. "We are known to have helicopters in the area, the Egyptians will think it was them that did it."

And the Dragon continued onwards into the enemy territory. The speaker was playing the Egyptian broadcasts for everyone to hear, and Adah was translating them in a mocking voice.

"No sign of the enemy helicopters yet," she translated after one particularly animated outburst. "But when we find them we will show them *the Egyptian way* of doing things."

"Ooooh," went everyone on board the Dragon, in a similarly mocking tone.

"I can't wait to get to the Channel and engage the Celtishians," translated Adah for their further amusement. "We will show them."

"Oooh," jeered everyone on board the Dragon again.

Sarah thought that this was a far cry from the reactions when they first arrived. Everybody it seemed, had grown stronger through the raids, and were ready now to take back the fight. The fear had been nearly completely destroyed. Yet the fact remained, they were in enemy airspace, and about to be outnumbered in a crazy but daring counter-raid.

But then Adah translated something from an enemy colonel that surprised her.

"The Pharaoh wishes to remind you all that deserters from Egypt will be shot. Rumours that Celtishia has a superior force are of course nonsense." Everybody booed. "And nobody needs to be afraid in our army. We all know that fear has always been the biggest problem in the enemy's ranks, and it is nonsense to suggest that they don't fear us still. Where would they get that new courage from?"

Sarah suspected that she was not alone, in not feeling as frightened as she used to be. And she turned to Denise in the hammock next to her.

"Are you ok?"

"Yes, I think so."

"You're not nervous then?"

"Are you kidding?" Denise asked. "I'm almost

messing myself here. Yet I am also confident as well. First time in conflict see? I didn't even get to go to Sark, as my dad wouldn't let me."

"You know that you have grown a lot, since then, don't you?"

"Of course. Kind of had too."

"I hope you don't blame us for your recruitment?" asked Sarah.

Denise answered this question nervously. "Well a little. But I am also very grateful to you, and Boudicca as well. Truth is, I hated the presenting role, and my days were numbered, as they like young women. I would have ended up in a back office, yet here we are making the news for real."

"I don't understand?" asked Sarah, wanting to know more.

"Look at it this way. My career is starting over, and now based on my own merits. Nobody can say, I got to where I am due to connections."

"I see," and Sarah remembered Freida telling her that Denise's parents owned the corporation.

"And if this goes well, I reckon, I will be able to rise even higher, and achieve more than I would have before."

"Funny how things work out, isn't it?" asked Sarah.

"Yes, now try not to worry, Sarah, because we are in the hands of the Whisper, and nothing really happens without his say so."

Sarah had not expected Denise to say that. "You truly believe that?" she asked.

"Yes, I do. And in time, you might as well."

"Thanks Denise. I needed to hear that." And Sarah turned her head away, and stared through the port hole, at the green mist, and the coast of Spain that was emerging before her.

And Freida's voice now projected itself through the speaker, in her capacity as the mission leader, and Captain of her platoon.

"OK all hands, get your weapons loaded, and keep the safety catches on. I repeat. Do not remove the safety catches, until we are on the ground."

There was a sound of the troops checking their guns, and making adjustments.

"Can all the officers, please check the guns of their people, because we don't want any errors."

Sarah and the unit all held their guns in the air, for Denise to look them over. The other units were doing the same. When Denise had checked her pistol, Sarah then placed her compound bow onto her back, and checked the knives on her uniform, while Freida continued to address all on the craft.

"Remember this is a conflict situation. When we dismount the Dragon, we are on a live mission. Our actions must be quick and decisive. To this end, I would like you all to listen carefully to any instructions, and acknowledge Adah, (my mother,) as second in command of the platoon."

"Most importantly," Freida continued, "we have three hours to do what we have to do, by that time, you need to be at the rendezvous point. If you are not there the dragon will have to leave without you. No Exceptions."

Sarah looked across to Adah, and saw her smiling in a way that said she could not be prouder of her daughter. Sarah wondered if all those years ago, when she was rescuing her from the Palace, in Palestine, if she had ever imagined this moment, and what her daughter was now doing? And it occurred to her, that as a mother, Adah had always believed in Freida's potential, and encouraged the best in her.

'We have some good news, however," Freida continued with her information update. "Our scanners confirm that the resistance on the ground is not what was prepared for. For some time, it has been suspected that many of the registered enemy troops are really ghost troops. This means that they take money for service, and march on paper, but never turn up when there is action is to be done. We also have evidence of mass desertions."

"Anyway, it seems that the actual body count on our scanners is much lower than we had expected. This makes things a lot easier for us, but do not get complacent. The guards there are ready to fight, and will kill given a chance."

"To that end, I would like to remind you all, that the success of this mission depends on the element of surprise, so gunfire is best avoided until necessary. Hand to hand weapons, or arrows, are preferred in the early stages, but please employ your common sense. Aim well, and remember to hit the right targets. We land in five minutes. Get ready, good luck, and keep your heads down."

As soon as Freida had finished speaking, there was a surge of noise from the engines, as the craft started to slow down quite decisively. There was a definite jolt, and they could see some flames coming from the Dragon. It didn't last long.

"Just a handful of enemy troops," explained Freida through the speaker system, "nothing to worry about. They are already dealt with."

The craft landed in a field, on top of a cliff. The engines powered down, and the doors started to open. There was a surge of fresh air from outside, and everybody took a deep breath.

"Ground troops secure the immediate area," ordered Freida. "Everybody else obey your leaders. And go, now."

"Follow me, now, and remain alert," yelled Adah, at the three units under her command.

"You heard her," said Denise to her unit, and they followed Adah out of the craft.

The grass smelled fresh, and there was a small breeze, which invigorated the entire company. The green mist, however, was thicker than usual, and helped to hide them and The Dragon from view.

They were on a kind of mini peninsular, of about

two hundred metres side to side. They were virtually surrounded by water, but across that water to the west was the City of Cadiz. It was surrounded and mostly obscured by the green mist, although the lights could be seen from the ships stationed there and the houses beyond.

Adah called over both Sarah and Denise, and got them to look through a pair of binoculars. They could see the city in more detail, and could make out that there was some kind of fiesta or riotous party taking place in the city, which was keeping the people distracted.

"Convenient," said Adah. "We couldn't have timed it better. They will probably party all night, and what with the alcohol consumed, will not be focused on defending the gate."

So Sarah looked at the battered wooden gate, and the ships that were stationed behind it. "The gate is badly maintained anyway," Sarah pointed out stating the obvious.

"That's right," said Adah, "our role tonight is simply to open it, for the others to enter. The ships we destroy are a bonus."

"Put your night vision on minimum setting only for now" instructed Adah to the troops under her command. This was now essential for it was late in the day, and getting darker than usual. They did so, and to the left, they could all see three badly burned dead bodies from the exchange before the landing. It was such a gruesome sight that even the bravest gasped, in shock.

"That's aweful," said Leslie.

"That's war, I'm afraid. Its ugly, and brutal," Denise replied.

"And now its real," said Sarah.

"I know," said Leslie to the group. "Or at least I am starting too."

And then Charlotte, who had been looking the other way, turned around, and saw the bodies for the first time. Her face turned a funny shade of darker green, and her cheeks puffed up. And then she was sick, to the amusement of the more experienced troops. Although to their credit, all remained silent, and just smirked with laughter.

21. GATE BREACH

"When you have quite finished," said Adah, as she approached the situation, and looked on with sympathy.

"Sorry," said Charlotte as she started to return to normal, and straighten up.

"That's ok. I guess that is your first dead body you have seen."

"Yes, it would be," interrupted Leslie, who was joining her. "My partner has lived a sheltered life that way." And with that Leslie placed a supportive arm around her.

"Well, there will be more before the mission is out, so toughen up," instructed Adah. "And we need to get going soon, as the deadlines tonight are tough."

Leslie did not look amused, but decided to say nothing.

"Can I freshen up?" asked Charlotte.

"No, you are going in the water soon, that will wash the sick off," offered a shocked but amazed Sarah. "Seriously?" she continued to everybody else. "We are in a middle of a war zone, and she wants, what: a shower, and a change of flipping clothes?"

The group looked on in shock and embarrassment. They all started looking at their feet.

"I'll go in before you," offered Louise. "To check on the water temperature."

"Avoid the vomit that is washed off more like," corrected Sarah, who was now getting irritated with her team.

"That is quite enough, all of you," ordered Denise, looking at Sarah with annoyance. And it was then, that Sarah remembered being sick on the boat.

"We are here to work together," Adah now pointed out, "so start doing so. Put your issues to one side, and try supporting each other."

"Sorry," said Louise and Sarah together.

"Good," said Adah, "because we will have no more nonsense tonight. Now teams 21, 20, and 19 follow me down the cliff. It is time to swim to Cadiz, and plant some explosives. Leslie, I understand that you are our resident lock-picking expert?

"That's right," Leslie said with pride, "there wasn't a safe I couldn't crack, before I was caught. Kept my hand in whilst in jail, opening cell doors for fun, and friends."

"Good, that will be useful," Adah pointed out, "picking the door lock will be quieter, and assist with the surprise element."

The team proceeded towards the cliff, where they started to lower themselves down with their equipment. But Sarah was having difficulties, and couldn't seem to focus as well as she might. Her head was hurting badly, and at one point, she even found herself suspended from the support rope. Swinging back in, she remembered the time, when the boys had made comments and Denise had fallen as a result.

Up above her, she could hear Charlotte ask her, "are you ok, Sarah. Can I help?"

"No I am fine thanks."

"Well, we are here if you need us?"

Now back on the cliff, she continued down to the bottom, and landed safely on the sand. She removed her winch and tackle, and sent it back up for the next group coming down. And looked out towards the sea. It smelt fresh, but for some reason did not provide her the usual pleasure she would feel from the coast.

The waves were lapping gently on the beach, and it was clearly a good day for the swim across to the gate of Cadiz. However, there was a lot of seaweeds, and they were going to benefit from them as cover from any watchmen. The mist meant that even though they were probably only four miles away, they were barely able to make out the destination, and the cheaply made wooden transport boats inside the gates, now left unmanned due to the festival.

"Remember, if we can't see them, they can't see us, especially; when they don't expect us," said Adah, to the three groups, under her command. "Come now Sarah, let's get a closer look."

As they inspected them in more detail, through a pair of super binoculars, Sarah's stomach once more churned out of fear, and something else. Revulsion. To her, the boats were similar to those used to smuggle refugees into Europe from North Africa, in her own dimension. They were long, made of wood, and had outboard engines on the back. Most had extra diesel barrels in them.

"Those things are fire hazards," she said. "Not craft to use in an invasion."

"The day gets better, and better," said Adah. "I do believe that the Whisper is with us here today."

"Now we need to get ready to swim across as quickly as possible. So, you lot can help me with that crate," and Adah pointed at a large wooden crate being lowered by winch from the Dragon.

Most of the group did what was asked, but for some funny reason, Sarah just stood rooted to the spot, next to Charlotte and Leslie.

And it was then, that Sarah was suddenly filled with guilt for earlier. And she just knew, she had to try and put things right, as her stomach was now tightening up, her head was hurting, and she was starting to sweat in discomfort. The guilt had taken on physical characteristics.

Approaching Charlotte and Leslie, she quietly

asked, "Can I have a word please."

"Oh, what about?" asked Charlotte.

"Are you feeling better now Charlotte?" asked Sarah to open up the subject.

"Yes, she is. Why?" asked a protective Leslie, who was looking at her with disgust, for what was said earlier.

Sarah went a darker shade of green, and responded. "Look I am sorry about earlier. I just didn't think. Others laughed and I just went along with it. The pressure and all that. But I should have known better, and really messed up. Sometimes I think I'm being funny, when I am not."

"That's ok, we forgive you," said Charlotte to Leslie's astonishment, "just don't let it happen again."

"I won't I promise, and I'm sorry. And I apologize, to both of you that is."

"Its ok," Charlotte repeated, as she and Leslie gave her a hug. And as they did so, she could see Adah, giving her a look of approval. And, Sarah remembered Adah quoting some words from The Book of Comparisons. "Gently saying sorry, is like the finest honey and good for your body and spirit." And true enough. the stomach pains now subsided, along with the sweating and headaches.

The crate contained thirty small green handheld underwater scooters. They were electrical devices designed to be held out in front of the swimmer, like buoyancy aids, and were shaped like dolphins to ensure maximum speed through the surface water. Their oxygen filtration systems meant, that their users could also travel underwater for limited distances.

"It should take us no more than half an hour, to get there with these. I believe you have used the "Sea-Fish" in training and are competent in steering, underwater travel and firing at targets." And Adah looked at the group, before continuing. "Remember however, this time, it is real. Misses could be fatal."

"Remember they are the enemy, and they won't hesitate to kill you if you let them. We are expecting casualties as it is a secure base. However, do not be phased by that. As I have said, we have the element of surprise and can take down the stronghold."

The group looked worried, but tried not to show it. So Adah spelt it out for them as simply as she could.

"The plan is as you are aware, to swim with our "military 'Sea-Fish' for the first mile. Then we submerge for the rest of the journey, coming up just before the gate. Leslie, you pick the lock, and Charlotte you can use your explosive skills, just in case plan A fails. When the lock goes, team 21 will focus on opening the gate, and everybody else, swim or jet through the reeds and place as many explosives as you can. The more boats we get the better."

"But what happens then?" asked Louise.

"That's simple, the rest of the squad will follow on Seabikes and attack the harbor from inside. They will focus on its boats, and then its facilities. We have one hour maximum to do as much damage as possible before we head back here for the rendezvous with The Dragon."

"Please set your headset audio band to frequency seven, so I, and the other officers, can pass on orders though the headsets. Now let's get going, and good luck"

And Adah grabbed a 'Sea-Fish,' and dived into the water. The troops under her command followed her, Sarah being among the first to hit the warm water, and press on its engine, which silently hummed, and pulled her forward through the waves, with her basic equipment on her person.

They continued for about a mile, before Adah ordered them through their headsets to submerge. Then the machines released a tube that connected to their helmets, and instantly oxygen was filtered through, as they went lower and lower below the waves. They continued to follow a set route, that waved sometimes left, and sometimes right. But always heading roughly in the direction of the Gate of Cadiz.

The view was fantastic below the waves of the sea. The water being fairly clear, and the seaweeds growing high from the bottom upwards towards the surface, it made for a slower than preferred journey. However, as they neared the city, it was obvious that other ships had come this way before, as now the weeds had been disturbed. This made for clearer travel.

Adah however was straight on this, and giving everybody instructions through channel seven on the head sets.

"Keep to the planned route. It may seem like slower progress," she said, "but if anybody is watching us on radar, they are more likely to mistake us for fish. Probably too busy with the party up above anyway. Seems a shame to be crashing it really."

And it was then that Sarah noticed that there were indeed fish around her. Only up to this point she hadn't noticed them as she was so busy concentrating on steering the 'Sea-Fish' device, that propelled her through the water. And her first impressions of these fish, was that they were absolutely amazing. Slivers of silver flashing in and out, between reeds and rocks, at great speeds.

"Of course," she thought, "I could never swim at this speed. The radars would see us as seventy large fish, or a small shoal, as they would mistake my craft and I, as two separate creatures."

They continued to swim on, until they reached a point where the seabed was starting to rise.

"Ok, slow up," said Adah. "We are about to surface at the gate soon. In about five minutes. Leslie, be ready to deal with the lock. Charlotte you are on back up. Everybody else, get ready for battle, and keep calm."

Even underwater, Sarah could sense that everybody had got very tense, and the nerves of the three units were going to be crucial to the mission's success. Adah was trying to control her people and the situation.

"And just so you know," she continued, "Freida has notified me that the rest of our troops have started their journey over. They hope to arrive as the gate opens, maximizing the effect of the attack."

And with that she gave an upwards signal and the rest of the group followed her up to the gate.

They arrived just outside the great wooden gate, and from under the water started to look up. Hidden among the reeds, and seaweed. as best as they could. Leslie and Charlotte however, swam on hand in hand, towards the gate. Leslie climbed up, and very quickly started using a hairpin to pick it open.

The rest of the unit listened nervously through their headphones, as Leslie set about the lock.

"Left a bit. Right a bit. Got you."

There was a small click, and the gate started to move inwards, while Leslie fell back into the water as quietly as she could. Clearly her days of safe cracking, and general crime had taught her great break-in skills. Charlotte was seen to kiss Leslie quickly under water, as the rest of the unit surged on the gate pushing it open. But as it opened they were spotted.

An alarm started to sound, and some gunfire rained down on the unit. However, because they were under water the effect of the bullets was almost zero. This changed as they surfaced to exchange fire.

Two of Sarah's unit were struck, and bullets had missed Sarah by inches. Now two of her friends, Nigella and Donna were floating on the water. Her colleagues killed in battle right in front of her, and she started to feel a little sick.

Despite the early casualties, it was not all lost, because it seemed that they were outnumbering the enemy guards. And the returning fire using the Sea-Fish were effective in eradicating this opposition.

"Keep alert" yelled Adah, "and set some explosives. Unit 19 focus on guarding everyone else." And they planted explosives as the remaining troops from the Dragon were starting to arrive. Sarah watched with relief as they jetted past in their Sea-Fish, also opening fire from the surface on anybody who appeared to be a threat.

"Now let's light this place up," yelled Adah. And then there was an almighty blast, and a small fireball, as the first of the explosives took off setting a wooden boat on fire. And as the fire burnt the rope securing it in place, the breeze blew it gently into other craft. They in turn also caught fire.

The locals, it seemed had been surprised and delighted to see all the craft they hated on fire. This caused them to start taking sides and join in with the Celtishian Forces. Now they were grabbing any Egyptian or sympathizer they could find, and turning their own weapons on them.

The party was descending into an insurrection, as Egyptians panicked and opened fire on the crowd, killing innocent civilians. The attempt to intimidate had failed and the uprising was now growing.

As the situation progressed, it got worse for the Egyptians. In their confusion at fighting two enemies very suddenly, they could no longer tell who their enemies were, and started opening fire on each other. Freida's company however were better prepared, and focused on taking down the Egyptian resistance only.

Freida's company was able to seize the docks easily, due to the commotion elsewhere that was now developing. The loss of life in the company being kept to a minimum, as the troops gained positions of cover in the chaos, and the Egyptians were left performing acts of friendly fire on each other. Sarah's unit led by Denise was able to join them, in this advance.

Meanwhile, Sarah suddenly heard Freida's voice speak into her earphones. "Attention all troops. Attack the red command centre on the left, with the snake drapes on the outside. Set it on fire, and let's get to the rendezvous point, A.S.A.P."

"A good idea," thought Sarah, who then realized that somehow she had ended up in a key location. And she had her bow, with two flame arrows. Taking cover behind a wall, she took them out of the quiver, and slowly lit them both. "We'll cover you," said an enthusiastic Louise, pointing to Leslie and Amber, and with that the three of them positioned themselves in a shield formation, covering Sarah from gun fire. Their shields deflected the bullets.

Sarah took her chance, and positioned herself. She then quickly and safely stringed the first arrow into her bow, and launched it through the air. It landed in the middle of the left drape. The second shot hit the drape on the right. Both caught fire, and the building started to burn, while Sarah ducked back behind the wall for safety, as the few remaining Egyptian guards responded by firing on them. And a grenade came flying through the air in their direction.

The girls providing the shield wall, saw it like it was in slow motion, and disbanded as safely as they could. Attempting to join Sarah in safety. Leslie, and Amber both made it unharmed, but Louise took a load of the blast. She fell over and did not move from where she had fallen. From her position of safety, Sarah could see that she was breathing, but only just.

"Return fire," yelled Denise to the rest of the unit. And so the troops opened fire, forcing the Egyptians to take cover, until a grenade was thrown wiping them all out. The remaining Egyptian guards died seconds later, ending the siege of the base, and leaving the team safe enough to get to Louise.

Louise was lying on the ground, and clearly in a lot of pain. Her breathing was getting laboured and it looked like she was going into shock. Martha Zing was at her side, in her medical capacity, as soon as she could get there, trying as best as she can to offer help.

Sarah was also over at her side, holding her hand and trying to offer help, as Louise started to cough up blood. She went a very pale shade of green, and started look worryied.

"Hang in there," said the Medic, "Try not to panic. Help is on its way," Martha continued to try and reassure her. Then turning to Denise, she said, "Quick, she is feeling very cold to touch. Just get me a blanket, they're in the back of the Seabikes."

And with that Denise rushed to get a blanket. And was on the way back to Martha, when they all heard the words they feared from Louise.

"Tell my parents, I am sorry", and then she spat up some more blood, before going limp. She died there in front of them, leaving the team feeling totally helpless. Time seemed to slow down for Sarah, who had just seen a good friend die. She had even trained with her. And at that moment, she didn't have a clue what to do, except mildly cry, and grieve her loss. Martha closed Louise's eyes, out of respect. And Sarah straightened Louise's torc, as she liked to look her best.

The other units, had sealed off the area, and were now starting to gather around. As the officer in charge of three units, Adah appeared to both commiserate at their loss, and to congratulate them on their success. "Good shot, Sarah. And well done that shield team. And poor Louise. Such a brave girl, and such a brave act." she reflected. "But let's get out of here. Jump on the back of any Seabike, and we will get out of here." This was sadly short lived.

"Adah," said Denise, "I think you should turn around quickly, there is something you need to see." Denise was pointing at the building, and Sarah had a sense of foreboding, and that things were about to get weird.

22. GRUDGES

S arah's suspicion was soon proved right. For she could now see what Denise had seen.

In the near distance, one of the units had made a high profile arrest in conjunction with Spanish locals. However, the identity of the prisoner was a mystery to her. A huge giant of a woman, was being led at gunpoint, by another unit.

The giant green woman was about eight feet tall, and clearly in handcuffs under arrest. Sarah looked at her, but couldn't make out where she had seen her before. She wore an enormous zebra skin dress, with sexy curves, and a series of expensive gold necklaces were adorning her neck. Adah soon set her right though.

"Great Whisper," she exclaimed, "you must be joking? Princess Bloody Phillipa? And my daughter has seen her." And Adah started to run in that direction, as if a nightmare was coming true.

Matters were made worse, when local TV cameras started descending on the scene. The importance of these two captures was not lost on them either, and they were clearly desperate for a major story.

Sarah realized that Adah was right, about Freida though. In fact, not only had she seen her, she was now standing in front of her, and confronting her as her prisoner. Freida had a knife drawn, and was heard saying four words. "Remember me, do you?"

"You," was the staged reply of the Princess, in front of the cameras. "Well I be... The food mistress? Used to sleep with the Chief Prince. His bit on the side. A mere insignificant runaway slave. Now, what do you think you are doing? Let me go now, I have diplomatic immunity. You can't hold me."

"I can when you are under arrest," Freida said, "for human trafficking. Diplomatic immunity does not cover that."

Phillipa looked stunned, as she clearly hadn't grasped that fact until this moment, and could think of nothing to say, while Freida pushed home her moral advantage.

"And as the leading officer here.." She paused to make the point. "I. Captain Sophie-Smith of the Kingdom of Celtishia, place you, Princess Phillipa under arrest for war crimes, and the human trafficking, exploitation, and cruelty towards children. And there will be more charges to follow."

And with that she spoke into her tech tab, to Captain Abraham Beer of the Dragon.

"Captain, please bring the saucer over here. All enemies are defeated, and the mission has exceeded expectations. It is safe to land. Authorization. Freida Sophie-Smith. And by the way, there will be two high profile prisoners for you to take into custody, for a hearing at the League of Nations."

"Yes Captain, coming over now," replied Captain Beer.

The princess was not, however, going quietly, and started to question her arrest.

"Under arrest," she protested with great indignity to the cameras. "Why? Who is accusing me?" Princess Phillipa demanded for the benefit of the cameras.

"I am," said Freida bluntly, and as Company leader, "I am arresting you for trafficking, and war crimes."

"A runaway? A fugitive? And a slave?" Princess Phillipa was laughing at Freida. "Pretending to be a captain?"

"A runaway now turned prosecution witness, who adds your confession." interjected Adah, holding up her Tech-Tab, indicating a recording. She also pointed to the television cameras for effect. "And I am a second witness of your crimes which include assisting with murder. And I am now coming forward".

"Why, who are you?" asked the Princess. And it was clear by her tone of voice, she really didn't know.

"I was one of the chefs at the time of Prince Asama's death. I worked in the kitchens, and vanished that same night for safety reasons."

The Princess looked stunned by this revelation, but tried to act calm. "This will never stand up. Not when I am about to take the throne as the only rightful heir of Chief Prince Asama."

"Well that's the thing," said Adah giving her, what could only be described as the most cunning smile, Sarah had seen in her life. "What you said, isn't entirely true. The late chief Prince Asama has a direct son and daughter".

"No, he doesn't," laughed the snooty Princess.

"He does," interjected Freida, "I should know. I bore them."

The Princess looked stunned. So did everybody else except Adah. Sarah had not expected that revelation at all. Everywhere around them soldiers were looking stunned.

"And a direct son or daughter is always considered greater than a daughter-in-law, even when the mother was his personal slave," Freida pointed out. "I conceived them by him on the same night, that he died. His death was the reason I fled, and eventually claimed sanctuary in the City of Devonport under Ancient International Law."

Adah made her way over as quickly as she could, and getting hold of Freida, pulled her into a hug, that only a concerned mother could give.

In her head, Sarah repeated the words, that Freida had said. "I conceived them on the same night." Meanwhile some of the unit looked at her, as Freida's best friend, hoping for some kind of clarification in the confusion.

She looked across to Adah and Freida, caught in a parent and child embrace. Out of the corner of her eye, she could just about make out a look from Adah towards her that indicated it was true. And then Sarah started to put things together in her head.

It all made sense, Enoch and Ruth were her children, not brothers and sisters. They had the same slightly darker skin of Freida, and even the same birthmarks. In addition, their ages matched the time when Freida had come from Palestine, and then Sarah remembered what Adah had said, "you wait ages for a child, then three come along at once."

And of course, Freida was damaged emotionally by what happened, Sarah recalled. And she would be in no fit state to look after twins, and aged only eighteen. Especially as the official age of consent was twenty one.

"So," thought Sarah, "Adah must have then stepped up as mother to Enoch and Ruth. Covering the arrival of two illegitimate children, born out of wedlock. And having to pretend they were brother and sister, led in part, to Freida's conduct issues, and the intervention by Boudicca."

Over the next few minutes, of course, the cameras started to go wild at this news. A presenter was making wild guesses, and asking weird questions of Freida and Phillipa, who was demanding release and threatening to sue.

But Freida was still in charge. And she now turned to Princess Phillipa, with a look of venom in her eye. "And you as twice previously stated, are under arrest, for human trafficking, and war crimes. There are many witnesses to these acts, and lots of evidence. International law demands that you will stand trial. You are also under arrest for a false claim to a royal throne. You can expect a life sentence" And turning to one of the other officers, she pointed at Mustapha Sword, and the Princess, and said, "put them both in the brig in handcuffs, attached to the wall. Make them comfortable, and prepare for transportation."

"I demand the right to trial by combat," yelled The Princess, bursting away from her captors for a few seconds. It was said for everybody to hear, including the the World's Media. "And I challenge that scrawny little captain of yours, and choose knives as my weapons. It is my Ancient Right."

"And what do you place down as a guarantee?" asked Freida. "International Law states that 'Trial by Combat' is guaranteed at a cost?"

"The Egyptian claim on Celtishia," the giant Phillipa replied, to the gasps of everybody present.

Freida remained calm and simply pointed out for everyone in the media to hear, "you don't have the right to gamble that, on your false innocence. As you are not even the Princess of Palestine."

"Yes, I do, I am engaged to the Pharaoh himself," she replied in a smug way, holding out her hands to get the handcuffs removed. "I can act on his behalf."

And as the guards released the handcuffs for what was to follow, a few of those people present clapped momentarily, before realizing this was not a good thing.

"Really," asked Freida squaring up to her, "you think that is a good idea. I must advise you that, if you lose, and live, you will go to prison for life. You will lose all rights to a royal pardon. That's if you don't die in the process."

"The Pharaoh will appeal. He is my fiancé."

"He won't." Freida was laughing at her now. "He'll dump your backside in seconds! For losing him any international and diplomatic claim he had, on expanding his territory."

Freida was now in reaching distance of the Princess. They were looking at each other with what could only be described as pure loathing. And then the Princess made the first move, by grabbing Freida, and throwing her through the air in anger. Freida landed a few feet away, in a heap on the ground.

"But I will not lose, silly little slave," the giant green Princess laughed, as Freida picked herself up. "Don't you remember the beatings I used to give you in the palace? How I could pick you up, and plaster you against a wall? For fun? And now I demand the right to combat with knives. And in five minutes I will walk free. And you will be dead, I am sure of that."

"Then I accept," said a confident Freida, putting down her gun on the ground, and pointing to various knives on her person. "I have my knives. I assume you have yours?"

The Celtishian Guards let go of the Princess, and handed her a bag, that they had seized from her.

"Yes," said the enormously tall Princess as she chose three knives, the size of small swords. And assuming a fighting stance, she challenged Freida, "well slave? Are you ready to die?"

"No! But I am ready to fight," and with that Freida adopted her own stance, and started to circle her opponent.

Sarah looked at Adah, wondering how serious this could get, for Adah had been looking seriously worried. However, she was now starting to cheer and encourage her daughter, and could be heard shouting, "go on my girl, you can take the bitch." The rest of the troops, and nearby officials were starting to surround the opponents. The cameras were rolling, while Freida continued to slowly circle the Princess. Freida looked focused and determined against her larger opponent.

Denise came alongside Sarah, and nervously took her hand. The rest of the remaining unit was joining them. Charlotte was holding the hand of Leslie. The group all looked worried. Sarah could only get out half the question she had on her mind.

"Is this?"

"Yes," replied Denise. "A fight to the death, or serious injury at least. It only ends when one opponent is unable to continue."

"Oh!" Sarah stopped, and collected herself, wanting to get behind her friend, who was still circling her opponent and looking straight into her eyes. The bigger Princess Phillipa, for her part was trying to intimidate with threatening forward gestures. Both were trying to psych out their opponent.

"Be careful, Freida, and you can take the cow," yelled Sarah.

And Denise started to chant Freida's name, and the rest of the troops joined in.

"Cute," said Phillipa, "I see you have a fan club." She paused, looking at Sarah, then continued, "of losers."

"Fancy your chances then?" asked Freida.

"Yeah, I have been in many fights in the palace, as you should remember. In fact, I was often the favourite to win." The Princess was now looking very smug.

"I do," Freida countered, "and I remembered some of the opponents taking money to take a dive."

There was a moment's doubt from Princess Phillipa, and it showed on her face.

"Oh you didn't know? You were too slow, clumsy, careless, and…"

And with that Princess Phillipa, launched her first attack. She had gambled all on a surprise element, and was attempting a careless slash on Freida. But Freida had obviously anticipated this, and was able to get easily out of the way, causing the Princess to lose balance momentarily as she went forward.

Sarah could see that she was indeed slower and clumsy.

In response, Freida threw a knife at her, and it landed straight in her right buttock. It was now sticking out at an angle, with blood on the blade. The Princess, howled in pain, and the troops all cheered, including Sarah, who could feel herself being overtaken by some kind of blood lust.

"I was going to say 'Stupid'," exclaimed Freida, to Phillipa, to the amusement of the spectators.

The Princess regathered herself, as best she could. Then in shock, or perhaps desperation, she made yet another careless lunge at Freida. This time landing on the ground face down, the dagger remaining in her right buttock.

Again the crowd laughed at her, and cheered Freida on.

Only this time Freida wasn't feeling so easy going, and throw another of her daggers. This time it stuck into Phillipa's back. Again she cried out in pain, but she wasn't giving up yet.

Rising to her feet, she proceeded to make a series of strikes at Freida, who was keeping just out of her range. Freida was countering by coming in whenever the Princess looked tired or out of time. Phillipa's lack of fitness, and slowness of speed was giving her a disadvantage. The discipline that Freida was showing was starting to win over, and the two knives sticking out of the Princess were starting to take their toll. The Princess was slowing down even more. She was both tiring and loosing, and everyone knew it was going that way.

With one last effort, Princess Phillipa let out a scream of rage, and flew at Freida trying to stab her. Although she was able to graze Freida, she failed to make any serious contact, and fell over. Stupidly she lay there too long. And with that, she felt a third dagger stick into her leg. Then a fourth hit her best arm, effectively causing her to drop another of her weapons.

"Please," cried the Princess, looking helpless, "I yield."

And Freida, stood over her and said to one of her officers, "Take her away then."

And once more, she had her rights read to her, by the guards. They then handcuffed her from behind. And she was taken away towards the Dragon, as a prisoner. Freida was bleeding from her arm and clearly in pain. But she was just about standing, and staring at the captured princess in triumph. And everybody was cheering her victory, so much so, it was all turning a bit chaotic.

Luckily, Adah however, was on hand, and then with one wink at Denise, she did what needed to be done.

"Captain Freida Sophie-Smith," she interjected, "I am hereby temporarily removing you of your command, due to injuries, under article eleven of the 'Common Sense Manual for troop command.' You must see the doctor, as soon as possible." And she pointed at Doctor Martha Zing.

"Surely, there is no such law," yelled the desperately injured Princess Phillipa, in desperation for attention. But nobody seemed to care about her opinion any more.

"I wouldn't know," Adah scowled, back at the Princess, indicating she didn't care about her opinion. And turning back to her daughter continued, "I am also assigning you to hammock rest on "The Dragon". And for the benefit of the media, she pointed at the craft that was now landing. "As my daughter, however, I want to go on record as saying, that I am proud of you for coming forward of your own accord to assist in enquiries."

And the mother and daughter gave each other a hug. That is, until Adah pushed her away, and slapped her around the cheek. "But don't you ever put me through that again," she said. And she hugged her daughter close once more.

Adah now turned to the troops, and the cameras.

"Any questions, please feel free to ask our media expert Sargent Denise La-Rooche of this Company. She will answer them, or get back to you."

And with that she brought the company to attention, and told them to secure the position, and recover the dead, and wounded. "Work with the Spanish Authorities. Nobody is to be left behind," she said.

"Meanwhile, I will personally deal with the issue of the two prisoners, and all the paperwork it initially involves. This will all take about half an hour, then we will start the journey back to Celtishia."

Sarah accompanied Freida. She was determined to offer her support. Adah naturally, made no attempts to stop her, as she wanted her daughter with her best friend at this time. And Freida was relieved to have her best friend with her, as she was finally facing up to her past. And as she walked up the gangplank to salutes from her officers, she was able to raise a smile and a "thank you" in Sarah's direction.

Meanwhile, Princess Phillipa wept in front of the cameras, as she was led away. The evil Princess was now realizing that she had traded away everything in one go. Her freedom, her future marriage had both gone, and so had her right to become Queen. F for probably the first time in her life Princess Phillipa was on her own, and at the mercy of others.

She was escorted away by another giant woman,

namely Medical Officer Martha Zing. Her role being to ensure the welfare of the prisoner. The knives were sticking out of her awaiting removal, and there were wounds that had to be healed. Then and only then would she be handed over for trial. The Media were already speculating she would use ill health, and injury, as a reason to avoid justice.

23. WRAP UP

A s soon as the Princess was secured on board and ready for transport. Adah took to her Tech-Tab to electronically command all the troops onto the Dragon.

"OK, all troops," The message said, "We have performed our role with distinction. Captain Sophie Smith had previously given orders that I was the second in command, if she was unable to continue. So on that basis, I am assuming the command role, and ordering you all to get on board the dragon. Buckle up, and get ready for the flight home."

However, I have more bad news first. As you are aware we succeeded in taking Cadiz, and starting an uprising in Spain. But it has not been without casualties. I regret to inform you that our officers have reported our losses. It is now confirmed that the number of people killed in battle is forty-six. Their bodies are on board. However, one "Nigella Winter," was lost on the initial assault, and searches remain underway with local forces, for her remains. While all attempts to locate her remains will be investigated, it is believed that her body was burnt in the fire, and may not be recoverable"

The company's reaction to the loss of life among the crew was very severe. Everybody had lost someone that they were close too, and this was never going to be easy. But the idea, of a body unaccounted for was a real shock.

Meanwhile for Sarah the loss of Louise, had hit her especially hard. Louise had been so young, and stunningly beautiful. Sarah could also remember how brave she had been at that moment, when she had volunteered to provide the shield cover for her arrows. And indeed, she had then stood strong, as the bullets bounced of her rectangular see-through shield. Sarah could not at this stage imagine what that was like, trusting your life to a bit of advanced plastic, and watching the bullets pound against it.

Basically, what disturbed her the most was this feeling that she should be dead and not Louise, Nigella and Donna. And this was just the people she knew. In reality, there were another forty-three, who had perished in the attack on Cadiz. As the person who suggested it, she felt that their deaths were therefore her fault.

Freida also took the news of the loss of Louise very hard indeed, and shed a few tears for her, from the hammock where she was now resting. Freida had mentored Louise personally, and it was another blow to her.

358

Sarah had to deal with the question of how to best support her friend in this situation. Initially she had kept clear to allow the Doctor to examine her, and then assisted in helping her with the stitching of the wounds. She had then assumed a nursing capacity, fetching blankets and cups of hot chocolate to cheer her up. Adah popped in regularly to check up on her, and inform her of anything related to the team.

Eventually she decided that the best approach was to tackle it head on, and when the mother was visiting she decided to ask some questions.

"So what happens now?" she bravely asked them both.

"What with?" asked Adah.

"Your children? Freida's children?"

"Well we can make a claim for them, to take over the Palestine territory. Get them on the throne, so to speak. If that is ok with you, Freida?" Adah was looking at her daughter for direction.

Freida was looking uncertain, "Can we prove they are Asama's children? I know they are, but can we prove it beyond doubt?"

"Yes, D.N.A. testing will prove it," Adah replied cutting over what she was saying, "we can get the results sent straight to the League of Nations. It can be done within the hour. Their D.N.A is already on record."

"Do it then! They should not miss out any longer."

"What I meant was?" Sarah continued to question them. "Are you going to change the arrangements for their care. Now, it is out in the open?"

And both Freida, and Adah, looked uncertain at this point. After all the disclosure had clearly not been planned. And Sarah kept silent on purpose to allow them to make a decision. It was Freida who finally answered the question for them both.

"I guess the first thing we need to do, is talk directly to them before the media does."

"But what are you going to tell them?" Sarah enquired.

"The truth, of course. It is about time they knew all of it," said Adah. "But they will legally remain my children. This means that I will legally take all decisions with Freida's input. Basically no domestic changes. I hope?" And she looked at Freida with an air of uncertainty. Freida looked back with what looked like an expression of relief.

"Of course, that is probably the best thing for them. I didn't plan to become a mother, and was never ready for it at eighteen." Freida was crying a little now. "Their father was not a man I loved, so I can love them better in my role as an older sister."

"Then," said Adah taking charge, "Sarah, do me a favour, tell Captain Beer he is in charge until I return. Freida, my daughter: we must talk to Benjamin, and your siblings immediately. And tell Denise to get on with the press conference, she will work out what needs to be said."

And with that they connected their Tech-Tabs to the screen in the units barracks, and dialed back to the sub-holding. Sarah left the room, spoke to Denise, and updated Captain Beer.

24. JUSTICE

By the time, she had got back to the main room of the Dragon, the craft had been in the air for about an hour. This meant that they were mostly now in the lounge, and talking in subdued terms about all that had happened. Sarah's arrival, caused them all to turn and look at her. They were hoping that she could update them further.

Unfortunately, all she could tell them was that there was going to be a press conference. And Sargeant Denise La-Rooche would be taking it from onboard The Dragon itself. They only had to wait about five minutes until the screens came on, and The Dragon was broadcasting live to The Green World.

"Good evening, and welcome to this vital news update," said Denise, as she appeared on the screen, looking both official and stunning. "For those who do not know me, my name is Denise La-Rooche. I was formerly a presenter with the CBC, but am now a press sergeant in the Celt-ishian military."

"Firstly. Today has been a decisive day in the

war between Celtishia and Egypt, and the result is that in a period of three hours, we have seen an attack on the City of Cadiz, and the surrender of Spain by Egyptian officials. I must warn you, that some viewers may find the following images distressing."

Her face was replaced with images of some of the fighting, before Denise spoke over the video clips, showing them opening the gate, and smashing their way through the ships.

Eventually her voice sounded over the video, and started to give more information.

"The attack was a total success, and succeeded predominantly in giving confidence to the local people and forces to defy their Egyptian oppressors. Here we see them fighting back, and alongside Celtishian forces."

There was video of Spanish resistance,

"Things reached a head when Princess Phillipa of Lebanon was captured. In defiance Princess Phillipa challenged the leading officer to a duel gambling the Egyptian claim on our land in the process. You may find the following distressing."

The Trial by Combat was projected through the airwaves for the world to see. It was followed by an edited version of the fight, with a brief commentary of the key moments. Finally, the news clip showed the images of Phillipa, being arrested and taken away, while Denise narrated over the top.

Up to this point the scenes had all related to

things Sarah already knew, having been there herself. But there was this feeling that elsewhere things were also now changing. And so it came as no surprise to her that, the day's events were now followed by other scenes in France.

"Just in. The news of the Egyptian defeat seems to have now inspired others to also make their stand," Denise announced. "The CBC has since been informed that the Prince of Spain, and the Princess of Catalonia, have formerly declared independence. They have started resistance and had requested Egypt to leave their lands. The League of Nations have received receipt of their declaration of independence, and requests."

This has been followed by similar requests from France and Portugal. Conflict has broken out on the French coast between Egypt and the French. The French forces are now attempting to take back their coastal cities that are under Egyptian control."

"As we speak," she continued, "Celtishian forces are crossing the Channel to assist them in this liberation, and victory is expected soon."

"Despite the objections of the Pharaoh, we have not been invaded. Life goes on, and everything is far from over."

"The resurgence of France and Spain in particular, means that there is now an alliance poised against him. And we welcome them to the fight, alongside America, who have also announced their support. It is like things are just starting."

"Many months ago, the Pharaoh mocked us and the whisper. We all saw the speech. But the Whisper has spoken today, through the brave and decisive actions of others. Long live Celtishia."

The screens went off. And another screen indicated that there was at least another three hours travelling to do.

Back in the Hub, and all over Celtishia, there was now much celebrating and partying. Many raising toasts to Freida and 'Sarah The Great Destroyer." Others spent the evening, telling lewd jokes about the Egyptians. This was a notable contrast from when Sarah first arrived and everybody was scared to speak about Egypt. Now the threat was seen to have gone, and it was like the fear had been destroyed.

"Vincent?" asked Sarah into her tech tab, while trying to relax in her hammock

"Yes, Sarah." said Vincent, appearing in holographic form beside her in the hammock. "What can I do for you?" he asked.

"What does the rest of the media say about the mission?"

"Well Sarah, International Media has gone into overdrive. Basically they are repeating the news, using our clips, but putting on their own spin. The American media is calling it a humiliation of Egypt. They are supporting the claim of the twins to rule Palestine. They are also suggesting that the Egyptian forces return to their own land, and stay there. They have proposed an international task force to ensure that this happens."

"Meanwhile, Egypt are not talking about the battle at all. They are instead describing a withdrawal for diplomatic processes. They say they want to give others the chance to bid for peace with them."

Sarah laughed as Vincent continued. "Independent outlets are starting chat programs to discuss what should happen next. By the way, you have six invites already to appear on various shows?"

"Not interested," Sarah replied.

"Very good, Sarah. I will let them know."

"Other programs are just showing the fight, and Phillipa gambling away the Egyptian claim on Celtishia. But.."

"But what?" asked Sarah, suspecting she already knew the answer.

"They are also talking a lot about Freida, who has now been identified as the mother of the children. They are also speculating about exactly what happened back then?"

"Oh?"

"Yes, they are saying that she may have committed murder?"

"But that is ridiculous," Sarah objected in a hugely outraged voice. "They never even suspected murder before. Besides he fell and just banged his head. The fat slob experienced justice by his own stupidity."

"I know, we have Freida's memories, as evidence. I have taken the liberty of sending copies of these to the League of Nations. It will be used as evidence to acquit her, and to support her children's claim. But the politicians and conspiracy theorists are going to have a field day discussing all this. They will talk of little else for months."

"But there is no truth to the slurs?"

"I know," said Vincent, "however some people are already smearing her character, by referring to her as a loose woman, or a mistress. Even the lowest class of slave."

"But she was there against her will, and forced to do disgusting things." Sarah now continued to argue the defense of her friend. "For fear of her life, if she did not comply?"

"But unfortunately, for some, there is no smoke without fire, so to speak. They find it hard to believe that this goes on. They will even start to say it was her fault. Admitting this injustice would mean that they would have to do something."

In the headset, the holographic image of Vincent now showed great concern, as if he was trying to hide something. In time he spoke.

"They are also speculating about you, Sarah."

"Why? What about me?"

"They are mostly general speculations," said Vincent trying to evade the question, "very boring really?"

"Such as," said Sarah, making it clear she wanted to know the truth.

"Whether or not you are married? Have you really heard The Whisper speaking to you? Are you just the pawn of Boudicca? What skin colour are you now? Are you going to be safe after all this? Are you returning to the Mist-Less Dimension? Are you and Freida just good friends? Normal stuff, that is to be expected," said Vincent casually. "Just speculations on the planetary web."

Sarah was offended by the nature of some of these questions. And she wondered whether people really had that little to do with their spare time. And then she realized that back in her own dimension, she had engaged in such trivial issues, and things were near identical in this regard.

"Well I am not married? And yes I believe The Whisper has spoken to me, for starters," she replied angrily, "and you can let them know that if you like."

"Will do," replied Vincent. "Anything else, Sarah?"

"No that's all for now, I'll ask for you, when you are needed again."

And on that instruction, such as it was, Vincent vanished, leaving Sarah alone in reality.

Meanwhile, the troops on 'the Dragon" remained totally quiet. They were delighted of course, at the victory, but nobody dared to cheer. They were also suntil in grief. For them this was not a cheering matter. Instead they saw it as a hard won, and even lucky turn of events, which had resulted in the death of about a quarter of their group.

"Suntil," Sarah reasoned to herself about an hour later, "it could have been worse." But she did not dare say it.

Instead, she now sat on her hammock watching out for Freida who was fast asleep due to a sleeping tablet. Adah had left her in charge, and this had pleased her, although it was not the first time, she had guarded her friend when in need.

Leslie and Charlotte came in briefly to bring some hot chocolate, for her. And Sarah was glad to see them and talk about the things that had happened.

Charlotte was straight in with the update. "It has just been announced that, the French have started to reclaim their own territory. Our troops are assisting them, where necessary."

"Egypt has admitted their loss of the region, somewhat reluctantly," Leslie informed her. "He had no choice as the world has seen the challenge by combat, and the stakes that 'Phillipa' agreed to. She had a promise of marriage contract on her apparently. Denise has just issued another press release to show it.

Leslie then continued. "Of course, we all know that he now has only a small navy in the short term, and no means to transport his troops. Many of his forces are now trapped between enemies, and cut off from further help. He is regrouping his remaining forces in Tunisia."

"A necessary change of strategy then?" Sarah asked Leslie.

"Yes, The Pharaoh says they are "planning to withdraw" for the time being only."

"Of course" said Charlotte, quoting the news, as if she had thought of it herself. "Although a victory has been won today, this is just the start of something else. For starters, I suspect the price on Freida's head will soar now!" And she looked down at her Captain. "I guess that Boudicca will increase our Captain's security. And yours I suspect?"

Over the next few minutes Sarah sat with Leslie and Charlotte, and they discussed many things. Like their relationship, and Leslie's injury.

"What happened? and are you ok, Leslie?"

"A grenade went off, and I took the tail end of it. On my left arm. But it is just a burn," Leslie pointed it out, dismissing it as nothing. "Louise, took the full brunt of it." And she gave a look of guilt, "so how can I complain?"

But Charlotte looked a little more worried, "I had to tell my partner here get it checked out. The doc was concerned about infection; we have been told to keep it clean."

"Like I intended to let it get infected?"

"And I am more concerned about our mental health," Charlotte pointed out, to Sarah. "What happened back there was horrific."

"Honestly you can be such a woos at times," said Leslie, now getting up to leave the room. But looking at Charlotte, with a look that said "thank you." And Charlotte, who was joining Leslie, was about to respond when the news began. The screens suddenly came on, and the usual CBC jingle started to play.

They said "bye for now," and Sarah leant back in her hammock to watch. There was nothing on it she didn't already know.

When it was over, she took her Tech-Tab in her hand, and whispered for Vincent to advise her.

Vincent appeared as a holographic projection.

'How is the press handling the news, do you think?" she asked.

"I cannot think, for myself, at least not officially," replied the green holographic man. "But I would say, it is as to be expected. Mostly supporting Celtishia over Egypt."

"What about the revelation, of Freida's?'

"I don't understand, what do you mean Sarah?"

"That she had children via the Chief Prince?"

"Oh I already knew that, I was her personal assistant first, you see."

"What I meant is that they have a claim on Palestine?"

"I know that too, so what are you asking?"

 "And will the twins be allowed to rule?" asked Sarah, getting more exasperated with every question.

"Difficult to answer that one, I'm afraid," said Vincent.

"How so?"

"Well it means a lot of speculation, which is not what I am programmed to do really."

"Go on Vincent, you have my permission."

"In that case. I speculate that" and Vincent paused to compute, "there is a sixty to forty percent chance of it happening. The league of Nations are testing their D.N.A, and will soon verify the claim. Other circumstantial evidence also backs up Freida's story. But there are many things that will need explaining. The process could take about twelve months, and even re-sult in a civil war in the region."

Sarah had not expected that. And so she asked for clarification of Vincent's speculation, "Civil war? But why?"

"This has always been a disputed region, and politically it is a hotbed for alternating ideas. There are many factions with their own agendas. They also have their own prejudices."

"Such as?"

"Well, the oldest of the twins is Ruth. The female twin. And some of the people in the region prefer male, to female rulers. They were only accepting Phillipa because of Egypt's influence."

"Oh," said Sarah, who was only just starting to

understand the issue. "I see the problem now."

"Do you?" Vincent responded. "Because they are also Israeli, or Jewish, rather than Arab. The last thing Egypt will want is a Jewish run state. And the children have also been raised in Celtishia, so their values will be very different to theirs. Western values, in fact."

"What's wrong with that?" Sarah demanded.

"Nothing, Sarah. At least not in our eyes. But they have no "Royal Blood" on the mother's side, and unfortunately Freida is being portrayed as a rather dodgy slave. The local government officials aren't going to like these things at all. Many will oppose her."

"Ouch." Sarah now realized the immensity of what had happened. "Its a bit of a bomb waiting to go off, isn't it? But aren't these just excuses being offered to, you know, avoid dealing with the consequences?"

"And to retain control? I would guess Sarah," said Vincent, "that although Palestine may not be the richest region, it still brings in the revenue for Egypt."

"Money and power," said Sarah. And now she was angry. "The two things that seem to rule the planet, in both dimensions. The wheel just keeps on turning. Money buys the power, and the power gets you money."

"Don't forget sex," pointed out Vincent. "In this case, it has clearly put a spoke in the wheel. There is bound to be a counter claim of potential illegitimacy, when the D.N.A checks out."

"Furthermore" Vincent continued, "I cannot see Egypt just giving up their claim on the region. The children are young, they will argue, without the knowledge to rule."

"So," asked Sarah, as she brought the conversation to end, "what can I do to help?"

"Support Freida as a friend," he replied. "And let Boudicca push the case for the children."

The Dragon continued on its journey for about one more hour, before it touched down in Devonport, at the base where they had started their journey. Sarah had enjoyed the last few minutes of views, flying over Devonport Sound, observing what was the same, and noting what was different from the Plymouth she knew. But now the craft was coming in to land vertically, the appeal of flying by a saucer was wearing off. Once again her ears hurt, due to the change in air pressure. Denise had forgotten to hand out the sweets to the team.

Looking out of the craft's portholes, the unit could see a press and media storm erupting on the tarmac. Journalists and photographers alike scrabbled for the best locations to ask questions and take their photos. They were held back by a line of troops, and law enforcement officers, for their own safety's sake. Otherwise they would have been literally right underneath the craft as it landed.

"Attention all hands. Please remain on the Dragon," said Adah over the speaker system. "Our first job will be to hand over our prisoners. The Princess," she said with real scorn, "is going to the League of Nations. Boudicca is there with Military and Royal Transport to escort her personally."

Sarah looked out of the porthole window, at the scene below. Troops were starting to clear a space, and a path to the hangar. Officials with "League of Nations" badges on their lapels were waiting anxiously, with handcuffs by their side. They were clearly there to take the Princess into custody.

Five minutes later she was escorted off the craft. This excited the press into another media storm, as the journalists scrabbled against security to try and get an interview. The cameras clicked and clicked for the best photo of a humiliated Princess. Meanwhile Sarah tried to imagine the story headlines.

"Princess one day, prisoner the next."

"Engaged to Pharaoh, now in a cell."

The evil Princess was led to the guards, by Doctor Martha Zing, and handed over to the League of Nations. She addressed the authorities, for all to hear.

"I present the prisoner, Princess Phillipa of Lebanon. She is accused of child abduction, sexual trafficking, abuse of power, and being complicit in the murder of many innocent children.

We have confession, testimony and witnesses. We are handing her over for trial in New Yorvic, under the League of Nations' mandate. We can confirm she is healthy and in a right state of mind, and therefore fit to stand trial. We have also taken the liberty of ensuring your arrival by providing the transportation at our expense."

This announcement caused great enthusiasm on the craft, because many of the troops felt it was long overdue. They had also seen her brag about what she had done to Freida, and the very idea of child abuse was repulsive to them. Sarah reflected, that it was exactly the same in her dimension.

The Princess was re-handcuffed to great cheers from the media, and the troops, and then led away to another craft for transport overseas, and to face justice for all she had done. Five minutes later Boudicca also boarded with a security escort.

"She is the prosecutor. Apparently she is asking for a life sentence," Denise whispered in Sarah's ear.

"Good riddance, to the Princess" said Adah over the speaker to the laughter and applause of the entire company. "Now she has gone, we will offload our fallen first. We are loading coffins on now to transport their bodies in. I assure you all that they will all be buried with dignity."

"The injured will then be escorted off by paramedics, in reverse order of superiority. Captain

Sophie-Smith will go last. Then everybody else is free to disembark, and well done everyone, we have made a difference today."

There was a pause, and a silence, within their compartment. In fact, the whole craft was now silent.

"The fallen," remembered Sarah, in a quiet voice to the unit.

"Poor Louise. Have her parents been informed already?" she asked Denise.

"Yes, but I have the task of speaking to them directly," Denise replied. "Do you want to come with me? They are waiting for us in the hangar."

"Of course, but I am not sure what I'll say to help them." Sarah had never been in this situation before. She was worried that she would somehow make the situation worse.

"We can't help them, just extend our sympathy for their loss. And maybe…"

"Maybe what..?"

There was a pause before Denise answered the question. "Maybe, tell them some stories about the training, and how you got on with her."

"I'll do that." Sarah then looked at Denise and asked, "do we know when the funeral is? They do have funerals here in this dimension, I assume? I never thought to ask before."

"Yes, usually within three days of the death. They are quite noisy affairs though. Sometimes fights are even known to break out, I should warn you."

But before she could ask, her Tech-Tab gave an emergency ring. On the other end was Queen Boudicca herself requesting a private call with Sarah, as soon as she was able to do so.

"I had better take this now," she said to Denise, looking in the direction behind her, "I will use my office."

"Your office?" asked Denise, wondering what on earth, Sarah could possibly mean. Then she realized. "Ah, the toilet!"

The conversation took about ten minutes, and was made in very hushed voices.

When Sarah finally came out of the bathroom, she was very reserved, and non-talkative. The team knew that she was hiding something, but also knew better than to ask her about it. They all knew she had used the cubicle to take a Tech-Tab call, and that the conversation was with the Queen. And if Boudicca herself was involved, then they would probably find out sooner or later anyway.

However, before anybody could be tempted to ask, there was what sounded like a bugle being blown.

"Attention all hands, we are now disembarking "the fallen" from our midst."

It was like she had ordered everybody to be quiet. For all over the craft, people stopped what they were doing, and stood respectfully as the coffins were ceremoniously escorted of by other troops. The military presence it seemed had increased in the last ten minutes, and troops could be seen saluting the fallen on either side as the coffins passed by in the middle.

They were escorted to the main hangar, where other transportation awaited them in the form of helicopters and smaller saucers. Louise's body was ushered to the side, and into a small van where Louise's relatives could be seen crying.

"We had better go and speak to them as soon as we can," said Denise. And Sarah nodded, fearing the moment that was to come.

Thirty minutes later they had all disembarked the craft. Denise quickly hugged her family, while Sarah greeted her boyfriend Simon. After the reunions, Sarah and Denise made their way over to the hangar to speak to Louise's relatives. There were about ten present, and they stood around nervously, wearing black, and crying.

In the end, it was to be a simple conversation, and not nearly as scary as they had imagined it would be.

Sarah was heard to say things like, "I am sorry for your loss. I always liked Louise." Denise gave the younger of Louise's brothers a hug, and spoke at length with her parents sharing stories regarding the training.

All in all, Sarah thought they were a nice family. She even wished to have met them under different circumstances. She just saw them as another family from Devonport. Poor. Hardworking. Down to earth. And decent.

In their shared grief, the "dimension issue" meant nothing. Sarah knew that some things are multi-versal, and nobody should have to bury their young. Yet here they all were, coping as best as they could.

In the background, the craft now carrying 'The Princess,' took off vertically. It rose for about five hundred feet, and then jetted away horizontally for New Yorvic. The Royal Escort followed them as Boudicca, was also on board.

It was a good two hours, before the news came through, that the craft had landed in New Yorvic. Phillipa had been transferred into a cell, and could be seen on television, protesting her innocence.

Lebanon was the only country challenging the arrest. They had secured her some lawyers, and were actively putting on the diplomatic pressure, to get Phillipa a pardon. However, most countries were saying they were opposed to it, and she should indeed stand trial. Under the international pressure, even Egypt had disowned her.

One hour later, a familiar looking green faced man stood on the steps outside the court of justice. He was wearing an expensive suit, and spoke into a microphone. The man announced that a life sentence would be pursued, but the gathering of evidence was likely to take a few months.

Three days passed, and Sarah found herself standing in a clearing to attend the funeral of Louise. One of the many girls who had been killed in battle.

The unit has all turned up in uniform out of respect, and Sarah stood there crying next to Freida. Adah stood behind them, keeping a low profile.

It was the first funeral that Sarah had attended, in this dimension. It was also the first funeral since her fathers. And it brought back bad memories. Especially when the coffin was carried in, supported by members of Louise family.

They sang a song, under the direction of a well-known local Rabbi, called Wendy. Then they said some poem that addressed The Whisper, that was projected onto a screen suspended in the trees. Finally, they escorted the coffin to a hole in the ground, where it was lowered with ceremony.

Freida gave a final eulogy, over the grace. As her mentor, she described Louise as, "brave to the last, and a spirited individual. Popular with all she met." Then they took it in turn to throw on some flowers, and some dirt. The casket was covered to more singing of a tune, which Sarah knew well from the Catacombs.

And that was that. No more Louise, except she was still living on in their memories. They believed that one day they would be reunited, and the pain they were now feeling would get easier with time.

The party that followed, lasted all night. And there was much drinking. Cider seemed to be the most popular, and Sarah certainly took a lot of it.

"In honour of Louise," she kept saying with a slur, as she got another glass. It was the best way she could think of coping.

"You will regret it in the morning," advised Adah, out of concern.

"Let her drink, and forget her misery, just for tonight", said Freida, rebuking Adah a little in jest. Clearly, she had done worse in her time, and wasn't passing any judgement.

Later that night, the Sarah and Freida caught up with each other. It was the conversation that the two friends needed to have.

"Boudicca told me," whispered Freida so nobody else could hear.

"Told you what?" asked Sarah, although she already knew the answer.

"She told me, that you decided to return short term to your dimension. To get some things?"

"I knew she would," said Sarah. She knew that Freida and Boudicca talked about everything. And this was bound to have come up.

"You sure it is what you want?" asked Freida.

"Yes, but it is only for a short time. The portal

there opens in two days, and the first return is in three months, with a blood moon."

"You will miss the investigations," she pointed out pragmatically. "It is likely that The Princess' defense will rip me to pieces. But I am sure that Boudicca will still get the conviction at trial eventually."

This was what Sarah had been dreading. She wanted to be there to support her, but knew that it was necessary to get there and back as quickly as possible.

"I am sorry, I wanted to be there for support. But I must speak to my mother."

Freida was starting to give Sarah a look that indicated she didn't understand, but was not convinced it was a good idea. Eventually Freida questioned her friend. "But why?"

"To explain, why I am going to vanish forever. And she may never see me again."

Freida was starting to get it. "Yes, you need to explain that to her. Do you think she will understand?"

"Maybe," said Sarah, "because I think she knows something anyway. My dad had some Celtishian coins remember."

"I assume you have no regrets about leaving?"

"Only one."

Freida looked confused by this revelation, thinking she had Sarah figured out. "Really, what is it?" she asked. "Can I help?"

Sarah was looking downwards at her feet, as

she explained. "I fear I might lose my boyfriend Simon, when I am away. You know for three months! I really like him you know. I only realized, when we were under fire in Cadiz. He was all I could see. And I want to keep him for myself."

"Then take control," advised Freida, who was no expert in relationships herself. "Knock some sense into him. I can call his mother if you want. Do the diplomacy for you?"

"I am not sure I understand?" said Sarah, somewhat baffled by what Freida had proposed.

Freida looked amazed still didn't get this one, and explained, with a cheeky voice.

"Look at it this way! Do you have a hockey stick?"

25. MIST-LESS

S arah didn't like the idea of the hockey stick approach to getting your man, and decided to ask Simon directly. She didn't mind being vulnerable in this situation, but she did still have to ask the parents though.

Freida's negotiations were a total success. Freida's call had been accepted by Simon's parents with enthusiasm and puzzlement, as she was mildly famous in Celtishia for her military role. Although seen to be a girl with a past, thanks to the media, they were willing to hear what she had to say.

The news of the request had not come as a shock to them either. Simon's parents had already heard that he was dating "Sarah, (the girl from the Mist-Less,)" from his friends. And they all approved of her. Simon's parents felt proud of him, for serving the country. They wanted to give their blessing to the marriage proposal.

As it happened they were to have dinner with their son, at Midday the following day. They said that, "they look forward to meeting Sarah then." The 'meet up' couldn't come quickly enough.

The hardest thing for her was informing him, she would be away for a bit, and pretending she would be saying a temporary goodbye. But Sarah found ways to distract him, saying "let's enjoy this evening."

On the day in question, she went with Freida by PTM, to the rendezvous site. It was a simple restaurant, that served foreign food, mostly French. It was located near the shopping district, known here as "Downtown Devonport"

She entered via the door with a rabbi, and of course, Freida, her best friend. They spotted Simon sitting at a table with his back turned. However, the arrival of the war celebrities caused applause to break out all over, and the surprise element was lost. Simon had turned around and saw them as they reached the table.

"Hi babe, what are you doing here?" And he greeted her with a passionate kiss. Sarah kissed him back.

"I am here to see you all. There is something urgent to be discussed." Sarah was blushing with every word.

"Really?" asked a confused Simon.

"Yes," said his mother behind him, in a voice of exasperation. "And I want you to know that if you say yes, I approve."

"To what?" He asked looking from his mother to Sarah, and back again. He was totally confused by what was happening.

"I love this bit," said Freida laughing, "men are always so slow on the uptake."

"Well," said Sarah, taking his hand, "I am going home for a few months only. I must talk to my family, and explain things, if they will believe it."

Simon looked devastated. "You are leaving me?" She moved closer, and looked at him reassuringly. "Yes, but only for a short time, but when I return; within three months, I want to marry you. I want to love you, and I want you to love me. I want to take your body as my own? Until through death we eventually part? If you will have me?"

The restaurant clapped, and some restaurant customers shouted, "say yes: Dumbo."

"Yes," he said without hesitation. And without a sound of regret.

Sarah was overwhelmed with relief. But nobody else seemed to be. His mother was clapping her hands with glee. She then grabbed Sarah into a hug, and said "welcome to the family." The restaurant applauded loudly.

"Congratulations" said the Rabbi, when it had quietened down, "you are both engaged!"

The rest of the meal was like a celebration. The restaurant was very accommodating and made room for the extra guests at Simon's table, and allowed them to extend the bar-tab without question.

A magnum bottle of sparkling cider was brought in, and shared around the table. (The green bottle resembled a champagne bottle, like it had been designed to help celebrate good things).

"We haven't had much call for these in some time," the waiter pointed out. "Things were rough until recently. But with Egypt defeated, things will probably pick up."

The waiter handed the magnum of sparkling cider to Sarah, who cracked it open causing fizz to spray everywhere. Then the waiter poured it into glasses. And everyone drank lots, while Sarah got to start a meal the way she had always wanted. With the desserts. And nobody seemed to mind. It was the welcome to a new family, that could not have gone better.

During the meal, Sarah was leaning into Simon, her fiancé, when Freida joined her. The two friends had a lot to talk about.

"Congratulations, both of you."

"Thank you."

"Glad she asked me," said Simon.

"You really didn't see it coming, did you?" asked Freida.

"No, and I will miss her when she is gone."

And with that Simon, made his excuses leaving Sarah and Freida alone to talk some more.

"Just tonight then?" Freida pointed out. "How are you feeling?"

"Scared. Of course."

"Of what," asked Freida. "You know the technology works? As long as you don't get your dates mixed up for the return you should be ok."

"My Mother, she will think I have gone mad."

"But Sarah," laughed Freida, "you were always mad." She was joking of course.

"So tell me again," Sarah asked, "how do you open the portal to the Mist-Less Dimension"

Freida looked over her shoulder, before she answered. "Well it is top secret, and known only to a handful in our country. But basically, a storm is expected today that will last a few days. There will be rain and lightning. Using metal conductors, we direct that same lightning to a specific point. Using a 'dimension viewer,' we match a stone circle in this dimension to a stone circle in yours, and the lightning strikes here will open the portal."

Freida checked around her again, before continuing.

"You must be running or falling, when you enter the stone circle. Judah will be there to basically push you sideways if necessary, at the right time."

"Now remember, it is important that you are in the right place as agreed, in order to return. However, if you fail to make the rendezvous, we will send through a rescue party to check you are ok. If we believe you are having problems, we can enlist help even on your side. Furthermore, if you request it, we will extract you using all means necessary. The decision to return will be yours."

Sarah really wanted to return. And as far as she was concerned it was a short visit only. Back to her world. Make peace with her family. Get some stuff. Return and get married.

"Freida?" Sarah asked, "may I ask you a few favours?

"Of course?"

"I need you to help Simon locate a home for us to live in. Above ground, and a small holding. I have some funds he can access for a deposit. I also have a bank account previously belonging to my grandmother here. I traced it following Louise's advice. I trust you both, in this."

"Good to know. You can consider it done."

"He will have a posting overseas, when I am gone. Make sure he doesn't forget me?" Sarah looked worried as she said this, for she knew in her dimension, troops were sometimes known to stray when separated from partners.

"Don't be ridiculous," Freida said, looking really quite shocked. "He is not that sort of man. And the company would never stand for it."

Sarah was relieved at the rebuke. "And there is something else," she continued. "When I return I will need a bridesmaid. Someone I can trust. Someone, who can bridge the worlds for me. Will you do it?"

Freida blushed a dark green. "Of course. I would be honoured, but I get first choice of any spare boys."

The last night in the Green World, was a night Sarah would always remember. She went out to the Barbican with Simon, and they relaxed in a local fish restaurant. And for the first time they started to plan their future together, as they looked out over the boats in the harbour.

Sarah could not help noticing that there was a vibrancy about the dock and fishing area of the city. People she did not know were drinking and partying with their friends in every direction around her. Meanwhile lights could be seen that created an almost magical effect, as the green mist kept floating like vapour past their window.

At ten o'clock in the evening, however, there was a storm warning, and this was the sign that they should start to make their way back to base. And with that they shared carriage on the mono rail back to the base, where they descended on the staff bar for a few more rounds. At twelve o'clock, Sarah decided it was time to brave the storm. She put on a coat and made her way with Simon to the entrance to the female catacombs. It was here that she kissed him passionately good night, and then finally went to bed alone.

By the time she reached her room, Freida was already fast asleep.

Sarah slept well, and was woken early next morning

"Wake up, sleepy head," said Freida, "I have brought you breakfast in bed, for your last morning"

"Eh? What?"

"I said, I have brought you breakfast in bed, for your last morning." Freida loved to repeat herself. "It is green soda bread and duck eggs. And a kiwi smoothie."

Sarah was not feeling her best. "What time is it?" she asked.

"Almost eight,' said Freida, "We have just under two hours to the rendezvous. Now eat, get dressed, and let's go. Simon is outside wanting to share a carriage on the monorail. We have booked the entire section, for security purposes."

Sarah did as she was told, and got dressed into the clothes she had arrived in. Although things had changed for her, and they weren't really her style anymore.

After getting dressed, and brushing her hair. She grabbed a sandwich, and then made her way upstairs. The storm was in full effect, and lightning could be seen and then heard as it lit up the sky with its bright silver forks, over the green mist.

Despite the bad weather, the ride to the rendezvous site was dead easy. For starters, she was under a cover, and could see the city through the storm, as she rode above it. Eventually the monorail pulled into Downtown Devonport. The whole company was there to greet them, and guide them to the circular shop that had been requisitioned for the day. Despite the now torrential rain, they were friendly and keen to give her a great send off.

Judah was there to meet her. And Sarah was glad to see him.

"My Bou, is in New Yorvic, on prosecution business, of course," he told her. "I spoke to her this morning, and she said she is sorry she could not be here, but will see you soon. We will be married by then, I expect."

Sarah looked across at the house. It looked ordinary. Well for Celtishia. It was about twenty metres from side to side, and the typical round shape. The stock had all been removed and the area was cordoned off under the pretext of an Egyptian terrorist scare. The extensive rain meant that nobody was querying this.

This was probably a good thing, because Judah had rigged it up so that it looked like the inside of an umbrella. Metal wires could be seen coming down the sides, and now on the top of the dome was a large metal spike.

"To catch the lightning," Judah explained. "We need to keep the electricity it generates in suspension for about ten seconds. Enough to get you through."

There was a flash as a fork of lightning could be seen in the sky.

"It is a good thing I am not scared of this stuff,"

Sarah whispered to Freida. Freida was trying to keep the rain of her head with the use of a hood, on her coat.

"One. Two. Three." counted Judah, until the lightning crack could be heard. "The lightning is three miles away. Will be here soon. The devices are set up. Why don't you take a look?"

Sarah approached the device. It looked like a small box with lots of weird lights. It had two microscopes sticking out, and a screen on top. As soon as she saw it she laughed. Judah did not look impressed, but she was not bothered about this. She could not believe that this machine would work, and yet to her surprise she soon realized that it did.

Through the lens, she could see the Plymouth she knew. Specifically, she could see the town centre, and a ring of stones near a play facility. Shops were on either side. And it was also raining heavily there. People were sheltering in canopies outside of the shops.

"That is weird," said Sarah, as she hinted at Freida to take a look. "Come and see."

"So this is your Plymouth," said Freida as she looked into the lens. "I can't get over the pink faces. And the lack of green mist. Everything is so clear there."

"But remember, though there is only one human race." Sarah felt it was important to say that.

They were both brought back to reality by another flash of lightning. The sky was lit up, as the fork of lightning could be seen, coming down upon them.

"One Two."

And there was the crack of thunder.

"Two miles away" said Judah, "I would get into position, if I was you and get ready to run."

She only had to wait about a minute.

Another loud crack, and a third lightning fork appeared, lighting up the sky instantaneously. But this time it was different. The clouds and stars in the sky seemed for a few seconds, to turn the sky into a strong white light and Sarah could see plainly a planet, shaped exactly like the Earth she knew come falling down towards her.

Sarah did not know that only she could see this. To everyone else, the house was lit up like a giant glowing ball in the ground.

"Run like we told you Sarah," yelled Judah, and she started to sprint as fast as she could into the house.

As she entered she heard hand-bells ringing as the earth in the sky got nearer. The ground vibrated and ran into something.

The good news was that the mist had gone, the rain was falling heavily, and she was back in the middle of the Plymouth in the Mist-Less dimension. She was home.

The bad news was that Sarah had crashed into an old woman. The woman fell to the ground, and Sarah landed on top of her.

"Watch where you're going, you stupid tart" yelled the unknown woman, and looked at Sarah to see her green face staring back in shock. The unknown woman screamed and called for help.

Of course, the police were nowhere to be seen, when they were needed. So Sarah got to her feet, and started running. But the sight of a green face had alerted others, and some gave chase, leaving their shelters to run after her in the rain. They believed that they had witnessed an assault on an old woman.

Sarah ran around the corner into another street of shops. But it was proving difficult, as she was strangely and suddenly losing breath, despite being quite fit from military training. Her pursuers were slowing down for they could see something was wrong. People everywhere were staring at her, as she struggled to run in a straight line.

"Try drinking less!" shouted a bystander trying to be funny.

"And wash the bogeys of your face," yelled another.

Up in front, she could see some paramedics, and tried to run in their direction. But a pursuer now grabbed her, and she struggled. Both to free herself and to breathe. It was then she remembered the letter from her dad.

"I need better air," she exclaimed, and as she fell to the floor nearly passed out. The pursuer let go in horror, and called out to the paramedics to help. The last thing Sarah saw was them arriving with their equipment.

It was six weeks later that Sarah Salter awoke in a hospital, to see her mother there beside her, with her brother. They were clearly relieved, and worried. The mother also looked angry, but was holding back the urge to scold her daughter because of the nurses nearby.

She was wearing a hospital gown, and was in a small side room. There was a picture on the wall, of a boat in a harbour. The place smelled of disinfectant, like it had just been cleaned and sterilized.

Sarah soon realized that she was wearing some kind of face mask, which dug into her nose like a set of new glasses. She tried to take it off, but a nurse was there to gently stop her.

"Hello Sarah," said the military nurse, who approached her bed. Sarah acknowledged her with a nod. And the nurse dutifully went into a standard introduction. "My name is Dinah, and I am your nurse. You are in hospital, and you are safe. But you must keep the mask on."

Sarah let go of her face mask, and looked at her mother. Carly Salter just nodded at her daughter. "What happened," she said.

You were found in the street, with hypoxia. The paramedics gave you oxygen on the scene. "Apparently you knew, you needed air." The nurse was looking at Sarah with suspicion. "Furthermore, you have been missing for months, and nobody seems to know why?"

"I was elsewhere."

"Well that is obvious," joked the nurse. "I am here at the request of your mother. We are old friends. But officially, I here to look after you for other reasons." And she gave Sarah a mirror. Sarah looked briefly, and handed back the mirror, like what she saw was no big deal. The nurse took the mirror and placed it down on a side table, without a word.

"Have you never seen a person with a green face before?" asked Sarah jokingly.

"No, but I have heard of such things," replied the nurse, a little too knowingly for Sarah's liking. "Normally it would suggest a vitamin deficiency. But, we also fear an unknown virus, may be behind this. For this reason, you have been barriered by military doctors. This means that until further notice, you cannot leave the room. But there is an private bathroom if you need it."

"There you go then," she replied, perhaps a bit rudely.

The nurse seemed to just ignore this, and leant forward to indicate she was not about to be dismissed. Dinah replied therefore, in a way that suggested it was wise for Sarah to listen to her. "I said *normally*, Miss Salter. Because you have been calling out some weird stuff in your unconsciousness."

"Surely that is usual."

"Not the stuff you are said to be saying. You were mentioning a place called 'Celtishia.' And a boy called Simon, and.." The nurse stopped for a second. "Due to oxygen depletion: you apparently started to get violent. You caused mayhem on the ward, so we now have security outside the door. The military in the hospital was delighted to assist in this matter. They don't normally!"

"Oh,' said Sarah, realizing the importance of such a statement. The military were asking questions, that would take some explaining on her part.

"Oh indeed," said the military nurse. Dinah now strangely winked at her, while nobody was looking. "The police I am afraid will also want to speak to you, but I have told them all. They can't until you are well enough."

"What about?" she asked the nurse, getting a little worried.

The nurse gave a dismissive look, when she answered, with a very dry style of humour.

"Just the business of knocking over a woman whilst running wildly through town with a green face."

"What?" And then she remembered. "I didn't mean to. I didn't see her." Sarah was horrified by what had happened, and had never meant to harm anyone.

"That's exactly what I said would have happened," said the nurse. "You would not know where you were in that state, or who was there. And the TV surveillance mysteriously seems to have gone down that night, due to the storm. Inconclusive evidence some lawyers have advised your mother."

"We have lawyers?" asked a surprised Sarah.

"Yes, paid for by some mysterious business organization, involved in technology development. Very well connected apparently. And they seemed to know all about you, and were most insistent on helping."

"Oh, but I don't understand how?"

"How they knew about you, before you were even registered legally you mean? Now that is a mystery," Dinah pointed out. "But they have appointed a really good legal team to help you. It was them who got you out of the military hospital you were taken too, and into the hands of the NHS. They advise us both daily." Dinah motioned to herself and Carly Salter, (Sarah's mum).

"We will all help you in this," interrupted her mother, "whatever has happened."

And with that she felt the calm touch of the Whisper reassure her, that it was okay to trust her mum. And it was then, Sarah also realized for certain, that her mother knew something. So did the nurse, although it was unclear if she could be trusted or not. And although effectively under some kind of house-arrest, she was not alone, and had all the help that she needed.

N.R. Gurney

The story of Sarah Salter's journeys continue in "Green Mist Singularity."

42056292R00237

Printed in Poland
by Amazon Fulfillment
Poland Sp. z o.o., Wrocław